The Rise of Sturd

By Maria DeVivo

The Rise of Sturd

By Maria DeVivo

Twilight Times Books
Kingsport Tennessee

The Rise of Sturd

Paladin Timeless Books, an imprint of
Twilight Times Books
P O Box 3340
Kingsport TN 37664
http://twilighttimesbooks.com/

First Edition, December 2015

ISBN: 978-1-60619-218-4

Library of Congress Control Number: 2015957833

Cover art by Ural Akyuz

Printed in the United States of America.

For Babaysh – for your unwavering love, strength, devotion and support, even in the face of catastrophe and chaos.

For Doc – for planting the early seeds of my imagination. These tales have your influence written all over them.

For Mojo – it's always for you, and always will be for you.

Acknowledgments

Thank you to my husband, Joe — you are always there to guide me in ways that even I can't see sometimes. Thanks to my daughter, Morgan — your intelligence and creativity has opened new dimensions in my world. My parents, brothers, sisters, nephews, cousins, aunts, and uncles (so many to name!) — you all have inspired me in some way. Thank you to my publisher, Lida Quillen, for allowing my craziness to make it to print. Thank you to my editors for helping to flesh out my labor of love. Jan Kafka, you are my eagle eye, and Gerry Mills, your influence will stay with me through all my days. You are deeply missed. To Victoria Tomlinson for giving Ember her full name! Without artist Ural Akyuz, Ember and company would not have a physical form. Your vision is frighteningly in line with mine. Thank you Joel Dougherty and Nik Kolidas for bringing "Memo: Ember's Song" to musical life. Thank you to my writing partner-in-crime, Scott Eder — your enthusiasm for our craft is infectious. To my beta readers, Dennis Rooney and Justin Dougherty — your help is always appreciated. And to all my friends and people I consider my extended family — the outpouring of love and support is deeply felt, and I am extremely grateful for every ounce of it.

I am truly blessed.

Chapter One

IF THERE WAS ONE THING OGDEN CASTLEBERRY HATED ABOUT HIS LIFE JOB, it was not having a view of the sunset. His single office window was on the wrong side of the building, and only gave him the slightest indication that the twilight aura in the North Pole sky had completely vanished. Darkness crept its way in a semi-circle that engulfed the room, rather than giving a full frontal show.

Ogden loved sunset at the North Pole – when the sky wrapped itself in golds and pinks and the sun looked like an orange fireball ready to shoot its powerful rays at everyone and anything. As an elfling, he had marveled at this beauty, soaked in every last breathtaking moment. Norland had the best sunsets in the entire world, because Norland was the most sacred place to ever exist. Only the most special elves lived here. Headquarters was based here, and of course, it was the homeland of the one and only Santa Claus. But what should it matter now?

He began lighting the lanterns around the room, preferring the soft glow of the flames over the harsh fluorescence of the electric lights, the only sound his own footfalls.

"You shouldn't complain," he said, his voice booming in the room as he began to laugh. "It could be worse. You could be mining coal!" But his laughter ended in a long sigh, for as much as he was grateful to have such an easygoing job, he wondered if he would enjoy a more laborious one if it was coupled with some company.

There were multiple elves chatting away in the offices below and above him. They were sharing family stories, or working on projects, or commiserating about something. All Ogden could do was complain to himself.

If only the Council had let him have some company while he worked, then maybe all this wouldn't seem so tedious. If they had just let his twin brother, Orthor, work with him, then maybe he wouldn't feel the loneliness of his Life Job so much. But they didn't. No matter how many times he complained to Elven Resources about getting a new office, or at least having a companion of sorts, this was his fate. Sit. Wait. Watch.

He resigned himself to his swivel chair, propped his feet on top of his oak desk, and did just that. Sit. Wait. Watch. "I have the most boring job in all of Norland," he sighed.

He supposed it was a noble job, being entrusted with the most revered text in the Elven Realm. He and Orthor had been ecstatic when their mother announced they would be Book Keepers for the revered Book of Names. It was the giant magic book that held all the names of all the children in the entire world. The good. The bad. The boys. The girls. What elf wouldn't want to be privy to information of that magnitude? The brothers had been less ecstatic, however, when they had been informed that they would be split up. Orthor had to take the day shift, and Ogden had to take the night. "Divide the work, divide the spoils," their Master had said.

Ogden had been struggling with that concept ever since. What spoils? Where were the spoils? His spoils were awfully spoiled, because never getting to spend any time with his brother was worse than never getting to see a Norland sunset again.

He threw his arms above his head and yawned. His thermos, filled with hot cocoa, had been placed in its usual spot next to a brown paper bag that was filled with chocolate chip cookies. He was now prepared for another night of sitting, and waiting, and watching The Book of Names. Well, if he was going to be honest, sitting, and waiting, and occasionally glancing at The Book of Names, because nothing too dramatic really happened within the book.

The Book sat in all its glory within its rectangular glass case. The pages magically flipped forwards and backwards on their own. Colors of the scripted text changed from gold to red, red to silver, green to gold. This noble and esteemed job really didn't require him to do much of anything because the Book was literally a living document, and all Ogden had to do was sit there and let the Book do all the work.

When the spirit of The Big Night first entered a child's heart, their name was automatically written in The Book. Over time, the names changed in appearance – naughty girls were written in red, naughty boys in green, good girls in gold, good boys in silver. It is from this main source that the Lists for the elves at the North Pole were created. But when the time came, and a child no longer believed in the Claus, their name was grayed out and moved to the back of the Book where it eventually disappeared to make way for the new names of new children. Like a revolving door, the Book was in a constant state of rotation. Names come in, names go out, and whether the name was gold or red or gray was all up to the human child who carried it. Ogden had seen names gray out as early as five years old, others as late as thirteen. On average, a name stayed active in the Book for ten years.

The sound of the turning pages soothed him, and he closed his eyes, taking in the sweet rhythmic cadence of the "flip, flip, flip" of the Book. It sounded like the gentle flutter of Graespur wings flapping in the night sky, and he wished he wasn't confined to this chair, this office, this building. He longed so desperately to be free – to watch the sunset, to bask in the moonlight, to sit in a garden feeding the Graespurs, but instead he was confined here – this desk, this office, this lonely life.

The pages of the Book slowed down a bit, which was not unusual for this time of year. March was when things were the calmest. Children of the world were in what Ogden called a "lull-state." They were still coming down from their Big Day high, readjusting from their festivities, getting their lives back to a semi-state of normal. The months of February and March were typically the least active, not many color changes, not much graying. It wasn't usually until August when the pages of the Book acted like they were possessed, flipping sometimes violently back and forth. That was when the Good and Naughty Lists were finalized for the year, and last-minute decisions were made as to which List each child would ultimately appear.

Just thinking about a "lull-state" put Ogden into one of his own. His head sank deeper into the cushion on his chair, and he revisited his previous thoughts of the missed sunset. He crossed his arms over his chest, stuffed his hands in his armpits and grumbled, "It probably was perfect," before letting his body feel the first tingling sensations of a deep sleep. *It's only March*, he thought, *it's not like…* and he started to drift off to the sound of the gentle page turns of the Book.

The silence in the office startled him and his head snapped up from the side of his shoulder. It took him a second or two to collect his bearings. His hands were still firmly pressed in the deep cups of his arms, and the sides of his mouth were moist with sleep-drool. He looked around the room, making sure everything was in its proper place; the paintings undisturbed, blinds on the windows untouched, thermos and brown paper bag still in their spots. But something was amiss. Something was…

The Book.

The pages of the book stopped turning, and there was only one reason why that could happen.

In a near panic, Ogden jumped up from his chair to inspect the Book. His sweaty hands lifted the glass casing so he could get a better look. Sure enough, there it was – a black spot over a child's name, as if a smudge of coal had been forced upon it, stamping it out forever. There were some people in the world who just didn't believe in much of anything. Even though belief in the Claus might disappear, the true spirit of the season doesn't leave a person entirely. That's why the name is grayed out in the Book. Unless - a person loses all faith and love for the Big Day, and completely obliterates the spirit from their heart. Then they are stamped out, blacked, erased from the Book forever. A black spot over a name was not entirely unheard of. It happened, on average, two or three times a year. *But in March?*

Ogden stared at the name – *Ryan Black.* "The irony," he said. He touched the dark spot to acknowledge the eliminated name, which would free the book to continue its work. It felt like burnt paper, like a charred and brittle soul. He shook his head gently. "Poor guy," he whispered, removing his finger from the Book. Almost immediately, the pages began flipping back and forth again, quickly at first, then slowing down to a resting heartbeat's pace. He stood over the Book for a few moments, watching the magic ebb and flow, mesmerized by the changing colors as if they were strobe lights at a dance hall.

Just as he was about to put the glass casing back over the Book, the pages stopped again. The silence tied his stomach into knots. Before his eyes, another name was transforming from gold to gray to brown to black; the paper of the page bubbled up a smudge mark, branding the Book with yet another non-believer. Ogden was transfixed. He had never witnessed the transformation before.

Katharine Burnham.

Had this been the first black name of the evening, he would have chuckled at the irony, but this wasn't the first, and this was no laughing matter. In fact, this was unprecedented. He hesitated a little when he lifted his finger from the name, the anticipation bubbling over into his sweaty, shaky hand, the anxiety gnawing at his rumbling tummy.

Scared that it would happen again, he closed his eyes tight, praying to Claus to hear the pages of the Book start flipping again. "C'mon, c'mon," he said as if coaxing the Book, "you can do it!"

But there was silence. Only silence. The pages of the Book had not resumed rotation, and after waiting a few minutes, Ogden slowly opened his eyes to see the horror on the page before him – a third name had been blackened out.

For a second, he thought his heart had stopped. He took a deep breath, and without touching the smudge on the Book, quickly replaced the glass casing. He wasn't about to stick around to wait and see if any more names would be obliterated.

He went to his desk, grabbed his thermos, took a long drink of his hot cocoa, and began pacing heavily back and forth in the center of the room. "It's only March!" he said, wiping his mouth with the back of his hand. He tried everything in his power to remain calm. He told himself that maybe it was a mistake, maybe it was just a fluke, maybe it was a ramification of the Double Coal Night – the last Big Night when the bad kids had gotten two years-worth of coal. It could all be related. Couldn't it?

No matter how he tried to justify it in his mind, he knew that three black names in one night was something that needed to be reported, but the last thing he wanted to do was call Elven Resources.

He was probably the last elf they would want to hear from, but if he didn't contact someone, the consequences could be severe for him.

He reluctantly picked up the blue phone on his desk and dialed ER's number. He'd called to complain so many times, he had it memorized. When the operator picked up, he didn't even have to identify himself. He said, "Goldie?"

Goldie, on the other end, sighed heavily.

"Yes, Ogden."

He inhaled deeply, anticipating how he was going to phrase his next sentence. "Goldie, I think there's a problem over here."

"Ogden, you know they're not going to change your office. They're not going to add any windows or..."

"No, nothing like that."

"Okay, surprise me then."

"It's just that... um... the Book..."

"What's wrong?" Her voice was higher, alarmed.

"It's just that... well... there's been some... black marks on the names and..."

"What do you mean 'marks?' As in plural? More than one?"

He cracked his knuckles until there was nothing left to crack. "Um... like, say... three."

Goldie gasped. "I'm contacting the boss. Don't leave the room." And with that, Goldie hung up her extension.

The boss? He'd never met the boss before. Heard stories of the wrath of the boss, the apathy of the boss, the sarcasm of the boss, the magic of the boss, but had never actually come face to face *with* the boss!

He continued to pace the room for what felt like an eternity. A knock at the door made him freeze in his tracks. He was able to whimper, "Come in," in a voice that sounded like an elfling.

The door burst open and a figure stood in the doorway. The glaring light from the hallway and the darkness within his office cast a gloomy shadow around the figure that had materialized – the dark outline of the body coupled with what appeared to be a jumpsuit gave the figure the appearance of super elf height, taller than that of the Tree Elves from the Pole.

The boss.

"What's going on?" the figure said.

Ogden gulped hard, trying to clear the nervous lump that had formed in his throat. "I don't quite know for sure," he began. "The Book stopped turning pages and I saw the black marks. Kids names stamped out. I touched them and…"

"Three? Is that what you said?" The boss's voice filled the room. Ogden thought he heard the panes of glass on the windows rattle gently.

He wiped his sweaty hands down the sides of his pants. "Well… I don't really know. I… I saw the third one and I just called Elven Resources."

The figure's arms shot straight in the air. "Well, go over and touch the darn name, Ogden!"

Ogden winced a little, then made his way over to the Book. He removed the casing and touched the last black name he saw. *Abby Sutton.* He stepped back as the pages immediately began to turn in a violent frenzy. His eyes widened when they stopped as soon as they had started, and four more names burnt out to almost dust.

He could barely breathe. He could barely move.

"Castleberry," the boss called from the door, "talk to me."

Ogden turned from the Book and faced the doorway. "There's four more names," he said slowly. "Miss Skye? I think you need to see this."

Ember stepped out from the shadows of the doorway and into the light of the room. Her counterfeit appearance of height diminished as she glided across the wooden floor. She walked over to Ogden and the Book, and he could see her hands were caked with coal dust. Her eyes nearly went wild when she saw the pages burnt to a crisp, the names of the hardened children barely visible now on the surface.

"Great," she huffed. "Just what I damn need!"

Chapter Two

A N EMERGENCY MEETING OF THE COUNCIL WAS CALLED AT ONCE AND ALL
but one of the figureheads of Norland found themselves assem-
bled in the Meeting Room on the 13th floor of the Headquarters'
main building. From the looks on their faces, Ember could tell that
they were not pleased to be there.

While they waited for the last member, Ember did her best not to
make eye contact with the ten already present. Instead, she transfixed
her eyes on the baby blue sky just beyond the picture windows. Puffs
of white clouds lazily floated by as if they were nonchalantly saying,
"hello! goodbye!" Their dreamy movements mirrored the feeling she
had in the pit of her stomach. Hello. Goodbye. Get on with the show
and back to business.

A nudge on her leg from under the table got her attention. Ogden
furrowed his brow at her, and she realized she had been drumming
her fingers on the table top. The others were staring at her as well.
She curled her fingers up into fists and placed her hands in her lap.
"Sorry," she mumbled.

One of the rules of any type of meeting was to remain quiet until
all members were present. Every seat at the table was specifically
designated for an elf. Each elf sat at a high-back mahogany chair with
regal wood carvings along the sides and back, and at each spot was an
official wooden wedge nameplate that bore the elf's name and title.

The seat assignments never changed. Ember looked down the line,
reading the nameplates to herself to pass the time. The head of the
table was reserved for *Jolevana "Una" M'raz Ruprecht*, Councilwoman
#1. At the other end was none other than *Docena Frost M'raz*, Madame
Claus.

Docena M'raz: Mrs. Claus, the Boss's wife, Lady Frost, the Boss
Lady - many monikers for such a dominating force. Mrs. Claus was
second-in-command to the Boss, she did his bidding, operated in his
place at the Council, and most importantly, took the stress and worries off him (so all he needed to be concerned with was the Big Night
and delivering the goods to all the children of the world). And even

though Ember had been in her presence before, she still got a little star-struck to be in the same room with the legendary counterpart of the legend himself.

However, the missus was not at all the grandmotherly type that Ember had previously expected. The regal Madame Claus wore a pinstripe business suit, elegantly tailored to her svelte body. Yes, Mrs. Claus had silver-gray, almost white hair, pulled into a tight bun. Her round cheeks were rosy with a subtle pink blush, blue eyes carefully accented with black, and her lipstick a dark red, yet she oozed an aura of no-nonsense dominance.

Remembering the strong presence of Councilwoman #1, Ember wondered if there would be a power-play between the two alpha female elves.

Ember looked at her own nameplate at the table. It read *Ember Skye*, Coal Elf.

Of course it does.

She was the outsider at the table. She knew it. Everyone there knew it. She saw it in their sideways glances, hear it in their tones of voice when they spoke to her, sense it in the distance they kept when they stood beside her. The other Council elves were all connected – whether by blood or marriage. She had no ties with any of them. From the reception she usually got, she suspected the mere presence of a Coal Elf at the table made their stomachs turn – a Coal Elf who got special consideration from the Boss and got her Life Job changed, a Coal Elf who was now granted access to some of the innermost workings of their Elven Society. Someone didn't even have the decency to change her nameplate to *Coal Deliverer*, because in their eyes she was, and always would be, nothing more than a Coal Elf.

All of them made her uneasy, but the nameplate in front of the empty seat across the table made her squirm – *Sturd Ruprecht*.

Field Data Collector. His new position. Created especially for him. For some reason, the Council felt that his presence was a valuable one, and they had explained (in not so many words) that even though he had botched the whole "Coal-less Night" scheme, they were determined to keep him around in some capacity. What did *Field Data*

Collector mean, anyway? The shear ambiguity of the title just reeked of trouble. She had little doubt that the familial ties played an underlying role in Sturd's new position.

Speaking of reeking, the air in the room drastically changed when he bustled through the office door, profusely apologizing, shaking hands with his kin. Ember shook her head in disgust as he approached her, a pointy-tooth smile plastered on his face. "Miss Skye," he said cordially as he lifted her hands from her lap, cupped them in one of his, and gently patted them. Ember's skin crawled at his touch. His skin felt like hardened leather and his sharp nails pricked her flesh.

"Mr. Ruprecht," she said in return as she nodded at him, but she could feel the bile gurgling up in her throat.

Sturd took his seat at the table, grinning the entire time.

This was the first time Ember had seen him since the Council had mandated that he take some time off to "soul search" as part of his punishment. *Maybe it did do him some good?* she wondered. He actually looked refreshed. His posture was more refined – he wasn't as hunched over as she had known him to be. His demeanor was certainly different, and his normal body odor of rotted flesh had seemed to disappear. There was something about him that she couldn't quite put her finger on. *Maybe…*

A banging on the table startled her and made her stiffen to attention.

"Now that we're all here," Mrs. Claus said, "let's begin, shall we?" She placed her gavel in front of her as a collective deep breath filled the room. "Now, then," she continued in her business-like tone, "we all are aware of the situation that has occurred with the Book of Names. As of this morning, there have been fifteen consecutive burn-outs."

"Seventeen," Orthor Castleberry interrupted, his hand meekly raised in the air. Mrs. Claus shot him an angry look for interrupting, but her expression soon changed to one of deep concern.

"Seventeen?" she asked.

"Yes, Madame," he replied. "Right before I left for the meeting, two more names blacked." He paused. "I just left. There could be more."

Mrs. Claus ran her hands over the top of her gray hair, just stopping at the center where her bun began. She closed her eyes tightly and shook her head before addressing the Council again. "This is serious," she began.

"Yes, it certainly is," a strong and haunting voice broke through. It was Councilwoman #1, Jolevana M'Raz Ruprecht - wife of Councilman #3, Zelcodor Ruprecht; aunt of Sturd; sister of the Boss himself. *Una* to her closest friends and family members. "Madame, I would hate to think that…"

Mrs. Claus glared at her. "To think what? To think that the Council had anything to do with this? Because certainly anything that has happened after your so-called 'Coal-less Night' couldn't possibly be connected, right? Let's get one thing straight, Madame Councilwoman, the Boss is still upset about the whole debacle of the Coal-less Night, and he is still deciding whether or not…"

"Whether or not *what?*" Una barked. "The Council operated in full accordance with the Codex. We broke no laws. It clearly states in the Eleventh Provision of Regulation Two that…"

"You do not need to school me in the ways of the Codex, *Una,*" Mrs. Claus interrupted.

Una folded her hands in front of her at the table and sat completely erect. In a calm voice she cooed, "Then, please, Madame Claus, your insinuation of idle threats is not appropriate at this table. The Council has done nothing wrong, and if His Highness wishes to pursue any further action, then I suggest you tell him to speak to me… directly."

Una and Mrs. Claus locked eyes as an awkward silence sucked the oxygen out of the room - a deep, pulsating silence interrupted only by Ogden's sporadic knuckle crunching. Una held Mrs. Claus's strong gaze in a weird kind of standoff with neither one backing down. Ember wondered if one of them was going to lurch across the table and strangle the other.

Sturd obnoxiously cleared his throat while Mrs. Claus's assistant, Senara Calix, put a gentle hand on her mistress's shoulder, trying to coax her out of her death stare.

"We need order and balance," Councilwoman #2 spoke out. Her quavering voice was barely audible. "Order and balance, or else everything ceases to exist, turns to dust." Her eyes dropped down, and Ember remembered that Cerissa Lux, Councilwoman #2, was the weak one of the bunch - the emotional one, the one who cried real tears for the victims of the Coal-less Night. Ember's heart ached for the pitiful tone in Cerissa's voice. The children of the world had not been punished with coal that year, and it left the elven world in a wicked state of peril. Over-grown Nessie fruits touched the ground. Sickness and death blanketed the entire North Pole. No elf was left unfazed, and Ember surmised that Cerissa must have experienced the devastating loss of a loved one that winter.

Una adjusted the purple cords around her black robe. "Yes, Ms. Lux," she said coldly, still staring at Mrs. Claus, "that is really what this is all about, isn't it?" Her eyebrows raised in what appeared to be a silent challenge to the Boss's wife before she looked over at her female counterpart on the Council.

Ogden couldn't stop fidgeting, and it irritated Ember something awful. She punched his leg under the table and scolded, "Quit it!" from the side of her mouth. Startled by the disturbance from her side of the table, Sturd's red eyes immediately focused on her.

Mrs. Claus scanned the group and folded her hands in front of her on the table. She sat up straight, and took a deep breath as if to collect her thoughts. "We all know that blackened names are not good for business," she said calmly, matter-of-factly, and Ember admired her controlled manner in the face of yet another potentially disastrous event. "The total and complete absence of the spirit from the heart of any human should not be taken lightly. Our arrangement with the human world -- good, bad, naughty, nice – is predicated on the *belief*. If not in the Claus, then in the spirit of the Day in general. The hope that it brings. The light that it shines in man's heart to motivate him to greatness. The spirit has existed far longer than our Elven race, longer than the humans, since before the division of time. Now we can sit here and debate Nessie fruit and power balance 'til the snowmen come home, but without spirit…" She rubbed her face just underneath her eyes. "Ms. Lux is right. There won't be anything left to even debate."

Harold Pennybaker, who had sat in silence the entire time, began flipping through a notepad in front of him. "Castleberry, on average, how many black names a year?" he asked.

"Two," the brothers responded in unison.

"Two," Mrs. Claus stressed. "Council members, what say you to the recent wave of black names? Any thoughts? Any ideas for a solution?"

Thoughts lead to ideas. Ideas lead to plans. Plans lead to Lists getting ripped up and elves getting sick and loved ones getting hurt and worse... Ember wanted to scream, "No! No plans! No solutions!" They needed to figure out what it meant.

Zelcodor, Councilman #3, reached under his chair and produced a green binder. He slid it down the row of elves at the table until it reached Sturd. "Why, yes, Madame, we in fact have some interesting thoughts on the situation. My nephew, our newly appointed Field Data Collector, has been working on something that might help. For the last six months, he has been observing certain trends and habits in the human world, making notations – collecting data so to speak. With your permission, I would like Sturd to present his findings to the Council."

Mrs. Claus signaled for Sturd to proceed. Sturd opened the binder and rose from his chair. Smiling, he scanned the faces of the elves at the table as if waiting to receive applause or some form of recognition. He hesitated for a moment, and after realizing no such response was coming, he passed everyone a spreadsheet. "Timing," he began. "It's all about timing."

Ember's heart beat faster at the sound of his voice, and a sick feeling invaded her stomach. Having been privy to many of Sturd's over-the-top orations, she had a feeling this was going to be a real winner. She picked up the paper and stared at the color coded chart. It was divided by months, but separated into two columns – one column outlining the elven world, one column outlining the human world.

Sturd held up his paper, his gnarled forefinger pointing crookedly at one of the line graphs. "You see, this line here indicates the discrepancies in our time placement. The humans don't really start to take the Big Day seriously until mid-November, but by then it's too late for some of them. Our Lists are finalized by the last Quarterly Meeting in late August. That's a three- month gap between the final List and human interest. Who knows? A child can do much in three months. Go bad. Go good. Get better. *Get worse.*" His emphasis on the word 'worse' made Ember look up from her paper, instantly suspicious.

As Sturd continued to speak, the other elves were nodding their heads in agreement. Much of what he said was true, but Ember couldn't seem to make a connection between the black names and the gap.

"So," he continued, "I suggest we coordinate a larger, more aggressive seasonal campaign."

Ember cocked her head to the side, puzzled, as Mrs. Claus eyed the Council members slowly. She looked directly at Sturd. "Proposal?" She didn't look impressed, but her expression indicated that she would entertain just about any idea at this point.

"I envision it as Christmas in July!" he exclaimed with his mouth wide open. His pointed teeth flashed under the fluorescent light, giving them dark, elongated shadows; they looked like fangs on a nightmarish monster.

The Council members all smiled, but Mrs. Claus was not completely sold on the idea. "Again, I ask – proposal? How do you think this will be effective?"

Sturd closed his eyes for a second and inhaled. He was obviously annoyed that his plan was not immediately well-received.

"Well, Madame, by starting Christmas in July, we could plant the seeds of the Big Day much, much earlier. Children will be more aware, cognizant. The August deadline wouldn't seem so unfair then. We could help organize fairs, bazaars, dedicated mall outlets, advertising, all the bells and whistles humans thrive on. Let's set up the new reindeer, Zyklon, to be the breakout star of the season. There's so much we can do! The human perception of the Big Day needs a serious shake-up. They're tired of the same old, same old. If we don't try to implement something, the situation could have dire consequences."

Dire.

Ember's stomach dropped as bad memories quickly resurfaced. The last time Sturd had uttered that word, he announced a plan that had doomed many, many elves. It didn't feel right to her then, and it didn't feel right to her now.

Mrs. Claus looked back at the paper, back at Sturd, then to the Council members. "What says the Council? Your Honor?" she said to Una in a formal tone.

Una placed her hands on the table and smiled, "We, the Council, agree."

"Very well," Mrs. Claus acknowledged. "Mr. Pennybaker? Mr. Castleberry? Any objections?"

"Nay," the three answered at once. "Miss Skye?"

Ember's heart thumped rapidly in her chest like a newborn Graespur. Was this really happening again? Arbitrary plans not thought through, and implemented wantonly? Were they really going to go down an unplanned road that could quite possibly lead to *dire consequences*? Again? She knew that if she didn't say anything now, she would never get the chance again. It amazed her that no one else in the room had voiced this opinion. Clearly, this was a stupid plan! Why was she the only one who thought so?

"Yes," Ember blurted, and the faces on the elves at the table froze like stone. Sturd's lip curled up in a violent sneer, as if he were a rabid dog ready to attack. "This is bogus! It's a bogus plan!"

Mrs. Claus's eyes went wide with anger. "Young lady! How dare you..."

"I'm sorry," she said. "I'm sorry, Madame, it just doesn't *feel* right. I don't see how starting the season earlier is going to stop the names from blacking out. It's... well... kinda silly, don't you think?"

Mrs. Claus's eyes narrowed at the thought, and Ember thought she might actually have gotten through to her. "Mr. Ruprecht?" she asked. "Miss Skye does bring up a valid point. Would you care to address it?"

Zelcodor and Una exchanged fierce glances. Sturd cleared his throat as he calmly took his seat. "Well, Madame," he began, "as I said..."

"I know what you said, Mr. Ruprecht. Can you please present the cadre with your analysis on how this is going to help our current situation?"

Sturd licked his lips and breathed deeply. "But of course. The humans are distracted. They are all about the 'now.' Their scattered minds are no longer capable of holding on to long-term thoughts or goals. An entire year between Big Nights is becoming more and more of a challenge for them to keep in their hearts. By exposing them at an earlier time, it's more like a reminder for them, and will ultimately make it easier for them to keep the Spirit alive in their hearts. I've spent some time studying them, my friends, and I've seen the way they have *changed*."

Ember's face twisted in disbelief. She balled her fists and slammed them on the table. "No way!" she yelled in an uncontrollable outburst.

All eyes were on Ember. Una's head snapped sharply in her direction. "Do *you* have a plan? I don't see you presenting the Council with a solution."

Sweat dampened Ember's clenched hands. "Yes... I mean, no ma'am," she stammered, "I mean... it's just that... the last time the Council instituted some sort of *plan*, if I remember correctly, nearly half of our Elven population either got sick or died, and..."

Una's eyes went wild. "Hold your tongue, young one!"

Mrs. Claus extended her arm across the table to silence the Councilwoman. "Ember, I assure you, the Council does not dole out commands willy-nilly," she said in a stern voice. "And while we may not all agree on certain decisions made-" she paused, and gave a brief, sideways glance in Una's direction- "we are all held accountable under the strict guidelines of our Codex."

"All the more reason..." Ember began.

Mrs. Claus pointed her finger at Ember and continued, "And just because *you've* been promoted in your Life Job does not mean that you have the right or privilege to speak to anyone at this table with disrespect. Do I make myself clear, Miss Skye?"

Ember shrunk back in her seat, trying to hide from the staring eyes of the others at the table. "Yes, Madame. Perfectly clear."

"On that note, if there are no other suggestions at the table, it is settled. We will get the elves in order for a summer launch. Sturd, I want you to present to the Council a full-scale tactical report. We need to start informing the others as soon as possible."

He stood up from his chair. "Yes, Madame."

She waved her hand in the air, dismissing him. Sturd left the office, followed by Harold and Orthor and Ogden.

"Wait for me by my sleigh," Mrs. Claus said to her assistant, Senara, and she and Council members #2-5 exited as well. Left in the room was Ember, Una, and Mrs. Claus. Ember remained seated at the table, waiting for everyone to leave so she could be the last.

Una walked over to the opposite head of the table and waited for Mrs. Claus to stand up. "Oh, Docena, now you know what I was talking about. I presume that this is just the nature of the young one. Lots of growing up to do."

Mrs. Claus pushed in her chair and she and Una walked out of the office. Ember remained alone in the room staring at her nameplate on the mahogany table.

Chapter Three

EMBER WOKE UP WITH A FRIGHTENED GASP. THE DISORIENTING TERROR from yet another nightmare left her body shaking, and after a few moments she was able to come out of it like she usually did. She took notice of everything in her room just to be sure she was, in fact, awake. She was in her den, in her room. The velvet covers of her bed were thrown to the floor.

Another dream. Another nightmare. But it was always the same – a swarm of malicious pixies attack her during Banter's funeral.

The funeral for Banter and the other elves who had not survived the Sickness had been months ago, but the memories of that day were still fresh, like slowly healing wounds needing re-bandaging every once in a while. And while the dreams always turned bizarre and fractured, the memory of that day was as clear as a gemstone in Crystal Cave...

Through her watery eyes, Ember remembered watching the slow and steady movement of the wooden canoes drift on the Ignis River.

All were ablaze; the bodies of the fallen Coal Elves were covered in white garments, strapped to the stern seats, set on fire and pushed out onto the river in one of the oldest traditions in the Mines – the Funeral Procession. But this time was different. This time there were many bodies of the fallen, brothers of the Mines who were taken much too soon by way of the Coal-less Night. Consequence of the poisoned Nessie fruit. Sickness that had no cure. Death that had no rhyme or reason. So many brothers. So many fallen. So much smoke and dust and stench that made the onlookers struggle to see, struggle to breathe. For the ones who survived the carnage, this was the final reminder of the damage that had befallen them all. While those standing still had their lives, none of them had escaped the horror unscathed.

Tannen came up from behind and wrapped his arms around Ember's shoulders. He nuzzled his face gently in the crook of her neck as she reached one arm up and tousled his head of ashy blond hair a few times to acknowledge his presence. He gave her cheek a quick peck of a kiss before he lifted his face and rested his chin on the top of her head. Ember hated having to keep their newly formed relationship a secret, but at that moment, she didn't mind his open display of affection – it was what friends did for each other in times of comfort and need, and she didn't think the other elves would think otherwise. The majority of elves were mourning a loved one, a friend, a colleague, or all three.

The whirlwind of their relationship had come suddenly and unexpectedly. After her debut as official Coal Deliverer on the Big Night, she had returned to the Mines to begin preparations for the upcoming year. On her very first Catta-car ride back to her den, the sparks between them were no longer undeniable. There was no explanation for it. Despite telling herself that she would "keep him at arms-length --Catta-car rides only-" as she had for so many months, when their eyes met and Tannen got out of the trolley car to greet her with a warm hug, she just *knew*. And she knew that *he* knew.

From that moment on, the young couple had to keep their budding romance a secret, for it was forbidden for Coal Elves to connect and become involved on their own. In the Mines, elves were assigned their partners. That's just the way it always was in the Underground. Girls who lived and trained in the West Valley of the Mines were then assigned to be the elfwives of the miners. For whatever reason, Tannen had been deemed "ineligible" for a wife since he was sixteen elfyears old. Now, at twenty-two, it didn't seem likely that he would ever get one. And of course, Ember was not going to be assigned a male counterpart any time soon. They didn't train boys to be elfhusbands in West Valley. Ember and Tannen could have easily justified spending time together ("we're just friends"), but if they had been caught holding hands, or even, Claus forbid, stealing a kiss, their punishment could have been severe. The two were cautious with their public displays, but the sadness of the Funeral Procession struck her so deeply that Ember welcomed the affection from Tannen.

Tannen Trayth. Descendant of the Tree Elves, Tannen.
Blond-hair-green-eyes-love-the-way-you-hold-me-Tannen.
I-think-I'm-falling-completely-head-over-boots-for-you-Tannen...

The only elves who had been aware of her relationship were her best friends, Barkuss and the Reindeer Trainer, Kyla. Barkuss, who now stood next to her in a long line of his other brothers, tapped her arm. Ember looked at him and was met with his puffy, pleading eyes, half irritated by the smoke, half wrought with sadness. She wriggled her fingers below her waist, prompting him to grab her hand. Banter's blazing canoe would be approaching soon, and she was unsure how both she and Barkuss would react. Barkuss nodded as he interlocked his fingers in hers. Tannen gave her another quick squeeze, and she smiled to herself. No one said a word. The only sounds Ember could discern bouncing off the cave walls were the snivels of tears, the sporadic coughs, the crackling of the fiery canoes as they drifted by, and the chattering of Elvish.

Chattering of Elvish?

Like whispers, the words drifted to her ears with a circular motion. It was an almost natural, instinctual feeling, and she was quite sure no one else heard the words. They came to her deep and low, like they were resonating in her heart and mind, not her ears. She let go of Barkuss's hand, wriggled from Tannen's embrace, and began walking among the row of elves who were lined up on the bank of the Ignis mourning their kin. She was searching for the source of the conversation, hunting for its speakers, curious as to who in the Mines were even able to say the words of the ancient tongue.

"Do you think she's pretty?" a voice said in Elvish.

"Kinda. Do you?" another replied.

As she moved about the crowd, the voices became clearer and more distinct. "I just want to go home," one said.

"I know! I'm so hungry!" the other whined.

As she approached a rock alcove, the sounds were so loud, she thought the entire elf population would hear them. She peered into the semi-open crawlspace only to see two elflings huddled together in a corner. It was Juju and Bambam, Barkuss's twin nephews, his brother Bommer's little boys. They were precocious little things of eight elfyears old, always getting into some sort of mischief appropriate for boy elves their age. If anything, they resembled their Uncle Barkuss, with heads of red curly corkscrews, and chubby cheeks and hands. They still had their excess elfling fat, and coupled with their minimally ash-filled hair, they were identical little hellions.

"Boys! What are you doing here?" she scolded. "And why are you being so loud?"

The two boys looked up from their inner circle, eyes widened in a guilty expression. "We weren't being loud, Miss Ember," one of them said.

"Are you serious? I could hear you all the way over by the bank! Now come on!" She outstretched her hand to lead them out of the alcove. "Your father is probably freaking out that you're not with the family right now."

The boys gave each other a puzzled look and stood up. "I swear, Miss Ember, we weren't even talking," the other said.

"Just *shush*," she said as they walked in front of her. "You need to be with your father and uncles. This is important to them. You don't want to disrespect your family now, do you?"

They hung their heads low as Ember ushered them into the crowd of elves. "No ma'am," they sang in unison.

"Why is she so mean?"

"Yea, we weren't doin' nothing!"

Their voices again. In the pit of her soul. Loud, clear, distinct, familiar. Words of the ancients. *Elvish.*

"Wait a minute…" she started to say, but Bommer spotted her and the children and came rushing over.

His face was twisted, like how Banter used to look. He bent down low, pointing a finger from each of his hands into each of the boys' chests. "Bambam! Juju! Where in Claus's name have you been?" he reprimanded, trying to keep his voice to a low hush. "Your mother is worried sick, and your uncle's canoe is on its way!"

"Sorry, Poppa."

"Yea, sorry, Poppa."

Bommer placed a hand on Ember's shoulder. "How did you know where they were?"

She shrugged. "I don't know. I heard someone messing around behind the rock wall, so I thought I'd take a look. That's where they were."

Bommer snorted. "Yea, these two are natural hiders. He placed his hands on the top of their heads and roughed up their curly hair. "Now, go back to your Momma," he calmly instructed, and the boys dashed off to the bank's edge. Ember made her way back to her place next to Barkuss and Tannen.

Barkuss looked at her and mouthed, "Everything okay?" She nodded and grabbed his hand again.

Banter's canoe came into view, the flames dancing high, nearly touching the roof of the cave. Barkuss tightened his grip on Ember's hand and gasped a few times, trying to stifle the waves of sobs from his chest. Ember looked down the row of elves – Bommer wrapped his arm around his elfwife, Jacinda, as the twins clutched her housedress. Balrion and Bulder both had their heads in their hands, their shoulders rising and falling with each breath and muffled cry. Ember couldn't stop her own sadness from washing over her as tears were unleashed down her face.

"Goodbye, brother," Barkuss whispered as the canoe floated by.

Ember sat up in her bed, not wanting to remember the rest, but wanting to record yet another twisted pixie dream. She reached down on the side of the bed, picked up her covers, and threw them over her crossed legs. She was about to fetch her journal from her nightstand when she heard rhythmic pounding on her front door like a child's secret knock. It could only be one elf -- *Barkuss*, she thought, as she exhaled.

"I'm awake!" she yelled from her bedroom. "Come on in!"

She heard the front door open and close; the hum of the Graespurs' return for the morning got louder, then faded away. Barkuss was mumbling something to himself. As he got closer to her bedroom, she could make out what he was saying: "Leaving the front door opened?

Why, I should skin her alive! Never know what might come busting on in and... well, good morning!" he gushed as he entered her room. She stretched her arms over her head and yawned. "Ahh-nning." He handed her a stack of envelopes.

"Got your mail for you."

"Thanks," she said, placing the pile in her lap.

Barkuss plopped down onto the edge of her bed and grabbed at her feet from over the covers. He shook her legs back and forth and smiled a big toothy smile, his nose scrunched up, his eyes squinted shut. "Soooo," he sang excitedly.

"Soooo... what?"

"Big day today, E!"

Ember stuck her tongue out at him, grabbed at the covers, and threw them over her head. "No," she moaned. "*Not* a big day."

Barkuss laughed and pulled the blanket off her. Her hair had fallen forward and was a tangled mess in front of her face. She tried to blow a breath upward to create an open path for her eyes, but her hair kept falling in the same place. Finally, she gave up and pushed it back with her hand.

"Yes, a big day," he corrected. "Birthdays are always a big deal."

Ember shook her head. March 14th had not been a special day for her since she was an elfling. In fact, she hadn't even thought of her birthday since she was sent to the Mines. March 14th had become the anniversary of her slavery rather than a day to celebrate her birth. "Not for me. Not for nine years. Why would this one be any different?"

Barkuss furrowed his brow. "You really are clueless, aren't you? This is your *eighteenth* elfbirthday, E. It's kinda a big thing."

"Why? Do I like, get the right to vote or something?"

"Ha ha," he mocked dryly. "Super funny, E. Be serious. This one has a special meaning for you."

"Pray tell. I'm all pointed ears."

Barkuss crossed his arms over his chest and huffed. "Girl, I swear you are go'ne be the death of me! You got the world at your feet now, child. This is like a day of liberation for you! Re-birth. Your

first birthday in nine years without no more nasty heaving and ho-
ing. Your first birthday in a long while where you're *not* a Coal Elf!
It's your dream come true, so let's celebrate it! You're top dog, now.
Alpha graespur. Head…"

"Let's not get carried away, Barkuss." She rested her head against
the headboard. "Besides, you weren't at my last meeting. I certainly
wasn't top-anything then."

He waved his hand in front of his face and wriggled his nose. "Oh,
please," he breathed. "So Boss Lady slapped you in your place? Big
deal. You know your mouth can get you in trouble sometimes! So
what if they cut you down to size up there? Down here, you're still
our number one gal!"

"I don't know. All I know is that with the names disappearing from
the Book, everyone is completely on edge up there. And they come
up with these Claus-awful plans and schemes, and Sturd's involved
and heading up some wacky initiative, and…"

"Pish-posh! Let them deal with it. That's their job, right? You know
they're not gonna make any more mistakes like that Coal-less Night
debacle."

Ember gave a small smile. It was just like Barkuss to sweep an issue
under the carpet. He had helped her once with reconstructing the
Naughty List, and maybe he didn't want to get involved with Council
affairs again? Who knew? Christmas in July still sat unsettled in the
pit of her stomach. Her mind tried to get its wheels in motion, tried
to get a plan formulated so she could have something solid and con-
crete to present to the Council (instead of outbursts and fist-falls on
the table). Something was telling her she needed to thwart Sturd's
silly plan, and soon.

Barkuss smiled back and reached over to lovingly rub her hair.
"Look at this! Look at this! All this pretty blonde color coming
through!" he gushed. "Jeez, you've been going up Above so often,
soon you won't see any darkness on this lovely head. You should let
me give you a tail- braid for when…"

He stopped mid-thought, his face twisted to the side, and his
tongue extended in an "ick" face.

"What?" Ember asked, startled. "What is it? What's the matter?"

"Oooo..." he began. "Maybe one year older isn't such a good thing!"

"Huh? What are you..."

Barkuss ran his fingers through her hair and grabbed at a long fine strand. He tugged with some force and presented the hair in front of her face. "This!" he exclaimed, the single gray hair swaying in his excited breath.

She swatted at it. "A gray hair. Whoop-de-doo."

"It ain't just a gray hair, E. You know how fast those suckers can multiply? Maybe we need you to see the Stylist Elves or something..."

"I don't need a stylist, Barkuss. I'll be fine." She closed her eyes and leaned back on the headboard again. "Gray hairs and all."

Barkuss chuckled. "So, you gonna go through this stack of mail, or what?"

She cocked one eye open and smiled. "You do it. I'm still stressing over my one gray hair."

He reached for the envelopes in her lap as he mumbled, "Death. Of. Me."

Ember laughed.

Barkuss began flipping through the letters. "Junk. Junk. Junk. Do you want a 10% discount at the Candle store?"

"No." She paused. "Hey, Barkuss?"

"Junk. Junk. Uh-huh?"

"Do your nephews speak Elvish?"

"Huh? What?"

"The twins. Bommer's boys. Do they know how to speak Elvish?"

He continued leafing through the letters, not completely paying attention to her. "Uh. No. Not that I know of... hey! What's this Brotherhood thing about?"

"What Brotherhood thing?"

"I don't know. This." He held up a wrinkled flyer. "There's no envelope. Just this flyer stuck in with the other letters. Says there's a Brotherhood meeting in Sandstone Shelf next Friday."

"I guess it's junk. Besides, I'm not a brother, am I?"

Barkuss snickered. "When you're right, you're right. Junk. Junk..."
He paused, his silence causing Ember to lift her head and open her
eyes.

"What?" she asked.

His voice grew soft. "It's a letter from West Valley." He held up the
scalloped envelope in front of his face.

Barkuss extended his hand to pass her the letter.

She waved her hands at him. "No. You open it. You read it." She
curled her knees to her chest and placed her chin on the top of them.
"I got one the last two years: 'Dear Ember Skye, we regret to inform
you that we have deemed you ineligible to be an elfwife. Thank you
so much for your service to our community. Sincerely, Head Mistress
Shella. "

"You sure?"

Ember gave a quick nod then closed her eyes again. "I'm sure. It's
their yearly birthday card to me. Aren't I special?"

"Okay, then..." he said as he tore open the envelope and took out
the cardstock notice that was within. "'Dear Ember Skye,'" he began
to read.

"We regret to inform you that..." Ember chimed.

"'It is with great pleasure that we, the Council and the Magistrates
of West Valley, announce to you on the birth of your eighteenth
elfday, that you have been selected and approved, under the Fifth
Provision of Regulation Five, to be united in elf-marriage at a soon to
be determined date.'"

Barkuss stopped reading.

Ember froze. "Let me see that!" She lurched forward, grabbing at
the letter in his hand.

Barkuss pulled away. "No, Ember," he barked forcefully.

She narrowed her eyes at his foreboding tone. "Why not? It's my
letter. I want to know what it says!"

He tucked the letter under his bottom. "No, no, no," he said, trying
to make light of it. "Let's just forget about it for now, enjoy the day,
deal with this later..."

"Barkuss," she said, lowering her voice, "I swear to Claus that if you don't get your bum off that letter and read the rest to me, there will be another funeral on the Ignis real soon."

He sighed and brought the letter out from under his rear. With lightning speed, she snatched it from his grip and feverishly scanned the document. Barkuss remained silent as she mumbled all the words of the letter, and gasped when she got to the word *Sturd*.

Chapter Four

T HERE WAS A SHARP RINGING IN EMBER'S EARS, AS IF THE WORLD WAS
being tuned out and her brain concentrated solely on the blood
rushing throughout the arteries in her body. She felt dizzy and weak.
Barkuss was in front of her, waving his hands back and forth in her
face to get her attention, but it was no use. All she felt was numb.
Blurred. The word 'Sturd' hung heavy in the air, and a sudden bom-
bardment of images flashed in her mind.

Marriage? To Sturd? This had to be some crazy mistake. This had
to be part of her bad dream. *You can wake up anytime you like, Ember!*
She pictured herself standing at her kitchen stove preparing meals,
like all elfwives did, while Sturd was sitting at the table looking over
his work documents for the day. A gaggle of pointy-toothed elflings
chase each other throughout the den, screeching and wailing their
un-elflike cries.

She shuddered and felt an urgent sense to run, to flee, to escape...

Ember's eyes were coming back into focus, and her mind was formulating fractured, real- time thoughts.

Run. Flee. Escape. Defect.

The words replayed over and over instinctively in her mind.

Go. Now. Run. Hide. Defect.

Again and again. Over and over. Barkuss was still speaking to her,
but his voice was just muffled sounds mixing with the sound of her
heart beating from inside her ears and the voice inside her head telling her to

Run.

Defect. Go.

Go. Now!

As much as the words, the feelings, were screaming at her to move,
to act, to get up and leave, she was frozen still. Dazed. Still trying to
make sense of the letter with the reality. *Sturd?* She thought of the
poor elf from West Valley about a year ago. *"Pepper Brightly, her name
was Pepper Brightly."* The young girl couldn't have been more than
fourteen elfyears old when she was assigned to be Sturd's elfwife.

She couldn't bear the thought of spending the rest of her elflife with him, so the poor girl felt like she had no other choice but to run away. Run. Flee. Defect. But Defectors were usually caught, and it was no different for Pepper. And so the story went that at the end of her poor tragic life, Pepper was ultimately united with Sturd in the most visceral way. The words had become legend — a pitiful Defector elf turned into a tasty dish for Sturd's Sunday meal. Now Ember knew exactly how Pepper felt – that she would rather be food for the monster than be his mate.

Barkuss stood over her shaking her shoulders. "E! E!" He was yelling at her now, trying to break her from her trance.

"I have to go," she said calmly.

"Huh? What are you talking about?"

She stood up from the bed and pushed past him. "I have to leave, Barkuss. I have to run. Defect."

"No, no, no, no!" He grabbed her arm and turned her around so they were face to face. "You listen to me right now! There's nowhere for you to go but to West Valley. You hear me?" She started to turn away from him, but he cupped her chin in his hand and jerked her head forward again. "Do you hear me? You're gonna go to West Valley and straighten this whole mess out. There's gotta be some mistake. Ain't no way they gonna match you up with that one!"

"But... but..."

"Snap out of it, girl! You know me and your man got your back on this!"

My man? My boyfriend? Tannen... how am I ever going to...?

A wave of panic crashed over her. Her breaths became labored pants as the fear seeped into every inch of her body, making her hands shake and her toes tingle.

Barkuss took her hand and led her back to the bed. "Okay, okay." He patted her back in an effort to calm her down. "It's okay. It's gonna be okay. We'll figure this out." His touch was comforting, and soon Ember was able to take deep, lung-filling breaths. "There, there. We'll see this through. I'm telling you it's going to be okay."

"Okay," she exhaled. Her head was becoming clearer. Her thoughts were becoming less hazy and horror-stricken. Little by little, her heart slowed its pace and she regained control over her body. There was still the initial shock and confusion, but she managed to breathe in a form of composure. "Okay."

"You good now?"

She stood up again. "Good. For now. I think."

"Good. Do you need anything? Want some water? Something to eat?"

"No. No. I'm fine. I think I just need to get out of here. Need to clear my head. Get fresh air. Need to figure out what to do."

Barkuss's shoulders dropped and he sighed. "What do you need me to do, E? Say the word."

"I'm going to go Aboveground. If you see Tannen, tell him I needed to visit with Kyla, but please don't mention any of this."

Barkuss tipped his head forward. "Done, girl. Just don't do anything stupid like run away or anything."

"No worries. I would ask you to come along, but..."

Barkuss raised his eyebrows. "Girl! You know better than to ask me that! Sheesh!"

"I know. Just thought I'd be polite."

"Puh-leeze! 'Polite' my plump rear-end! You go do what you need to do. Tell Kyla I said 'hi'."

Chapter Five

BREATHING IN THE FRESH AIR WAS A GOOD START. THERE WAS A CRISPNESS in the mid-day air, as if the last remnants of the gray sky from the hard winter were trying ever so desperately to hang on. Soon it would be melted away by the spring sun, leaving flower sprouts and plant buds in its slushy wake. Ember's heart tore every time she visited Aboveground. Even though she had made the choice to remain in the Mines, there was something about the open frosty breeze that reminded her of her old life when she lived in Tir-La Treals – before the Mines, before the Sickness, before the devastation. And even though she was reconciled to calling the Mines her Home, there was always a gnawing sensation that she didn't actually have a Home. Not here, not there, not anywhere... *yet.*

The city of East Bank had been rebuilding quite nicely since the Sickness had caused so much death and destruction. It was a slow and steady process, but those who had survived were dedicated to bringing back the city to its former prominence and glory. Ultimately, each elf knew that his or her life depended on the balance of the worlds – both human and elven – and knowing that made the commitment to the reconstruction project more meaningful.

The Plumm Reindeer Stable had been one of the first reconstruction efforts. The community felt that since the Boss's newest reindeer, Zyklon, had been born and raised there that it was a worthy enough landmark to fix up first. And since Ember had helped Kyla get her training duties reinstated in a timely fashion, getting back to business was a priority.

The Stable was prettier than Ember remembered. The house and barn were repainted, the landscape freshly manicured with giant reindeer topiaries. Brand new iron gates to the grounds shone with a dark black lacquer highlighted with golden specks. Kyla was in the side field with a wooden corral fence, training with some of the new fawns. She looked up when she heard the gate clash shut. "Ember!" she exclaimed.

Ember smiled and ran to Kyla with outstretched arms. "It's so good to see you!"

"What a nice surprise! C'mon, let's go inside. I have some chocolate chip cookies in the oven with your name on them." Ember crinkled her nose. Kyla was a talented reindeer trainer, but her cooking skills left much to be desired. Kyla rolled her eyes. "I bought the dough pre- made from the shop."

"Hey! I didn't say anything!"

"You didn't have to."

Both girls laughed and they made their way into the kitchen. The Plumm house had been entirely remodeled and a fresh, new scent hung heavy in the air, but Kyla's almost haggard appearance – straggly blonde hair, heavy bags under her opal eyes – made her seem out of place in this house of newness. She looked older. Worn. Lucky enough to survive the Sickness, the after effects had surely taken their toll. Ember felt sorry for her in a way. Kyla's entire family had been over-come with sickness – her mother, father, and twin sister all victims of the poisoned Nessie fruit, and now here she was in a big house with nice things, and no one to share them with.

"Ya know, I really wish the Council would lay off me once and for all," Kyla said as she put out a set of fine china plates and cocoa mugs.

"What do you mean?" Ember asked.

"They won't leave me alone. They keep sending elves here as part of their Inquiry."

"I don't understand. You've been cleared to train reindeer again, why are they still bothering you?"

"Bothering? More like borderline harassment! They say they still need information on my family history. Guess it's taking them longer, considering my family is all gone." Kyla got a faraway look in her eyes and paused for a moment.

Ember ran her fingers through her hair as if trying to shake a thought to the front of her brain. "Is it because you speak Elvish?"

Kyla shrugged her shoulders.

"How is it that you can do that, anyway?"

Kyla lowered her eyes and shrugged again. "Me and Tyla always could. For as long as I can remember. And it wasn't like anyone taught us or anything. Ya know, how I was able to teach you? We just *could*. Maybe it's a twin thing or something."

Ember nodded her head. Elvish had come so easy for her, too. It was puzzling, because she didn't have a twin to practice with, like Kyla did. Kyla had just taught her some basic commands and phrases and the language just kind of opened itself up to her on its own. Like, it had always been inside her, lying dormant, waiting to be awoken.

"Even still," Ember began, "the Council has no right to come sniffing around here after all they've done! After all they've put you through and..." Heat from within rose up into her chest as if she was on fire. The thought of her dearest friend being bullied set off a spark that made her want to rage.

Kyla placed her hand on Ember's shoulder and gave her a soft smile. "So, tell me, Coal Girl, to what do I owe this pleasure?"

Ember breathed in deeply, relaxing all the muscles in her body. She hesitantly reached into her pocket. She handed the envelope from West Valley to Kyla. "This. It came today."

It was more than Ember could bear. Her muscles tensed again, and try as she might, she couldn't stop the tears from flowing. Between sobs and sniffles, she unloaded onto Kyla everything that had happened that day.

"Okay, okay," Kyla coaxed, handing Ember the envelope back, "not a very nice way to start your birthday, now, is it?" she said, trying to lighten the mood.

Ember composed herself and chuckled through her tears. "I don't think I can do it, Ky. I can't spend the rest of my life with Sturd. Barkuss seems to think it's a mistake, but I don't know what to think. He says I should go to West Valley and find out for sure. Maybe I'll just move back into Skye Manor. Now that my family is gone, it pretty much is my property, and it is abandoned and all..."

Abandoned. Nothing there. It actually didn't sound like a bad idea. There was a perfect place in the mansion where no one would ever find her. Long ago, she had accidentally stumbled across a secret room underneath the house that no one else knew about. Her father had used it to do his work, and only her mother and Nanny Carole had known about it. If she ran away to Skye Manor, she could hole up down there and develop a plan to get out of this. Or she could fade away into oblivion and live out the rest of her miserable life...

"Now you're talking silly talk. You're not running away to your old house. Maybe Barkuss is right. Maybe it was a mistake. Maybe they messed up. It wouldn't hurt to find out. I agree whole-heartedly with Barkuss. You should go and speak to the Head Mistress in West Valley. Find out what's going on. Voice your concerns. Tell them how you feel."

Kyla was right – running was not an option for Ember. Not now, and really, not ever. Ember rubbed her temples. "It's not the Head Mistress I'm worried about speaking my mind to. How the hell am I gonna tell Tannen?" She put her head in her hands for a few moments, then sat up.

Kyla cocked her head to the side. "Kinda odd timing, don't you think?"

"How so? What do you mean?"

"Did it ever cross your mind that the Council might have big plans for you... for both you and Sturd, actually."

Ember raised her eyebrows with curiosity. "Continue," she said in a stern voice.

"Well," Kyla began, "just hear me out. If you and Sturd are both recognized elves in the Council's extended group, maybe by marrying the two of you, they're setting you both up for future Council positions."

Ember did all she could to stifle a chuckle. "If you were at the last meeting, I don't think you would be saying that! Or maybe they're plotting one of our deaths because Claus-knows if the two of us are stuck together, I'll end up killing him, or he'll end up killing me."

"Seriously, Ember. Hear me out. You've lived with Sturd before. You apprenticed under his father and lived in a room in his home. You were practically suitemates! Who knows Sturd better than you?

Or rather, who could stomach living with Sturd, if not you?"

"I was an elfling back then. This is different!"

Kyla sighed and pulled her hair back into a make-shift bun. "So just don't live with him. Do the ceremony formality stuff, and then go your separate ways. If anyone asks, come up with a different excuse. Blame it on work. Blame it on the stress of your new position. Blame it on the Graespurs keeping you up at night! I don't know! Anything."

This definitely was an interesting point of view. Ember slowly nodded her head in time with Kyla's words. "In name only," she whispered. "That actually might be workable, but it still doesn't eliminate the real problem at hand — I'd still be his elfwife!"

Kyla clucked her tongue on the roof of her mouth. "The door is wide open for you to still be with Tannen. You two sneak around so much as it is, what would change, right?"

"Just my name."

"Exactly."

Ember rubbed her chin. "Then I could investigate, ya know? Figure out a way to get out of it or something. Maybe expose a loophole. Maybe march to the gates of The Boss's Manor and demand he revoke the decree."

"Now you're talking!" Kyla encouraged with a smile.

"Ya know, Kyla, my entire life has been determined by the written word. Everything that has happened to me has been outlined in a letter of sorts. My Life Job, when I got my Pass to come Aboveground, where I was assigned to work in the Mines. Now this. Everything is a decree, a note, a document, a regulation, or a provision of some regulation. How did that happen?"

"I guess the Boss has got it all figured out, right?"

"I guess," Ember replied, but she wasn't quite convinced. "I want to see Asche before I go," she said as she stood up from the table.

Kyla clapped her hands together in excitement. "Oh, I think he'd like that very much!"

Before walking out the back door to the barn, Ember spotted a flyer on Kyla's countertop. "Brotherhood meeting?" She picked it up and waved it in the air. "Where'd you get this?"

"Was mashed in with my mail the other day."

"Hmm. Me too. Weird."

"C'mon!" Kyla said, shifting gears. "Asche is going to be so excited!"

Asche was Ember's appointed Shadow Deer, the one who would pull her sleigh during the Big Night while she delivered the coal to the bad kids of the world. Technically, he was supposed to stay at the Main Stable in Norland, but after some bargaining, Ember was able to work out a deal with the Council that allowed him to remain at Kyla's stable.

"*Aschen! Aglia doon verdor!*" Ember shouted her arrival in Elvish when she walked in the barn. At the sound of Ember's voice, Asche leapt up and rushed to the door of his stall.

"Hey," Kyla said, "your Elvish is getting pretty good."

"Practice, practice, practice," she replied as she nuzzled against Asche's nose. "How's my boy? How's my big beautiful boy? I missed you. Yes I did. Yes I did."

Asche snorted and grunted as his head moved back and forth on the side of Ember's face. When they first met, there was an immediate connection, like electricity passing through Ember's fingers when she stroked his velvety nose.

"Have you heard any news from the Sled Elves?" Ember asked.

"Actually, yes. They should have your sleigh done in another month or so. Then they'll fit Big Boy here with his harness and all, and then they'll do the final touches. You should be ready long before the Big Night."

Ember continued stroking Asche's dark furry body and looked into his crystal blue eyes. "Great. It'll be nice to have something that's mine, ya know? Can't wait to take my guy riding proper."

Chapter Six

EMBER HELD ONTO THE ENVELOPE WITH A DEATH-GRIP AS SHE WALKED back to her den. Today was Tannen's morning shift work day. He would drive the Cattas until his mid-afternoon break, and meet her for lunch at her den in Ebony Cragg where they would have salty brundle sandwiches with peppermint tea and blue sugar-snaps for dessert. Then, when the Graespurs left the Mines at night, they would rendezvous on the Ignis for some late night fishing, some hand holding, and maybe a stolen kiss or two. It had become their normal, weekday routine, something she had quickly (and happily) grown accustomed to. Only today, the routine had drastically changed. The Graespurs were long gone, and she hoped that Barkuss had told Tannen where she had been so he wouldn't worry about her.

When she reached her den, she noticed the soft glow of candlelight emanating from the kitchen. *Barkuss probably waiting for me.*

Only, it wasn't Barkuss. It was Tannen who sat at her kitchen table waiting for her. There was a pained look on his face, and as she moved closer into the room, she noticed a letter on the table. A scalloped envelope much like the one she had received earlier that day. An icy sense of dread pricked the back of her skull...

He had gotten one, too.

"Tannen?" she said.

"I need to talk to you about something," he said in a low voice when she entered the room.

She reached inside her jumpsuit pocket, pulled out her identical envelope, and placed it on the table. She sat down in the chair across from him and slid her envelope next to his. "I need to talk to you about something, too." Tannen's green eyes widened for a second and he exhaled. Ember mimicked his action by exhaling as well; a strand of blonde hair gently rose up above her head and fell back on her face into the crease of her eyelid. Tannen couldn't help but chuckle as she swatted at it.

"Not funny," she pouted, extending her lower lip playfully. Unable to stand her innocent-like cuteness, he laughed out loud, to which she grinned and rolled her eyes.

"So," he began nonchalantly, "looks like you got mail of sorts."

She huffed again. "You, too," she said, and nodded her head at the two envelopes on the table.

"So," he continued, his voice piercing through the painful tension in the room, "what are your thoughts about this predicament?"

"Well," she answered as reserved as she could maintain, "the predicament, quite frankly, sucks!"

He reached his long arm across the table and made a motion for her hands. She willingly laced them in his, and he leaned in even closer to kiss them. She closed her eyes and let the warmth of his breath against her fingers penetrate the very deepest part of her aching soul. *Magic kisses.* Barkuss had told her once upon a time that his mother's kisses were magic. Back then, she had no idea what he meant, but now, with Tannen, she could feel the spark of his energy race through every pore of her flesh. And for a fleeting moment, she lost herself in the serenity of his breath, his kiss, his touch. She ran her thumb against the inside of his palm and watched the goosebumps rise on his forearm. It was in that one tender moment that she felt the tears start to well in her eyes. She released his grip and stood up, turning her back to him, not wanting him to see her sadness, her *weakness.*

"Don't do that to me, Em," he said, following after her. His arms swooped down and clasped around her small waist. She felt the warmth of his body through the burlap material of her jumpsuit and closed her eyes again. Tears began to stream down her cheeks, and he wrapped his arms closer to her face to wipe them away for her.

"Kyla says I should go to West Valley and plead my case," she said, her voice grunting between her sobs.

"That's not such a bad idea, ya know."

She swiveled her body around and locked her puffy eyes on his. "And risk revealing *us?*"

"Would that be so bad?"

She glared hard at him. "Who did you get?" she asked.

He tilted his head to the side, puzzled. "What do you mean?"
"Answer the question. Who were you assigned to?"
He shook his head. "No," he answered. "It doesn't matter. She doesn't matter."
Ember tried to wriggle from his embrace like a worm on a fishing hook, but he refused to let her go. "Let go of me!" she protested.
"Stop, Ember!" he pleaded.
"I'll stop if you tell me who she is!"
"Why? Why do you need to know?"
Why won't you tell me? What are you hiding?
Her mind began to race. The name on Tannen's letter was all she was fixated on. And then it dawned on her – he never asked who *she* was assigned to. A wave of suspicion and hurt washed over her, and she fought against his grasp. Fists balled. Crashing on his chest. Trying to push him away. Trying to punch the name out of him. Right now, it was just a name on a letter, but to hear the name – to hear him say her name – would make it real in some way. String the letters to sounds to an eventual face with skin and bones and ears and togetherness and apartness and elfbabies and... she couldn't bear to divine the future —Tannen's or her own. She remembered the butterflies in her stomach when she would see him in the Mines. She remembered the feeling of complete and utter timelessness during their first kiss on the raft along the Ignis River. She thought about how every time they stole away for their secret rendezvouses, none of those feelings died. He was her light in the darkness. The sun beaming through the Mouth of the Cave. His undying trust and loyalty helped get her through every Claus-forsaken day, and to think that he was now going to be someone else's...
I just want something I can never have...
On her last chest-blow, he grabbed her wrists and held them tightly. "Listen to me," he continued, "whoever she is, she's not for me. You know that. You have to know that." She relaxed a little and he let go of her arms so he could brush the stray hairs away from her eyes. "I remember the first time I saw you, ya know? Sturd was a good two or three feet in front of you and you were following him to the platform.

You came bopping up from behind him with your bouncy little walk, like a ray of sunshine in this Claus-forsaken dank hole."

She smiled at his choice of words. *He must be reading my mind.* "Oh stop it!" she muttered as she swatted at his chest with less force and anger than she had before.

He smiled at her. "No, I swear! It's true! There were all those other elves there, all despondent and wretched looking. Don't get me wrong, you looked as pissed as all get out, but there just something *there.* A light. A spark. A flicker. An *ember.*"

"Okay, okay! Now you're just being one of those hopeless..."

He pulled tighter around her waist, drawing her closer to him. "I mean it, Em. I always waited for you. Always hoped that you would ride the rails. Always hoped that I'd be able to catch a glimpse of you on my shift, maybe try to make you smile or something."

"But I hardly rode!"

"Yea. That much is true. But I always waited for you anyway. So, you see, if I had the patience to wait for a rider who rarely took my car, I think I can be patient enough to ride this ordeal out. The name on my letter doesn't mean anything because I'm going to take you to West Valley like Kyla said, and we're going to straighten this all out. And if it reveals how I feel about you..."

"And how I feel about you..."

"Then so be it. If you could go ahead and get your *Life Job* changed, I have all the faith and confidence in you to pretty much get whatever you want."

Ember smiled. Tannen always had a way of coloring her world with the prettiest colors of the rainbow. He leaned his face down and tried to kiss her, but she backed away. "But wait," she whispered, "what if it doesn't work. What if..."

"Let's just take it one step at a time, okay?"

"Okay," she replied, and this time when Tannen bent down to kiss her, she didn't pull away.

Chapter Seven

T HE NOCTURNAL GRAESPURS WHO DWELLED IN THE MINES MADE THEIR
nightly trip Aboveground. Their humming filled the caverns
like an alarm, a signal to all the Coal Elves that night was now upon
them. Stop working. Get home. Prepare for yet another day. Sensing
the fall of day, swarms of the bat-like creatures rose up from their
nests and took flight, instinctively rushing to the Mouth of the cave.
Once Aboveground, the Graespurs would spend their time frol-
icking in the open night air, flapping their wings against the bright
moonlight, dancing for any Land Elf who cared to watch. But most
importantly, they went to work. As with anything in the North Pole,
Graespurs were vital to the chain of life. Upon their nightly arrival
Aboveground, they flocked to the Nessie Groves and ate any and all
insects who dared taint the precious fruit.

All Graespurs were now out tonight. *All but two.*

Sturd sat in the ruins that had once been his mother's night-bloom-
ing garden, holding two Graespurs tightly in both his paws. The area
had not been cared for in many years and had become a dilapidated
shell of its former self. Green and brown kissle leaves grew wildly
from under the rocks; the mossy substance invaded the flowerbeds
where the purple Alcanthia flowers had once flourished. Kissle leaves
grew up and over the broken remnants of his childhood graeviary.

He examined the Graespurs in his hands, turning them from side
to side, inspecting their delicate wings and fingering their gray velvet
fur. They wriggled and squirmed, trying to break free from his grip,
but every time they moved or squeaked, he squeezed his hands, closing his fingers tightly around their defenseless bodies. The pain would
silence them, and they would be still for a few moments, but when
they calmed down and he eased his grip, they would sense that they
might be free and would begin squirming and squealing again. To
which, of course, Sturd squeezed back even harder. He rather enjoyed
this little game of squeeze and release, and he would play it until
there was no longer a push back from the Graespurs. It was a lesson
in control for both parties involved – the Graespurs being dominated,

and his hunger being suppressed. *These two Graes will make a great meal tonight*, he thought. However, it wasn't often that Sturd played with his food. He was feeling off today, enraged by events that had transpired.

Stripped of his position as Operations Manager in the Mines, Sturd's new job was "Field Data Collector." *Field Data Collector.* Brand new job, with a brand new title, accompanied by brand new rules created especially for him. It was a result of his so-called punishment for the Coal-less Night. But when Sturd looked deeper into the significance of the position, what he saw was a Life Job that essentially had no boundaries, no limitations, and no rules. *No rules.* A free pass to do as he pleased, and to continue to create chaos the way he saw fit. The Council hadn't really given him much of a punishment at all.

This new position forced him to spend much of his time in his home in Welfort Den. He was fine with that as he had already begun plans for reorganizing and rebuilding. The new job gave him more time to think and plan and plot. His 'Christmas in July' idea was starting to come to fruition after its approval by the Council and the Boss Lady, and there were other projects he was working on… other plans he had for the elven community.

When he had first heard of a group of elves banding together and calling themselves The Brotherhood, he had been skeptical – brushed it off as a bunch of disgruntled loons commiserating with each other. But when the buzz and hum didn't seem to die down, his curiosity had gotten the best of him, and he had clandestinely attended a so-called meeting. It didn't take long for him to recognize these elves were in such a misguided state of anger and confusion that it would be easy for him to swoop in and take over.

However, he had known that appealing to the entire Brotherhood was an impossible task. There had been many elves who mistrusted or hated him, and he would never be able to convince them all to get on board with his plan. The Nim'sim brothers were the leaders of the fraternity, and if he could just finesse them with his Ruprecht charm, he just might be able to amass the army he needed for his back pocket – to unleash when he was ready to make his move, when he was ready to take charge and lead.

The Nim'sims were ugly elves who lived in a den just outside of Raker's Cove. They were named Nim and Sim. Nim Nim'sim, and Sim Nim'sim - *Stupid names for stupid elves!* - and they had once been part of Sturd's crew when he was a Manager. Their dusty dwelling had reeked of rotted plants and sour milk — an odor almost too strong for Sturd to handle as he approached the den. He had to hold his breath as he entered and slowly exhaled, trying to adjust to the stench.

When he had pleaded his case to them, they had been tentative at first to agree. He told them a litany of lies and half-truths about the Council and the laws and life Aboveground, that it must have certainly added to fuel to their fires. Sturd was slick and fast with his words. He told them because he had worked so closely with the Council he was privy to their nefarious ways. He told them he believed the Council was trying to overthrow the Boss, and that the Boss had a personal vendetta against the Coal Elves. "You have a chance to do real good here," he proclaimed. "Regardless of your feelings toward me personally, think of all the elves you'd be helping. What a great way to rally up your boys to greatness!"

The brothers looked at each other with so much hope and promise in their eyes. "This can be it, if Sturd has all the insider info, we could use that to our advantage," Nim said to Sim.

"Foil the plans of the Council," Sim replied.

"We're in," Nim said to Sturd. "What do you need us and our boys to do?"

And that was it. Easy as a snap. He had his secret agreement with the Brotherhood, that he would use to his advantage whenever the time came. How ignorant they were! How easily swayed! Bile worked its way into his throat as he thought about his race. Elves. He hated them all —the whole damned lot of them. His hatred burned like soupy acid in his stomach. He detested them all and everything about them – their grimy faces, their hands worn and caked with coal ash, their songs and food. To him they were all nothing but sheep – mindless, useless, worthless, blindly following some stupid ideology until the day they died. And they were all so easily convinced and controlled, like the day he tore up the List and the Coal Elves had all gone berserk with happiness.

He chuckled out loud, remembering the scene.

Even the Council was misguided and useless. They had asked him long ago, before the Coal-less Night, "Sturd Ruprecht, if you were in charge in the Mines, what would you do?" He had gotten very giddy at the question because as long as he could remember, he had always dreamed of taking control, running the show, being the one that everyone feared and revered. He practically blushed and began spouting off his long laundry list of shake ups and new rules, a frightening doctrine for a "New Age" in the Mines. A chaotic vision of a controlled elf. And they had all nodded their heads, but he had never asked them any questions. They just replied, "Under the Fortieth Provision of Regulation Thirty, you are permitted," and dismissed him from their office. It was all so ambiguous, so random, so chaotic, and it filled him with a surge of power that felt like a fireball pulsating in the center of his chest.

And when the day of ripping up the List had come, he had no idea that he was going to go through with it until he actually did it. He hadn't prepared that speech, or the gestures, but when he had stood there on top of the rock shelf, hundreds of black-rimmed eyes practically begging him for a miracle, the fireball in his chest had exploded from within. And he *acted* – revealed the List and tore it to shreds. Oh, how they all clamored for a piece of it. Their bony bodies gyrated in ecstasy as if they had been set free from a cage. He had felt as if he were floating on air that day. The power of the chaos lifted him up, filled him with his own twisted sense of goodness. But looking at the crowd below had made him sick, made him want to wrap his hands around every one of *their* throats and squeeze the life out of *them*...

He looked down at his hands and realized the Graespurs were no longer struggling, no longer moving. He set their lifeless bodies next to his feet, next to the scalloped envelope sticking out from under his black boot, and growled —the fleeting happiness of his dinner prospect shattered by his disgust over the letter from West Valley. The front door of the den slammed shut. Sturd clutched the envelope and quickly rose to his feet.

"Sturd?" It was his father, Corzakk, returning from work. "Where are you, son?"

Sturd clenched his pointed teeth and sucked in a breath, the air making a sickening slithery sound that echoed against the cave walls. Anger made his head throb and his vision became hazy, like a sheer mesh veil falling down over his eyes. Every fiber in his body urged him to pounce and pummel his father at first sight. *Get on top of his gangly body and with both hands smash his head against the rocks. Smash. Smash. Smash. Smash.*

But when Corzakk appeared in front of him, Sturd was released from his violent trance. "Son, are you okay? I've been standing here in front of you…"

Sturd forcefully pressed the envelope against his father's chest, causing Corzakk to stumble backward. "No, Father, I'm not okay. What is this all about?" he hissed.

Corzakk handed the letter back to him. "This upsets you? Isn't this what you wanted? An elfwife?"

Sturd's red eyes flashed. "Not Ember. They're assigning *Ember* to me."

A slow grin tugged on the corners of Corzakk's mouth pulling them upward in an unnatural way. Deep lines cupped the sides of his cheeks that created uneven shadows on his face. His chest heaved up and down and a low grumbling sound from his stomach worked its way up and rattled out his throat like the sound a chugging stone blaster makes when low on fuel. It was his signature laugh – one that didn't happen often, but was quite alarming when it did. The sound irritated Sturd. *Jump on him! Force him to the ground. Use the side of that rock to smash…*

Sturd could no longer contain his rage. "You promised me!" he screamed uncontrollably. "You promised me when I was an elfling. When mom left! You told me that her sin would not punish me.

But it has! I've done everything I've ever been told to do. I'm publicly humiliated by being sent away for six months, and then *she* goes against my plan at the meeting. Then to make matters worse, I come home to find *this*!" He threw the envelope back at Corzakk's face. "An engagement to the one elf I would love nothing more than to crush with my bare hands!"

Corzakk's bizarre laughter segued into a body rocking coughing spell. He flailed his hands up and down trying to catch his breath. His pale face turned a sickly shade of gray, and with one last lurch, he coughed up something into his mouth and spit it onto the ground.

Sturd smirked at the white worm slithering in a small pool of his father's blood. "Serves you right for laughing at me. You aggravated your Coppleysites."

"Watch your tone." Corzakk wiped his mouth, leaving a dark red stain on the back of his hand. "Are you finished now?"

Sturd drew in his anger and tried his best to regain composure. "It's just that…"

Corzakk, frustrated, placed a hand on Sturd's shoulder. Sturd flinched from the initial touch, jerking his arm back instinctively. "When are you going to learn, Sturd?"

"Learn what?" he said through gritted teeth.

"For one, did you ever stop to think that there was a valid reason why they would pair you and her together?"

Sturd's eyes narrowed. "Wait a minute." He pointed a gnarled finger at his father. "You knew about this, didn't you?"

Corzakk nodded.

Jump on him now! He betrayed you! Ball up your fist and smash. Smash. Smash. Smash.

Sturd's rage flared up again. "How dare you!"

"Stop," Corzakk commanded. "Stop and think about the logical explan…"

"There is no logical explanation for this!"

"Then how do you ever expect to be more than what you are if you can't step back and examine the situation from an outside viewpoint?

Your failure to read between the lines will be what holds you back from greatness."

But Sturd had read between the lines. He was able to recognize the hidden meaning in the ambiguous meeting with the Council, and he was able to see past the inexplicable new job assignment. However, when it came to Ember, all he felt was emotion. There was no logic — just his undying animosity and repulsion.

"Think about it," Corzakk continued. "She's the wild card for all of us. She had the jump on you and you didn't even know it. She's volatile and a potential threat to all of elven society, not just us Coal Elves. And who would be best suited to keep her contained under a watchful eye?"

Sturd paused, absorbing his father's words. "Me," he finally answered.

"Exactly. Who would be the best elf to rein her in? Put her on a leash?"

Sturd smiled. "A literal one, Father?" And the both of them gave a small chuckle.

It did seem to make sense to him — his new position, working at home, not having to be in the field keeping tabs on other Coal Elves. And with Ember's new position, she too would be spending many days in her den, poring over paperwork more than anything else. She wouldn't be able to do much of anything without him knowing about it. How stupid he felt now. He should have seen that all along.

Corzakk placed a hand back on Sturd's shoulder, and this time Sturd didn't back away. "I know what I promised you long ago. I promised you would rise to greatness beyond your wildest dreams, and I intend to make good on that promise. You are my son and I only want the best for you. I know that you will accomplish many great things. I never wanted this lonely life for you, and I blame that on your mother." He paused, and crinkled his face up as if the memory of his former wife had been like a punch in the stomach. "But you have to understand, your life, this life, has been set in motion for quite some time."

Sturd nodded. He knew the story. He knew that his father had been married to someone else before his mother.

"Zoranna was a good elfwife to me," Corzakk continued. "And I loved her very much. What happened to her was so horrific; I didn't think I could stand to live alone. But I was assigned a new elfwife right away, your mother, I'len."

"But she was already married, Father," Sturd interrupted.

"Yes, but the Council has their reasons for doing what they do. And whatever the case may be, they deemed it necessary to remove her from the Dwin'nae home and from those mongrel children she had. With good reason, I'm sure! Look at how those elves turned out. Bommer, and Banter, and the other B's. They're despicable! And look at how she treated me. You. She abandoned us, Sturd."

Sturd wanted to reply, "I know," but no words would come out. The pain of his mother leaving, even though it had happened thirteen elfyears ago, was still fresh.

"And that is why, you will see, her sin is *not* punishing you. It will take some time to see the larger picture, but trust me, when you do, when it all falls into place…"

"When what falls into place?"

Corzakk closed his eyes and smiled. The crooked nubs of his small teeth looked like tiny white pearls strewn together haphazardly. "Your Uncle Zelcodor and Aunt Una are great elves, Sturd. Because their pairing of me and your mother didn't work out the way we had all planned, they made a promise to me. They promised me that you would be taken care of, that you would want for nothing, that you would uphold the Ruprecht Clan name with the highest of honors. I trust them, Sturd. I trust in their plan, and you would be wise to do the same. But you must also trust in yourself as well. It was your instinct, your drive that prompted you to destroy that List. That was pure and guttural. Don't ignore that, son."

Sturd raised his eyebrows. *Oh, don't you worry, Father. I can't ignore the chaos.* "I won't."

The two stared hard at each other for a few moments. "Sturd," Corzakk finally spoke, "what is it that you truly want? What is the one thing that you truly desire?"

The question wasn't a hard one. *Vengeance. Destruction. Chaos.* All words that flashed brightly behind his eyes. The letters of each word blazing like firestorms deep in the Mines. He put his hand up to his face and rubbed his temples.

What *did* he really want?

He breathed in deep, closing his eyes and accepting the dirt and dust into his lungs. His body shivered when the letters of all his emotions rearranged themselves to form his true intention in his mind. "To rule," he finally exhaled. "To rule all."

Corzakk smiled again. "Good. Let's go eat, shall we?"

Sturd bent down and picked up the bodies of the dead Graespurs and dangled them in front of his face. "I was thinking the same exact thing."

Chapter Eight

Sturd hated traveling beyond the gloaming of the Mines. It took him out of his comfort- zone of darkness and wrapped him in the sunny open-air of the world Above. The warmth of the orange fireball stung his pale skin, its light blinding his sensitive red eyes. He was used to the enclosed cavern walls with their oppressive heat and ash, and being in the openness of the Aboveground made him shudder. It was cold. It was wet. It was sunny, and happy, and full of hope and promise and spring air and music and smiles and... *It's just for a little while*, he thought, trying to coax himself out of a near panic attack. *Do your job, get the information you need, get home.* At Headquarters, his plan was to present his final report with instructions for *Christmas in July* to the Managers, check in with the Book Keepers, and get the hell out of there. The Managers were all on break, so he left the manila folder on the desk and rode the elevator to the thirteenth floor to see the Book Keepers.

Christmas in July... one of his more thought-out schemes. He couldn't wait to see the reaction this one would bring in both the human and elven worlds. It was all too perfect — start the holiday nearly six months earlier and "save" the spirit. Every elf bought it! Every elf agreed that this would work, but Sturd knew better. If anything, Sturd surmised, this would make even more blackened names appear in the Book. If there was one thing he had learned about the human world, it was timing. Oh yes, timing was everything for humans. He realized that they grumbled around that pumpkin holiday when the first storefront decorations for the Big Day were displayed. "Too soon!" they had hollered. They grumbled when the first TV ads for the Big Day were aired. "Can't we get through one holiday at a time?" they had groaned, feeling rushed to put up their own decorations, cook their own huge feasts, buy their own multitude of gifts gifts gifts. Overall, they were tired of the marketing ploys to push the Big Day further and further ahead. It was as if the Big Day were being shoved down their throats, and they ended up being resentful, angry, willing to forget the day altogether. If the humans were disgusted with a two-month head start, what would be the result of Christmas in July?

The Managers ate it all up. Gobble gobble. Swallow. Gulp. "The blackened names are undeniably a product of the loss of the spirit," he had proclaimed to them. They thumbed through his prospectus, nodded their heads. "This jump start on the season will allow them maximum exposure, but we must be wise to implement slowly. Start with their most adored televisions. Allow them to shop from the comfort of their own homes. Plant the seed and watch it grow. We'll need extra stock on specific merchandise; I'm sure you can create a comprehensive supply list." They mumbled to each other. Wrote down notes. Nodded some more. Sent Sturd on his way.

His giggle was almost maniacal when he went back to the elevator. He was hungry for the fallout, thirsty for the end result, craving the chaos he was sure this would create. Could it possibly be that he was the only elf who recognized the disastrous possibilities?

No.

He wasn't.

She knew, too. *She* had protested his plan. *She,* who had opposed him in a public forum. *She,* who would soon be bound to him in elf-marriage. *She,* whose strawberry scent made him crazy with hunger and rage. No sooner had the elevator began ascending, it stopped at the tenth floor, the heavy metal doors opening with a sweet sounding *ding.* A sweet *ding,* followed by a sweet smell. Strawberries. *Ember.*

Their eyes locked, and the smile on her face that he had briefly caught a glimpse of morphed into the scowl he had come to know and hate. Her dirty blonde hair was pulled back into a tight braid that dangled over her right shoulder, her face clean of any dirt or coal dust, her oversized black jumpsuit laundered and pressed. He couldn't be certain, but were her cheeks starting to fill out into plump glowing apples of health? She was a vision of horrific loveliness, carrying herself with an air of insecure confidence. She stepped into the elevator, keeping her gaze on him. She clenched her fists and he could smell her newfound power radiating from her. He breathed it in, inhaled the newness of it, let that insecure confidence wash over him. He wanted that power for his own. Strip her of it. Rip her arrogant stride from her spine. Teach her a lesson or two about being in control.

He wanted to rattle her, throw her off guard, make her feel nervous and shaken up. "Good morning," he greeted with an oversized, overly phony smile. "Going up?"

Ember looked him up and down, unwavering. "What are you doing here?"

"My job," he answered politely.

She snorted and shook her head. "Thirteen."

The elevator doors closed with a thud. "Great. Me, too."

"Fabulous," Ember replied dryly, and the elevator began its flight up.

"So, I assume you got your letter from West Valley," he prodded, knowing full well that engaging her in conversation would upset her.

Ember stiffened for a second, then rubbed at her temples. "Yea. Don't get any bright ideas or nothing, cause I'll tell you what – it ain't happening!"

Sturd clicked his tongue on the roof of him mouth with a slurpy *tsk tsk*, and the way she cringed at the sound of it indicated to him that his quest to annoy her was definitely working. "If the Council says it's happening, oh, you bet it's happening."

"Yea, right. Over my dead body."

Skye's dead body! Now there is an uplifting thought!

"Oh, what's wrong?" he goaded. "Don't like the way *Ember Ruprecht* sounds? I think it has a distinguished ring to it, don't ya think?"

They stopped at the thirteenth floor and the doors opened. "Think again, Sturd," she spat over her shoulder as she exited the elevator. "I requested a meeting and am going to West Valley, like right after here, to clear up this whole debacle. The Head Mistress *clearly* made some sort of mistake, and I'm going to take care of it."

He followed right behind her. "Oh no, no mistake was made, I can assure you. You really don't like the way *Ember Ruprecht* sounds?" he taunted.

She ignored him and continued walking faster down the corridor.

"Okay, okay, what about Ember *Skye* Ruprecht? I'd be okay with you wanting to keep your own last name in the mix, given your new powerful position and all. Ember Skye Ruprecht. Works for me. What about you? Does that work for you? Sound good?"

"Actually, it makes me want to vomit." She picked up her pace and he followed right behind.

"Oh, don't be that way! The Ruprecht Clan is one of the oldest clans at the Pole. We are a noble clan. A respectable clan. A high-ranking clan. My grandfather, Zerk Ruprecht, was a chief advisor to the Boss back in the day. My father, Corzakk, is a great Coal Mining Master. And my uncle, Zelcodor, a Council member married to none other than the Boss's sister. We have good roots. Strong roots. Any elflings you bear will be…"

Ember stopped short and turned on her heel, her braid whipping in Sturd's face. "Elflings? As in children? With *you*? You must be crazy if you ever think that…"

Sturd raised his crooked forefinger and wagged it back and forth. "Now, now. You know it says in the Codex that elves committed in marriage must at least have one elfling. At least. How else are we to ensure the survival of our race?"

"The Codex sucks!" she barked. "There needs to be some serious changes made to that thing!"

"Yes. I agree with you on that." He looked up at a clock in the hallway. "Oh, look at that. I have one more stop to make before I need to get home. Ya know, Welfort Den."

Ember rolled her eyes in disgust.

"See you very soon," Sturd growled.

"Don't count your Graespurs…" She turned her back to him again and continued down the hall. He watched her until she turned the corner and was out of sight, taking note of the lack of confidence in her step. He had gotten to her. Mission accomplished.

One last stop and then I can get out of this bizarro land.

He gently opened the door of the Book Keepers' office, and quietly stepped inside the large room. Even though it was mid-day, the office was dark – thick drapes drawn over picture windows, the only light in the room coming from a few lit oil lanterns. The only sounds from within the room were the gentle turning of book pages and the slight snoring of the elf sitting at his desk. His legs were crossed on the top of the desk and he was leaning back in his swivel chair with his mouth opened. Every time he breathed in and exhaled with the deep sound of sleep, his head bobbed up and down in gentle rhythm.

"Hello?" Sturd called in a loud voice.

Startled by the sudden boom echoing in the room, the elf snorted a few times, then jumped up to attention brushing at his sleeves. "Yes? Yes? Who's there? How can I help you?"

"Ogden Castleberry? It's me, Sturd."

The elf's eyes widened and he came out from behind the desk. "Um... hmm... why, yes," he stammered. "Mr. Ruprecht. What can I do for you? I'm Orthor, by the way."

"Pleased." Sturd said with his lip curling. "I'm here to examine the Book."

Orthor pulled back in hesitation and cocked an eyebrow. "Examine the Book?" he repeated.

"Yes. I want to cross-reference the names. See if there's anything that we can use as far as information about these humans. Were they connected? Related? Did they have the same experience base? That sort of thing, and..."

"Um... I don't know," Orthor hesitated, eyeing Sturd up and down. "You don't have clearance and I wasn't notified of this."

"Clearance? I don't need clearance. I'm Field Data Collector. I'm here, in the field, and I need to collect data!"

"Um... I don't know." Orthor moved to his desk and picked up the handle of the phone. "I think I should just call upstairs to double check."

Sturd slithered to the desk and pressed his finger down on the receiver. "Ogden," he began.

"Orthor," he corrected.

Sturd sucked in a wave of fury between his gritted teeth. "Mr. Castleberry," he continued in a smooth, calm tone. "Do you really think it is wise to bother the Council right now? I just delivered to the Managers, not even ten minutes ago, the plans for Christmas in July. It's probably sitting on the Council's desk right now. They're probably in deep conversation over the beginning stages of the plan. There's so much for them to deal with to get this launch done proper. Do you really think they would appreciate being interrupted right now?"

Orthor gulped and his hand wavered a little.

"Now, Ogden," Sturd said as he easily took the receiver from Orthor's hand and placed it back in the phone cradle.

"Orthor," he corrected again as Sturd gave a slight smirk.

Sturd grabbed Orthor's wrist and yanked on his arm. "Orthor. Orthor." He sighed, trying his best to remain composed. "I just want to take inventory of the names. Nothing more, nothing less. Now, you can call the Council, but I can guarantee my uncle and aunt will give me all the clearance I need to do my job. Will you let me just do my job, Ogden?"

Orthor quickly nodded his head. "Orthor."

"Just take me to the Book!" Sturd screamed.

Orthor's body jolted and he walked over to the glass case that covered the Book. "Here," he said as he lifted the case up and set it aside. The pages of the Book turned rhythmically back and forth. Sturd moved closer to the Book and reached his hand to touch the pages. "No!" Orthor admonished. "Don't touch. Just look. There hasn't been too much activity the last few days. Things have been rather quiet. The pages have been steady and the color changes have been normal. You'll be able to make out the names of the black spots just right."

Sturd tuned Orthor out. It was spell-binding the way the names changed colors and the pages danced. Each time a page turned and Sturd spied a black ashy spot, he felt his heart flutter with joy. *Sydney Gray. Eddie Peralta. Anthony Bower. Abigail Hall. Evan Rozet.* Blackened out. Non-believers with no rhyme or reason. It was a work of art. A thing of beauty.

"So far, we've had twenty-one names go dark. And that's a record high, considering there's less than a handful per year."

Names go dark. Lights out. To believe no more. The words were music to Sturd's ears. The blackened names made him swoon, made his fireball power nearly explode in his chest. If he knew how to, he thought he might cry. He swayed his head in time with the motion of the pages, committing all the names to memory. *Jill Jariwala. Ryan Matthews...*

Suddenly, the motion of the Book stopped. Orthor gasped. "No, no, no! Not another one! Not now!"

Sturd stopped his swoon-like trance and observed the Book as the page seared out another name. Just like that, *Seth Santiago* was silver, then copper, then brown, then black. A dark black smudge against the yellowed paper. An ink stain among golds and greens. The blackness filled him with an indescribable sensation that made his toes tingle. He wanted to touch it, he wanted to run his fingers over the burnt paper and feel the jagged edges of what was once a soul's name. Gone forever. Lights out. The death of hope and innocence. The birth of chaos — living, breathing chaos right before his eyes. A tangible manifestation of everything he felt in his own blackened heart. As if on instinct, he reached his fingers out toward the Book to be one with the stain, but Orthor slapped at his hand.

Orthor was frantic now. "I have to call Goldie. Every black name must get reported to the Council as soon as they happen!"

"Everything okay?" Sturd asked, still half in a trance.

"Okay? Okay? No. Nothing is okay! Don't you understand? If the humans blacken their hearts to the spirit of the Day, there's no more need for a Claus! Without a Claus, what would we do? What would we become?"

"We'd be free, wouldn't we?" Sturd said, without missing a beat, the words coming to and out of him as if they were always there and just waiting for a moment to be properly verbalized.

"Free? Free? What in Claus do you mean by that? No! That would be chaos! Elves on their own, left to their own devices, no purpose, no function. You think the Nessie Fruit Sickness was bad? Oh, man, if this ever goes down, you just wait and see. No holds barred, my friend!" Orthor quickly turned from Sturd, picked up the phone and began dialing.

Chaos. The way he liked it. The sound of the word. The implications behind the word. Chaos was good. Chaos he could handle. Eliminate the figure-head, let the mistletoe hit the fan, step in to save the fate of the elven race. It was a beautiful plan. Restore his own brand of order. He liked the chaos. If he could control it from within himself, he could control it, manipulate it in others.

Orthor was speaking on the phone in a heightened tone, the timbre of his voice at least an octave higher than its normal cadence. Sturd ignored him and began moving about the room, taking in the décor, reading the titles of the many books stacked in the bookcases. *A Study in Elvish, The Graespur Protocol, Barter and Trade in East Bank, Barter and Trade in West Bank.* Nothing too exciting. Rather boring reads, to be honest. Sturd wondered if the brothers were required to read these books as part of their Life Job. *Twelve Songs to Ring in the Big Night, Coal Mining Field Guide, The Codex Companion, The By-laws of Parish Estates.* Nothing worth stopping for, nothing worth his time reading. Orthor was still pleading with the other elf on the phone, and just as Sturd was about to turn from the bookshelf, a thin paperback tucked between two large hard covered textbooks caught his eye. The spine read *The Dublix Santarae* — its name alone piqued his interest, but what was even more curious was its placement on the shelf, as if it had been deliberately shoved in between the thick and unassuming books. *Hidden.*

He pulled it from the shelf. It had a red cover with green lettering. As he flipped through the pages, they were delicate and worn, almost brittle to the touch. He knew right away this was an ancient document. *An extremely significant document.* And when he opened to the first page and read, "In regards to the Claus..." he knew he had stumbled onto something beyond his wildest, twisted dreams. *The Dublix Santarae.*

Orthor slammed the phone down, and Sturd tucked the book under his shirt and spun around to meet him. "They're sending someone now. Did you get everything you needed?"

"Oh, yes," he answered. "I'll be going now."

Sturd left the office and headed back toward the elevator. With the book safe against his chest, he couldn't help but smile the whole way home.

Chapter Nine

R IDING IN THE CATTA- CAR WITH THE WARM CAVE-WIND BLOWING
through her hair, Ember realized she had never truly appreciated
the full expanse of the Mines. They ran further and deeper than she
had ever known. She had never been to West Valley, or anywhere
close to it for that matter. Her world had consisted of the small vicin-
ity to which she was confined – her den in Ebony Cragg, the dens of
the other elves she knew, the various caves where she was assigned to
work, the meeting points. The farthest she had ever ventured was up
through Barrier Holt, the cavern where the Mouth to Aboveground
was. But all that had been to the East. Now, they were headed West,
through unfamiliar terrain. West Valley —home of the future Coal
Elfwives! Ember hoped to get answers, maybe some sort of explanation or justification – anything to reconcile the turn of events both
she and Tannen had been presented.

Her recent encounter with Sturd still bothered her. Probably the
only reason why he would have been Aboveground was to go over
plans for Christmas in July. She clenched her fists and breathed deep,
seizing a breath in her chest as if to punish herself for her blatant stu-
pidity. She let him rattle her. She let him taunt her. But most importantly, she let him *distract* her. All that talk of names and elfbabies
clouded her mind when she should have been inquiring about the real
problem at hand — the blackened names.

Let's get this over with, so I can focus on all that.

Her eyes squinted from the fast motion of the trolley; she struggled
against the motion to take in and absorb the different territories they
were passing through, but it was as if Tannen drove at an unusually
fast pace on purpose. *To get this over with?* Since the night they had
revealed their engagement letters, they hadn't spoken much about the
situation except for the unified decision that Tannen would accom-
pany her to West Valley in order to confront the Head Mistress. She
had scoffed at his undying optimism when he smiled and said, "Don't
worry, we'll work this all out," his green eyes gleaming with so much
hope and faith. *How the hell does he do it? How in Claus's name can*

he be so positive and assured? And the more she thought about it, the more she realized that his confidence, his happy-go-lucky nature, was part of what drew her to him. The way he jumped in to help her when she had defected Above – *Almond tall struthers* —"I'll stall the others." She hadn't even told him what was going on, and still he did his best to protect her. And there were other things — little things —that showed his genuine and good soul. Holding the door for her, pulling out her chair at the dinner table, waiting (sometimes hours) for her to finish up her work just so he could say goodnight. He was comforting, warm, *real*, and every moment spent in his presence made her fall a little bit more, a little bit harder.

The only other time in her life she could remember having any type of romantic feelings was when she was back Aboveground in Tir-La Treals. At eight elfyears old, Jordy Pines was her first real crush. He was a boy in her class. His white hair shimmered like ice in the sunlight, and his frosty blue eyes reminded her of the summer sky. Jordy was sweet, not like most other boy elves their age. They had sat together at lunch and played games together on the playground. He even held her hand under the table during art class. But all that changed the following year when Jordy was assigned to be a Banker Elf, and Ember a Coal Elf. What a crush it truly turned out to be when Jordy's summer sky eyes turned to cold steel as he ignored her and would barely look at her the entire year before their apprenticeships. Her little heart had been broken those many years ago, but what she had with Tannen was different, a life-time possibility. Not the simple eye-batting puppy-dog love of young Jordy Pines. Tannen accepted her, cared for her. And now, all of that was threatened. The life she had just begun to envision with Tannen was quite possibly never going to come to fruition. Instead of becoming a *Trayth*, the black cloud of the *Ruprecht* name loomed on the immediate horizon.

Tannen Trayth. Descendant of the Tree Elves, Tannen. Forever-smiling-warm-hearted, Tannen. I-don't-know-if-I-can-live-without-you-in-my-life, Tannen...

The landscape of the Mines transformed as they moved farther west. A crackling sound in her ears alerted her to an altitude change, and the air seemed less suffocating. The stone walls took on different tones of blacks and deep purples. She wished that Tannen would have given her a guided tour of the area, but she knew when Tannen was driving, he wasn't much for talking. And right now, he drove with purpose, a determined energy that could be felt all the way back in her passenger car.

It seemed like the end of the line as they approached large, purple rock fortress doors. The doors met together at the center and were covered in callixus —thin black vines with spirally tendrils. Neon green flower buds grew from the vines, giving the cavern a misty, black-lit glow. The fortress doors were attached to rock columns that jutted out from the top to the bottom of the cave. They had a crystalline coating on them, and it reminded her of the crunchy fairy dust she had seen at the Mouth of the cave. Could it be that there was another Mouth somewhere in the west?

Tannen slowed the trolley to a gentle glide, waiting for the doors to open. "We're here," he called. "Hold on." When they did, he revved the engine once, lurching them forward and beyond the doors.

When the Catta came to a stop, Ember's breath hitched in her throat, producing a low gasping sound that echoed in the cave. She stepped onto the platform and approached the driver's car with a surreal slow-motion gait. Tannen remained seated, and when she was at arm's length, he handed her the letters. "You might need these when you plead your case," he said with a weak smile.

Her stomach turned with nauseated fear and she narrowed her eyebrows. "Wait? You're not coming in with me?"

"Can't. No male-elves allowed. Kinda their company policy, so to speak."

It was obvious he was trying to make light of the situation, but it was a feeble attempt and it only added to her nervousness.

She nodded, understanding the circumstances. "What now?"

"Well, we're actually inside the compound. This is the farthest west you can go in the Mines. We designed the car-run to go right into their gates this way so the drivers couldn't be seen, and West

Valley could be safeguarded. Look up and around. The compound is actually a thing of wonder. A world within a world, if you think about it."

Ember tilted her head up to view the monolithic cave walls. The platform of the Catta- car was, in fact, in the center of a semi-circular structure that seemed to stretch up and past the Mines. "How high up does it go?"

"To the Aboveground. The mountain in West Bank was hollowed out, and that's where the girls' dormitories are. They have windows in their rooms so they can see the sunrise and all that Aboveground stuff."

Ember sighed. *Yea, like a last hurrah before they're destined to darkness.* "How do you know all this anyway?"

Tannen pointed his thumb at his chest. "Tree Elf. Mine construction. Kind of a family business." He chuckled.

Ember relaxed her shoulders and chuckled with him briefly before her nerves came knocking at her knees again. "You'll wait for me here, right?"

Tannen revved the engine again. "Nah, I was thinking of driving around for a little bit. Maybe go home, maybe get some lunch. Oh, I know, I'll go to that Brotherhood meeting all the elves have been talking about. Who knows when I'll be back!"

"Brotherhood? So that's like a real thing?" she questioned.

"Yea. Apparently there's this group of elves who have these meetings and stuff. Like, they want things to be different in the Mines, and they're trying to rally everyone up to join their cause or something."

Ember raised an eyebrow. "Well, maybe you should go and see if there's anything they can help with this." She raised her hand and swatted her letter back and forth in front of his face.

Tannen grabbed her wrist and pulled her closer to the car. He stared into her eyes before leaning up to kiss her. Not caring if anyone was watching, she kissed him back, pressing her lips forcefully, almost desperately against his.

If only I could stay here, right here, in this moment...

Her heart sank when he pulled back and ended the kiss. "Do you think they knew about us? Do you think they did this on purpose?" he whispered.

The thought hadn't even dawned on her. Afraid to speak, afraid to hear the crackle in her voice, afraid to burst into hysterical tears, she just shrugged her shoulders. "I don't know. I don't see how." She paused. "I thought you were ineligible?"

"Hey! I thought *you* were ineligible!"

"I am! I mean, I was. I mean… I don't know!" She stepped back from the car, creating a few inches of distance between them. "Why won't you tell me who you got?"

Tannen stared at the floor. "It doesn't matter."

"Sure it does. Who did you get?"

"Really, Em, it doesn't matter."

A deep burning sensation began to work its way from the center of her stomach and up through her chest. For a moment, her nervous knee-knocking ceased, replaced by an unfamiliar sensation throughout her entire body. It was an alien feeling for her, one that made her want to scream in anger and cry in sadness at the same time. "No. Really. I wanna know who it is? Is she a Ceffle? One of the prestigious Coal Clans? Is she an Abovegrounder? Is she my age? Younger?"

Tannen put up his hands palms out. "Stop, Em. Just stop. We don't know her, if that's what you're getting at. And we can get crazy jealous all we want, it's not going to change things."

Ember shook her head in disbelief. "So, you're saying you're okay with this?"

"No. That's not what I meant." He made a motion as if to stand up, but Ember backed up even further.

She was stunned at his words, the pain in her chest a stabbing feeling. "If you were okay with this, then why didn't you say so? Why did you drive me all the way out here to clear something up that you didn't even care to be fixed?"

Tannen shook his head. "No. That's not what I meant, Em. I meant regardless of what happens, it's not going to change the way I feel about you."

Ember exhaled loudly. "You never asked me who I got. Don't you want to know?"

"No. Not really. Like I said, it doesn't matter."

Her shoulders slumped forward in defeat. For the first time she saw a thin veil of acceptance on Tannen's face and was able to read between the lines of what he said: No, he didn't like the situation. No, his feelings for her were not changed. But what she couldn't figure was this — if he was going to accept the fate that was presented to them regardless of how either of them felt. "But it does matter, Tannen. It all matters. I thought you of all elves would understand that."

"I do understand, Ember. We'll get through this."

"You've already said that, and you're not very convincing this time around." After a few moments of silence she said, "I should probably go in."

"Yea," he mumbled. She turned her back to him and started for the entrance to the compound. "Holly Adaire," he called to her.

She smirked. He was right, she didn't know who she was. The name alone sounded like an Abovegrounder. When she reached the entrance, she breathed in deeply and raised her fisted hand to knock. Before she did, she replied, "Sturd Ruprecht," without looking back. She could only imagine the look on Tannen's face.

Ember was warmly welcomed at the door by a young female elf. She had short strawberry blonde hair with shaggy bangs right above her eyebrows. Her eyes were a startling shade of ice blue, and she wore a yellow button-down dress that resembled sunshine. With heart in throat, Ember looked down at the name tag, wondering if she would read the name of Tannen's future wife. The name on the girl's breast pocket wasn't Holly, but rather one she noted as being quite familiar. *Kiffer Gulch.*

"Come and sit in the waiting room, honey. Mistress Shella is in a training session right now and will be with you shortly." Kiffer's smile was infectious, and Ember found herself smiling right back at the spirited elf as she took a seat on one of the plush couches.

"Thank you, Miss Gulch." Saying the name out loud rang bells in Ember's memory. *Gulch. Kipper Gulch. The nasty little Enforcer Elf in Norland with the high pitched voice who had bound her and Asche with his magic tether and tripped her on the roof of Headquarters.* "Oh, you can call me Kiff, Miss Skye!" she gushed.

"Ember."

Kiffer raised her hand to her mouth in a nervous giggle. "Okay. Miss Ember." Then she scurried back to her desk.

The West Valley compound was unlike anything Ember had seen in the Mines. It was as if it was its own separate entity – like Tannen had said - *a world within a world.* There was nothing "Mine-like" to be found here as the inside was the lavish home built for a princess. Pastel painted rock walls, bright pink rugs, dangling crystal chandeliers… all the trimmings for a royal highness. Unlike other apprenticeships, potential elfwives spent a minimum of two elfyears (sometimes longer) here in luxury – one apprenticing, and one practicing — only to be cast out into the real world of darkness and grime. *Like covering reindeer droppings in chocolate – cause at the end of the day you still have…*

Girls came in and out of the waiting room with their colorful dresses and neatly groomed heads of dustless hair. They all stopped and stared when they noticed Ember sitting there. Some gasped, some giggled the nervous "Kiffer giggle," and some even pointed and whispered. Slowly but surely, Ember was becoming agitated. She clutched the envelopes in her hands, making the paper damp with her palm sweat. It was obvious that word she was there was getting around the compound, as more and more girl elves filtered in. Stopping. Staring. Pointing. Whispering. *Giggling.*

Ember could no longer stand the gawking, and could no longer control her tongue. "Um, Kiff?" she called over. "Wanna explain to me what in Claus's name is going on with all these girls? Why am I getting the feeling that I'm some kind of animal in a cage?"

Kiff straightened up and rushed over to Ember with a serious face. Her loafers shuffled on the shag rug. "Oh, no, quite the opposite, Miss Ember," she said, kneeling beside her. "They are just in *awe* of you."

"Me? Why?"

Kiffer giggled. "Why?" she repeated in surprise. "Well, for one, you're the only Abovegrounder they know of who was not sent here to the Valley. And of course, you're the great Ember Skye! You're fearless. You confronted the Council. Got your Life-Job *changed*! Why, you're an inspiration to all elves, everywhere. You're the light and the hope."

Ember soaked in the coldness of Kiff's words. *If only they knew.* If only they knew the struggle, the plight, the constant beating she gave herself on the inside every day, the way she wrestled with her moral self and her sense of duty towards others. Did she even have a sense of duty toward others, or was she simply a selfish being with closed-minded intentions? Would she be here right now if she wasn't driven by her own egocentric motivation?

"Where is she? Where is Ember Skye?" A voice boomed from the overhang balcony. Ember looked up to see Shella Arabighymm, the wild-haired, eccentric Head Mistress of West Valley. She leaned forward on the rock balcony, her arms crossed on the ledge. Her gray hair was tucked behind her pointy ears, exposing her dangling ruby earrings.

"She's right here, Mistress," Kiffer called.

"Good. Great. Splendid. Show her up, Kiff."

Kiffer led Ember up three flights of stairs and into an enormous suite. "This is Head Mistress's personal lodgings," she said, excitedly. "Hardly anyone is allowed here."

"You don't say," Ember replied as she looked around.

"Good luck!" Kiffer said. She touched Ember's shoulder and walked out of the room, closing the door behind her.

"Come in, come in," Shella called from one of the inside rooms.

Ember followed the sound of her voice to an opened door. It was a bedroom, and in the reflection of a mirror, Ember saw Shella standing in a closet with her back facing her. She removed her blouse and quickly pulled a red turtleneck sweater over her head.

"Darn girls," Shella grumbled as she came out and met Ember by the bed. She spoke quickly, and loudly. "No matter how many times

I say it, they simply can't understand the concept of forks on the left, spoons on the right!" She smoothed her hair back behind her ears and reached for Ember's wrists. "Ah, but I digress. Come, child. Let's talk." And she led her to the bed. "Please excuse the informalities of this meeting. I've just been swamped with new assignments and graduations and such. This is a rather busy time of the year for us, and..."

"Well, Mistress," Ember began, "I won't take too much of your time. I wanted to ask you about these." She held out the dampened letters.

"Oh, yes! Your pairing. I must admit I was a little shocked by the Council's decision at first. I said to them, 'The girl hasn't been properly trained!' but that didn't seem to matter much to them. So, we can schedule you for some basic courses today and get you good and ready for August."

August? Four months...

Ember rubbed her hands together and stammered, "It's just that... no... I haven't been trained, and I have new duties and all, and I didn't think I was eligible..."

Shella gasped. "Not eligible? Why, who at the Pole told you that? Every elfmaid is eligible! It's just a matter of..."

Ember swallowed hard. "Let me guess. A name being pulled from a cap."

Shella chuckled. It sounded forced and empty. "Silly, silly. It's not as easy as you make it sound. It's a bit more complicated and involved than that."

"Well, can it be undone? That's why I'm here, Mistress. There has to be a mistake in my assignment, and in..."

Shella looked down at the envelopes and nodded at Ember's. When she flipped to the second one and saw that it was an envelope for Tannen Trayth, her honey eyes opened wide with a sense of knowing. "Oh, I see," she sang out. "Say no more." She placed the envelopes in Ember's hands and closed her fingers over the parchment. "I understand where this is going, and unfortunately, there's simply nothing I can do. You know that elf-pairings are arranged, Ember. The Council is solely responsible for marriage assignments because nothing good has ever come from a self-match. I can count on both hands how many self-matches I've seen in all my years, and on one hand I can count how many have worked out in the long run. Two fingers, to be exact. If the Council deems this proper, then it's in their hands to say so. This Tannen elf will be fine with his pairing. And you will be fine with yours." Shella lowered her voice with concern, "I think it best you keep your distance from Mr. Trayth from now on."

"It's just that..."

Shella stiffened up and shot Ember a look. Instinctively, Ember's hands balled into defensive fists, readying themselves for a battle of sorts, the letters crumpled with a threatening crunch. "No!" she screamed uncontrollably as Shella's eyes widened. "I can't accept this! This is craziness! You don't even know the elf I'm assigned to. You don't even know the extent of his... his... his *disgustingness!*" The heat of her anger flushed her face to the point where she actually saw red through her tear-swelled eyes.

Shella glided to the doorway of her room and hovered next to the white box with a red button that was perched on the wall. Ember was able to see through her rage for a split second and understood that Shella was about two seconds from radioing for help, so she lowered her fists and clasped her arms behind her back.

"You don't understand," she said after she forced herself to calm down. "Please. You have to help me. If you don't, I'll have to take this up to the Council, and..."

Shella's shoulders relaxed. "This Trayth elf," she said calmly, "do you love him?"

The question took Ember's breath away, and she struggled to fight against her tears. All this time she knew she cared for him, but those feelings, those butterflies... it wasn't like with Barkuss, or Kyla, or even Nanny Carole. It was a different leveled feeling – a different kind of connection – and although she'd never said it to either him or herself for that matter, she shook her head, 'yes.' Yes! Yes! She did love Tannen! She loved him in a way that made her heart smile and her soul sing, and the thought of being without him nearly drove her to do crazy things like punch a gray-haired Mistress Elf out.

Shella gave a soft smile that quickly melted to a scowl and her face darkened with hideous annoyance. "Then if you love him like you say you do, you'll be wise to keep your mouth shut about this issue, Miss Skye. Do not inundate the Council with this... this *frivolousness*. You've churned up enough waters to last an elflife," she admonished. "Now go downstairs, mingle with your *adoring* fans, regale them with your wondrous tales, have something to eat. But speak no more of this. It is what is is."

Pulling a name from a cap.

Ember pulled back a little at Shella's shifting tone. Her admonition was enough to perk up any upset elf's ears, and she thought it would be best to close her mouth and consider this battle lost for now. "No, I think I'll just see my way out," she replied dejectedly.

"Very well, then. I'll have one of the girls escort you. You can find your way to the waiting room, I presume."

Ember nodded and walked past Shella into the hallway. The door to the Mistress's chambers slammed quickly behind her, the sound shattered through the silence of the cave and caused the chandelier in the great hall to rattle in its perch. She was in a daze as she made her way down the stairs back to the waiting room.

All for nothing. All for nothing.

There was a gaggle of elfmaids by the front entrance waiting for her to return. She didn't have the heart or energy to engage them in conversation, so she extended her hand and waved goodbye. They were whispering (much louder than before), pointing (more conspicuously than before), and giggling (more wildly than before). She overheard one elf gush, "She's my hero," and when Ember looked up and into the crowd, her eyes met the gaze of a pretty elfmaid with curly golden hair and pale pink eyes. Her cheeks were plump and rosy and her eyes were filled with so much wonder and *life*. The elf, who couldn't have been older than sixteen elfyears, smiled at Ember, who in turn, smiled back, but when Ember's eyes drifted to the girl's nametag and read "Holly Adaire," her smile slithered from her face.

Chapter Ten

Ember was trapped. She wasn't quite sure how it had happened, or when it had happened, but the important thing was that it *had* happened. The bubblegum pink walls closed in on her, surrounded her in a sparkly bad dream. Each tiny window was outfitted with baby blue curtains (that matched the living room furniture) and had pink polka dots to match the nauseating color of the walls. The light fixture that hung over the dining table was a dome of a freakish combination of brightly colored glass and rhinestones. In fact, everything was covered in shimmering rhinestones, creating a constant glittering effect all throughout Barkuss's den.

The girls in West Valley would surely love all this.

Actually, it reminded her of the circus that used to travel throughout the Pole. Nanny Carole used to bring her to the East Bank Town Square to see *The Amazing Poppeldote and the Silverstar Circus*. Big colorful tents would be erected in the center square, and elves from all over the city would come to witness the dazzling show. As an elfling, Ember was amazed at the elaborate decorations and flashing lights. Nanny Carole would buy her chestnuts and redcandy coated popcorn, and she would stare intently as Poppeldote, the alluring magician and master of ceremonies, would present all of the spectacular events of his Silverstar Circus. He had clown elves juggling glass jars, and acrobatic elves on high wire trapezes. There were pretty lady elves who wore rhinestone covered leotards throwing flaming batons in the air and catching them in their mouths. Everything was exciting — colors, lights, sparkling and mystifying acts. Then Poppeldote added animals to his show. Fantastical creatures from every elf's wildest fantasy. Giant Koolshlekkers with their pink feathers that extended for miles. Light blue Peetiepons that did high dive flips into pools of water. Flying Aplidoks that could repeat anything an elf said.

And the legendary Chyga with his burning red eyes and powerful claws. Of course, to an elfing's wonder-filled eyes, it was all real, all of it. But one year when the "Koolshlekker" got loose and revealed that the "Chyga" was really an animatronic robot operated on the inside by three worker elves, Poppeldote was pretty much finished, and the circus didn't return the following year. In retrospect, Ember realized how something could look so desirable and perfect on the surface, yet be so rotted and broken on the inside.

Now, she was stuck here in Barkuss's circus den – a blue and pink sparkle hell. It wasn't so much Barkuss's taste in décor that was the issue, it was the fact that she was here *babysitting* the twins.

She couldn't remember the actual words, as Barkuss had approached her while she was in the midst of working. "Could you? Would you? Bommer won't stop bugging me about going to... and they're really well-behaved, and..." She had just kind of waved her hand in the air dismissively, more concerned with the spreadsheet in front of her, and huffed and mumbled a barely audible, "yea, yea." He had squealed and kissed her cheek before she had a chance to realize just what she had agreed to do.

She couldn't help feeling a little bamboozled by Barkuss, but he was right, the boys were super well-behaved, and besides, being here with them was much better than going to the Maidens' Brunch in West Valley that she had been invited to. Bambam and Juju stayed in Barkuss's office and pretty much kept to themselves. As a matter of fact, they hadn't come out of the office the whole time she was there.

Ember listened to them play. They were building a fortress with Barkuss's collection of colored stones. The two chittered and chattered, completing each other's sentences, getting angry at the other for doing something "wrong," and laughing at each other's ridiculous "war general dialog." She couldn't help but smile. They had each other, and that was the most important thing in the world. Even though she'd had a sister of her own, she had always felt like an only child. She and Ginger had always been at odds, right down to Ginger's very last days. Growing up, Ginger had always been so different from Ember – they never had much in common, and she could honestly say that the only thing that bound them together was the fact that they shared the same parents. Ember never felt like she *knew* Ginger. Ember always felt alone.

The only other elf who could vaguely understand her feelings of loneliness was Tannen. Many nights, the two had discussed Ember's strained non-existent relationship with her sister, as well as Tannen's status as an only child. Tannen had always said that he didn't mind not having siblings – that it allowed him to have a better bond with his parents and there was no in-house competition for family status or clan recognition. Although she could just mildly relate, she was thankful that they were able to bond over parts of their vastly different pasts.

Tannen Trayth. I really miss you, Tannen.

I-thought-we-had-a-shot-at-happiness,Tannen.

I-don't-think-I-can-bear-the-thought-of-you-with-another-elf-Tannen...

After her unproductive visit to West Valley, her relationship with him had ended. Much like when she first kept her distance from him not so long ago. But this was different. Back then they had not been in any kind of relationship. There was no prospect of 'could we end up together?' Then things changed. A relationship bloomed. She caught those butterfly feelings for him on a deeper level. And in two fateful letters, it was over. After her meeting with the Head Mistress, Tannen had vowed to make things right. He said he would do everything he could to get a reversal. He said he would find a way. But at the same time, there was an unspeakable tension between them that drove them apart, and she doubted that he was even pursuing the issue. She wasn't entirely off the hook, either. As much as she cared for him (her first love, call it what you will) she still had many walls – rocky walls that surrounded her small heart. And while he had chiseled away, torn down a lot of her defenses, there were still many untouched caverns that were wrought with stone.

She peered her head around the hallway corner when she heard Barkuss barge through the front door. "E? Where are you?" he frantically called. He was with his older brother, Bommer. The two were returning from a meeting of the Brotherhood.

"Here. Right here," she said as she walked into the living room.

Barkuss ran his hands through his hair. His eyebrows were raised and he kept shifting his weight back and forth on each leg. He was upset, unnerved. "Ooo, girl. They're talking about some crazy stuff over there! They're scheming like fiends!"

She chuckled. "What could a bunch of Coal Elves possibly be plotting? New pickaxe techniques? How they're going to bypass the ban on fishing in Onyx Alley?"

Bommer huffed under his breath. He sat down on the couch and rubbed at his temples as if he had returned from a long and frustrating day of coordinating and overseeing and working. He was a Manager of one mining crew in a western cavern called Lignite Gorge — one of the most dangerous caverns in the Mines. The coal there was highly susceptible to catching fire, and a single spark from a pickaxe could ignite a monstrous blaze in the seam that could burn for weeks. It must have been physically and mentally draining to have to check, double check, and triple check his crew's safety gear, and helmet size, and pickaxe blade density, and "hey, don't you dare light that lantern down here!" To add insult to injury, his own father, Borthen Dwin'nae, had worked - and died - in Lignite Gorge.

"Don't joke! I'm serious, E. They're talking about organizing up. Starting a revolution. You gotta go hear them."

"Oh yea?"

Barkuss rubbed at his own temples. "We left early. Weren't sure how long they were gonna keep going. But it was sure getting heated!"

Bommer looked over at Ember and nodded in her direction. "You're 'in' with the Council, right? Maybe you can alert them or something," he said, his voice deep and grumbly.

Ember exhaled in exasperation. "First of all, let's get something straight- I'm not 'in' with anybody. Second of all, I'm not so sure we can fully trust the Council with much of anything. What if they're really behind this Brotherhood nonsense? At this point, after all of *their* schemes, I wouldn't put it past them."

"I doubt it," Barkuss piped in. "Right before the meeting was going to break for recess, I overheard some of the elves talking, saying some real nasty stuff. Saying 'The Council's going down,' and all that. No. I don't think the big C is involved in this at all."

Ember didn't respond for a second, unsure exactly what Barkuss was saying, or what he was asking her to do. "How many elves were at this meeting?"

Barkuss's eyes widened and he threw his hands in the air. "Tons! Bommer said when he first started going, there were only a small handful of guys. Right, Bom?"

Bommer closed his eyes and nodded.

"But now!" Barkuss continued. "Girl, I couldn't even begin to count how many heads were there."

Ember imagined the scene — a throng of elves rallying together so their voices could be heard all the way to the northernmost point of Norland. The image intrigued her. Perhaps, if there were enough of them screaming for change, she would have just the right avenue for her voice to be heard. A voice that would cry and scream about the injustice of her upcoming wedding to Sturd! Something inside her clicked, and her pointed ears listened more carefully to what Barkuss was saying.

"I don't know." Barkuss shrugged his shoulders and locked his gaze on hers. "But I think you need to at least hear what's going on for yourself, cause when the reindeer droppings hit the fan, I don't wanna be the one to tell ya 'I told ya so!'"

Whatever he had seen and heard at that meeting had obviously shaken him up enough to seek her opinion or help or whatever it was he was seeking from her. In his eyes, she recognized a familiar look, a longing, a certain hope. It reminded her of the way the wondering eyes of the girls from West Valley had stared so longingly, so wonder-filled, so hopeful, in awe. Everyone must now see her in a different light, through a different lens.

She swallowed hard, and thought about West Valley. Tannen wasn't allowed on the premises because he wasn't female. How would she be perceived as the only girl elf there? Would they even allow it? "There's kinda one problem, Barkuss," she said. "It's a *Brotherhood* meeting. I'm not exactly a brother, now, am I?"

Barkuss clapped his hands together and gave a small squeal. "You'll come to check it out?"

Ember nodded. "Yea, yea. I gotta know, ya know?"

"Then don't you worry about a thing, sugar! I know just how to fix you up! We'll just need to pin up your hair and stick it under a helmet or something. That's not a problem at all. Bommer, do you think we can come by your place and use some of Jacinda's makeup tools?"

Bommer grunted and nodded his head.

Barkuss squealed again in delight. "Bam! Ju!" he called to the boys. "Pack up your things, we're all heading for your den!"

Back at Bommer's, Barkuss went to work on Ember's make-under. "This," he said as he waved Jacinda's makeup case in front of her, "this is where the magic happens. I'm gonna turn you from strikingly beautiful to downright manly."

Ember scrunched her nose. "You think I'm pretty?"

Barkuss huffed. He swept her hair up into a tight ponytail and inserted tiny pins to hold it in place. "Please, honey. Let's not get into that whole self-conscious-I'm-fishing-for-a- compliment-routine. You're gorgeous. You know it. Everyone knows it. Now, I'm gonna make you ungorgeous."

No, I don't know it, Barkuss. Ember shrugged, but Barkuss swatted at her shoulders to stay still. "Ya know, I'm not even going to ask you how you learned to use all that makeup junk," she said, changing the subject.

Barkuss laughed. "And if you did ask, I don't think I'd tell ya!"

Bommer's wife, Jacinda, stood at the kitchen sink washing up the greens for their dinner. Her back was slightly hunched over as she worked, and Ember couldn't decide if it was from physical pain, or some kind of sadness that was plaguing her body. The boys played tag around and through her legs, laughing wildly, before she raised her hand in the air and yelled at them to "scoot." They punched at each other, and took a seat at the table. Ember shuddered as she thought this scene could one day be of her and Sturd and their brood of elflings.

"Why did you guys even go to the meeting in the first place?" Ember asked through tight lips as Barkuss shushed her to sit still.

"Monsters," Bommer mumbled, and the twins gave each other a frightened look.

Jacinda rolled her eyes as she set the dinner table. "Here we go again," she said in a musical voice, "tell them all about your Chygas." The twins stiffened in their seats, and Barkuss winked an eye at them as if to calm them down. "Monsters aren't real," he assured them. "Your Uncle Banter and your dad used to tease me and your Uncles Bulder and Balrion. They used to tell us stories of the deadly Chyga — a ferocious beast with red eyes, sharp claws, and a sharp twisty tail that stalked the Mines. Their magic was said to be so powerful, Chygas could disappear at will and hide within the rock walls, waiting for their unsuspecting victims —who were always elflings, of course. A Chyga had three prickly horns on its head, and if they ever grazed your skin, you would fall into a deep coma. Me, and Balrion, and Bulder would be scared out of our minds! And of course, Papa would scold Uncle Banter and your Dad, and declare, 'Monsters aren't real,' hoping to quell our terror. Uncle Banter and your Dad would roll on the floor laughing at us, but sometimes, just sometimes, his own imagination would get the best of him, wouldn't it Bom? Your Dad would find himself up in the middle of the night with the covers drawn up over his head, praying to Claus the Chyga wasn't in the walls of his room waiting to attack."

Jacinda set plates of food down in front of the boys and wiped her hands on her burlap apron. "Barkuss, please stop scaring the children," she said with a frustrated sigh.

Barkuss laughed. "What? What did I do?"

"I still don't understand," Ember said as soon as Barkuss eased up on her face, "what do Chygas have to do with the Brotherhood?"

Bommer rubbed his temples and shook his head. "I don't know. I can't explain it. There are other elves who are just as frustrated and fed up, like I am. And they are willing to do something about it. There are others who are like-minded and want serious change. And I don't mean some cutesy perks like a Light List, or some Adam's Day festival. I'm talking major stuff. Life altering stuff. So, I guess the thought of having a voice was appealing."

"Hasn't there been enough change these last two elfyears?" Jacinda sighed, again. "What more could you possibly want? I don't know why you ever agreed to move up to Manager. You saw the stress it put on your father. And there was a reason why Banter never moved up. He always said that staying in his Supervisory position was the one thing that was keeping him alive."

Bommer slammed his fists onto the slab, shaking the table against the rock floor. "But he's not alive," he growled in a low voice.

Jacinda bowed her head and turned to face the sink again, cowering at the volume of Bommer's voice. The boys kept their hands under the table, but Ember could sense they were pawing at each other's legs for comfort. Ember felt sorry for Bommer — sorry for all of them. They had all lost something or someone to the Sickness, and it was clear to her that Bommer saw the Brotherhood as a means to closure. But there was a tinge of guilt in the pit of her belly, because her excitement about the Brotherhood meeting was purely self-serving. There were no wounds to heal, or dead brothers to mourn for. She had made peace with the loss of her family, and even the loss of her dear friend, Banter. Right now, she was praying to Claus that this Brotherhood meeting was to be the opportunity she had been hoping for.

"Bom, it's been a while now," Barkuss said calmly. "You have to let go at some point."

"Let go? Let go? Our brother died and you're telling me to let go?"

Barkuss leaned over the table and reached for Bommer's hands. "I get it," he said in a gently, "I do. Truly. You're the oldest of us all, and there was a part of you that felt like you needed to protect him. Us. But you can't, Bom. You couldn't. It was a freak accident. A sickness that we couldn't control. I'm not saying *not* to mourn, but there comes a time when…"

"You let it go?"

"Exactly."

Bommer pushed his chair back and stood up. "Well, maybe you can. Maybe you can let it all go — Mom, Dad, Banter. But I can't. I just can't." He walked over to Barkuss and pointed a finger in his face. "I was the one who claimed Banter's body. Not you. Me! You didn't see the look on his face. The way his skin was blue and crackled." He closed his eyes for a second and shuddered at the memory. "It was horrifying! I'll never be able to get those images out of my mind!"

Like a dead monster, Ember thought.

"But you *have* to!" Barkuss squealed. "You have to at least try. If we let every loss we've suffered through eat away at our hearts, there'd be nothing left of us! And what would become of your wife? Your boys? They'd all be walking around with some shell of a Daddy. Some monster behind an elven face. Do you really want that for them?"

Bommer waved his hands in the air as if to discredit what Barkuss said. "What do you know, Barkuss? You sure know how to turn a blind eye. If you had seen Banter..."

"I didn't have to." Barkuss looked at the floor. "Don't you think I wanted to help him, too? He was my brother, too. But what could we do? Our hands were so tied up. So twisted with that Sickness..."

"What if I told you I didn't think it was the Sickness that killed him?"

Barkuss's head shot up and he locked eyes with Bommer. "What? What do you mean?"

"Forget it," Bommer mumbled. "She ready to go?"

Ember stood up, shaky on her feet. "Ready," she said, smoothing her nervous hands down her jumpsuit. "How do I look?"

"Like a brother," Bommer said before he turned and walked out the door.

Chapter Eleven

THE SECOND HALF OF THE BROTHERHOOD MEETING HAD ALREADY STARTED, and if there were as many elves there as Barkuss had said, Ember was hoping to just slip into the crowd and remain inconspicuous. She felt extremely out of place among the male elves. Her small frame looked disproportionate next to their taller builds, and the makeup Barkuss used to create a mustache and beard on her face was starting to itch. Badly.

The cavern was lit only with soft helmet lights strategically placed in an outside circle, giving this Brotherhood meeting a clandestine feel. She and Bommer took a spot in the crowd next to a large elf. He grumbled and shoved a piece of paper in her hands. On it there was a chart with twelve boxes. Each box was numbered and had a different picture to represent something. There were no words anywhere on the page. Boxes 1-6 were X'ed out with deep coal marks.

Balrion, Bommer's younger brother by four elfyears, came up and stood in between them. He narrowed his brow at Bommer, as if to say, "Who's that?" Bommer closed his eyes and shook his head.

An elf made his way to the front of the crowd and stood on a wooden crate. Beside him stood two other elves dressed in un-Coal-Elf-like garb. Their cheeks were rosy, as if they had recently been Aboveground.

The elf on the crate cleared his throat in order to get everyone's attention. "Ahem!" He called, and the elves stopped their chatter. "We are so grateful to our organizers, the Nim'sim Brothers, for taking the time and energy to put together this twelve-point plan." He stepped down from the crate, and one of the rosy cheekers got up to speak.

"Brothers," he said in a hushed voice. "We're so glad that you decided to come out tonight. We understand this was a long meeting, and we appreciate you waiting for my brother and me to return to wrap things up. Hopefully, you will take back the message and share it with the others. Our hope is that we can achieve a united front for change."

Balrion nudged Ember with his elbow. "I know those guys," he said out of the side of his mouth. "They're the Nim'sim Brothers."

Ember, taken aback, just grunted. She figured it was an appropriate male elf response.

"Some of you mined with us in Raker's Cove," the crate elf continued, "but many of you know us because you attended parties at our den when the List was abolished and mining stopped. I'm Nim Nim'sim, and this is my brother, Sim." Nim motioned to his brother, who bowed his head respectfully.

Some Coal Elves nodded, Balrion included. "They gave the best parties," he whispered to Bommer.

Bommer waved his hand to silence his brother.

The brother elf not on the crate raised his arm high in the air. "So, during that Lull time, when all of us were free to go about our business however we saw fit, my brother and I had many lengthy conversations about lots of things, the biggest topic being – life. Life, in general. Most importantly, the life of a Coal Elf."

"What does it exactly mean to be a Coal Elf?" Nim interjected, looking at his brother. "We thought about this over and over again, and the answer is really simple. Being a Coal Elf means you mine the coal for the bad kids in the human world. Or, you collect that coal. Or, you oversee the elves who mine the coal. Or, you drive the trolley that takes the elves around to mine, or collect, or oversee. Or you train the elves to mine, or collect, or oversee. Or you build structures for the miners, collectors, and overseers."

"Or you import goods for the miners, collectors, and overseers. Or you harvest crystals for the Importers to use as currency for the goods for the miners, collectors, and overseers."

They were going back and forth, practically talking over each other.

"Do you see where we're going with this?" Sim said with a raised voice. "What we have to do is dictated to us. We're all told what we can or cannot do. We're told if we're even going to have an elfwife or not. What choice do we have in anything? What say do we have in any aspect of our lives? Do I want to mine? No! But I have to. Because someone told me I have to."

"And do I want to mine?" Nim added. "Sure. It's okay. Not a bad job. But I'd like to go to the surface every once and awhile without having to get written permission from a group of elves who think they're better than everyone else."

The Coal Elves in the circle were starting to mumble and grumble in agreement. Ember looked down and saw that Balrion was anxiously rubbing his hands together.

"Where is the equity between the Abovegrounders and Belowgrounders?" Sim said. "Why are we the ones destined for dust and darkness, and the ones up there are free to come and go as they please in the sunshine?"

"We need to band together," Nim added. "We need to make so much noise down here that they hear us up there."

"And not ignore us!" someone in the circle called out.

Bommer clenched his fists in excitement, and Ember felt a rush of adrenaline race through her. She was quickly becoming convinced that this was the exact avenue she needed to ride down in order to save her future. This was exactly the course of action she needed to capitalize on. She scanned the faces of the other Coal Elves in the group, and their eyes spoke volumes to her. She was not alone in the way she felt. They all had their independent reasons for being there, but they were all there for the same basic needs: Change. Freedom. A better way of life for himself. A better way of life for their families.

She looked at Bommer —his fists jammed in his pockets, his eyes closed tight. Was he thinking of his boys, his twins, his most precious children? Did he not want to see them grow up hacking and slashing at cave walls for their entire lives. *Not unless they really wanted to.* But who wanted to? Bambam and Juju were bright and playful and so full of life. Ember couldn't imagine their hearts growing dark like so many in the Mines, or suffer from uncontrollable illnesses, or become indifferent, or complacent, or worse, apathetic. She was sure he wanted his boys to be able to have a choice. A say in the direction their lives were to go. If Juju wanted to be a Toymaker Elf, he should have that option. If Bambam wanted to be a Banker Elf, then why not?

"Bulder had so many dreams and desires," Balrion whispered to Bommer. Ember strained her ears so she could hear their conversation. "But his mind was sick, and when Momma left, something inside him snapped."

Bommer didn't open his eyes, as if to ignore what Balrion was saying. Ember gurgled in her throat, "Who's Bulder?" hoping he would turn his attention, and his head, in her direction.

"My brother," he continued, as she had hoped. "One day, while going through a typical round of Coppleysites, he had indulged on too much grulish, and Bommer and Banter, our other brother, almost couldn't bring him out of the coma. When they did, the life, the spark, from Bulder's eyes was gone, replaced by a desperate look of a trapped animal who had been beat into submission." He turned toward Bommer again and lowered his voice. "I know you never want to see that look again, especially not in the eyes of your boys."

She could feel the energy pulsating throughout the cavern. Nim raised his hand. "Our twelve-step plan is bound to get us noticed. The elves Aboveground have their plans and their decrees, and dole out their letters and directives. Well, no more! It's our turn to take back the paths of our lives. We are now preparing for the next phase. If you look at your handout you'll see that this phase, phase seven, is going to be a pivotal one. The seven elves who have been chosen have volunteered their services in good faith. This is certainly not going to be an easy task. Our seven "swans" will covertly cross the Ignis, get to the Mouth, and meet with our contacts Aboveground. There, the process of organizing the Aboveground faction of the Brotherhood with us down here will begin."

The throng applauded with a thundering sound and Ember felt a sudden alarming rush in her body. Barkuss was right. All of this "organizing" and heated energy in one concentrated place couldn't be good for any of them. Her eyes darted back and forth across the crowd, trying to see if she recognized any of the Coal Elves, but stopped when she realized she was the only elf who wasn't clapping. A few of the others around her took notice and were boring their eyes into her body. She quickly brought her hands together in an over exaggerated applaud, lowered her voice as deep as she could, and let out a dramatic, "Whoo-hoo! Yeah!" It was so unnatural sounding that the second it left her mouth, she wanted to crawl into a rock shelf and hide. More eyes stared, their faces questioning her. Ember's hands went slick with sweat and tiny beads began to form on her head underneath the helmet and on the top of her lip. The top of her lip where Barkuss had artfully drawn a semi-believable mustache now threatened to be smeared by the dampness of her paranoia. *They're staring. They're staring. They're staring.*

"The Council has told us about their plan for Christmas in July," Sim chimed in, his voice rising above the mumbled echoes of the other elves. "But, doesn't anyone find it odd that they never told us why? Remember the Coal-less night, brothers? Did they ever explain why?"

"Of course not!" someone from the crowd yelled.

"No, no," Sim agreed. "Of course not, is right. But we know the truth now. We have connections."

Ember turned her head in his direction. The timbre of his voice on the word *connections* sounded… off. Up until this point, this meeting had been semi-innocuous — just a group of riled up Coal Elves. But the way he emphasized the word 'connections' made her stomach twitch.

"The names in the Book are being blackened out," Nim continued. "And you all know what that means for us. We have it on good authority that there have been thousands of names that have burned away like dry leaves under a hot summer sun."

Ember raised her eyebrows. *Thousands? No. Not yet, at least. But how did they know…*

"And our contact Aboveground is a solid one," Sim added. "He knows what he's talking about. He says that even Madame Claus herself is fearful of what's to come."

"So, we need to act in a timely manner," Nim said. "That's why we're letting our voices be heard gradually, in twelve steps. This way, when the situation becomes dire enough…"

Ember froze.

Did he just say 'dire'?

This whole Brotherhood thing reeks of Sturd.

She turned her nose upward like a bloodhound, inhaling the different scents that wafted throughout the crowd, hoping to get some indication that maybe - just maybe - Sturd was possibly behind the organization. There was no other way that they could have known about the blackened names. It had to be Sturd. He had to be behind this. Then, she looked around the crowd again, scanning the faces of the elves, searching for his royal ugliness. The other elves looked so hopeful, but there was an anger plastered on their faces. An anger that swelled inside them and festered until...

The situation becomes dire enough.

And like a ton of bricks it all became clear to her. She had been focusing on setting the wrong situation right. The Blackened Names in the Book. While there weren't thousands of them like the Nim'sim elf had said, there was enough to cause a stir in the ranks. More frighteningly, the number was growing beyond what any of the Council could have imagined. Her eyes swept to the back of the pack, and she saw him. *Tannen.* He was standing, taller than most elves, listening intently to the elf on the crate saying something about "our time down here" and "things need to change." Things did need to change. But the issue of her impending marriage to Sturd was not the "thing" she needed to fight for or change. She smiled to think that Tannen was there trying to figure out a way to fight for her, too. But she soon realized that the Brotherhood was of no help to her, or Tannen, or any other elf for that matter. If Sturd is in fact involved with them, then there's a much larger problem brewing at the Pole. Is the Council involved? Does the Boss know what's going on in his proverbial basement? Coming to the meeting had opened her eyes to a scenario she hadn't even dreamed possible. Her 'marriage issue' was secondary compared to this, and while it pained her to think that, she was able to recognize the larger problem at hand.

She continued to stare at Tannen for some time, but when he looked up and over in her direction, she turned her head, slumped her shoulders forward, and turned her back on him.

Her chest tightened as she felt the sweat streaming down her temples. It wouldn't be much longer until all her camouflage would be nothing but a smear of black and beige inky-ness. She tried mapping an escape route so she could duck and cover her way out before anyone exposed her for being a fraud.

The Nim'sim brother stepped off the crate, replaced by the elf who introduced him. One of the crowd members shouted "Nim'sim Power!" The Coal Elves gave a quiet applause. The Nim'sim brothers moved to the outside of the circle and began shaking hands with each elf as he left.

"Thank you so much for coming," Nim said to Bommer as he heartily gripped his hand.

Bommer nodded at both of them. "Our brother, Bulder, wanted to be here, but he was working late tonight," Balrion said excitedly.

"Well, not a problem at all," Nim responded with a smile. "We will have plenty of other meetings. I think our message is a strong one. We're not alone, and we're going to see a change, very soon."

Sim extended his hand in Ember's direction. Shaken by his puzzled expression, she awkwardly grumbled and waved her hand in a 'goodbye' gesture.

Bommer nodded again then grabbed at Balrion's work suit to move him along. Ember hurriedly followed behind. As they moved past the circle of faint light and closer to the darkness beyond, Ember caught a glimpse of something. A shape? A shadow with two glowing red eyes and prickly horns lurking in the darkness of the cave?

A Chyga?

"Did you just see that?" she asked Balrion.

"See what?"

"Nothing. I... uh... I thought I saw something over there in the corner."

"Like what? A monster or something?"

"Or something," Bommer said under his breath.

"Oh, big brother!" Balrion laughed and patted him on the back. "Monsters aren't real!"

But aren't they? Ember thought. *Aren't they alive and well and roaming the Mines right now? Aren't they hiding their monstrous faces and bodies in the guise of an elven shape? Aren't they in plain sight issuing laws and decrees for their own selfish benefit? And the masses would be none-the-wiser for it. Taught from birth to never question, taught from birth to always obey, all elves at the Pole knew that no one ever dared going against Santa Claus. Right? But even when he forces them to work jobs they hate, or marry elves they despise, or traps them in a hole for their entire existence while wicked monsters prowl in the darkness? What kind of leader lets that happen? What kind of leader lets names in a sacred book go poof, knowing full well the ramifications it could have on his people? What kind of leader lets his people eat poisoned fruit and suffer from a horrifying Sickness? A monstrous one?*

At least the Brotherhood has the right idea. And if Sturd is behind the Brotherhood, well, then maybe he has the right idea, too.

Something needs to give.

Something needs to change.

The monsters both Above and Below need to be vanquished.

Chapter Twelve

I T WAS SOME TIME SINCE THE GRAESPURS HAD LEFT THE MINES, AND WHAT should have been Ember's time for sleeping was interrupted by the endless thoughts in her mind. Once again, she found the weight of her life's circumstances uneasily resting on her shoulders. She tossed and turned until she finally gave in and sat up in bed. There would be no slumber tonight. *No rest for a Coal Elf.* To pass the time, she reached over to her nightstand and pulled from the top drawer her trusty Journal. Thumbing through the pages was like thumbing through a lifetime in a matter of ten seconds. This book had kept all her pain and suffering for the last eight elfyears, but the pages weren't all doom and gloom. There were moments of clarity, goals, dreams, and yes, accomplishments. In a way she felt a kind of privilege to have seen so much in such a small span of life. Feeling compelled and overwhelmed with thought and emotion, she picked up a pen from the drawer and began to write on a clean page:

I can't sleep this off. Was it not enough?
Time goes by in a blaze... Am I

Everything they want? Am I
Everything they need?

What would you do if your life was full of coal?
And with everything I know
Should I go?

I break through the rock, But I'm not broken.
I just scream at the top of my lungs.
Am I...
Everything they want?
Am I...
Everything they need?

E.S.

Right there, right in front of her, was everything she needed to know. Clarity. Truth. And she had to accept it. She had to accept a fate she was in no way prepared for. As much as it pained her, she had to accept her marriage to Sturd because there truly was no other alternative. The blackened names were the priority. An alternative to the nonsense also-known-as-Christmas-in-July was the priority. And marrying Sturd? Well, that was now part of the plan...

She had cried over it, prayed to Claus over it, talked about it with Barkuss and Kyla, and every time, Ember came to the same undeniable conclusion: Sturd cannot be trusted, and if he is mobilizing the Brotherhood for his own gain, the Brotherhood cannot be trusted. She can't go to the Council with this because if the Council was behind the Coal-less Night, then *they* cannot be trusted. Hell, she even had her doubts about whether or not the Boss himself could be trusted!

Marrying Sturd was the only way she would be able to get close enough to him to figure out just what in the hell his intentions truly were, and put a stop to his schemes.

She smoothed her fingers over her initials on the page – 'E.S.' 'Ember Skye.' The letters of her name looked alien, unfamiliar. On the opposite side of the page, she began scribbling her name over and over and over again, alternating between print and script, big and little letters, sloppy and neat... all different ways to see if any combination would feel like herself. Big, jagged 'E's' with miniscule 'mber's' attached. She even went so far as to write her entire name, the one given to her upon her birth by her mother – Ember Autumn Skye. Nothing looked right. More importantly, nothing *felt* right.

As if her hand was acting of its own accord, she began writing *Ember Trayth*. The words seemed to pour from her hand and out onto the page with a gentle fluidity that had a calming effect on her. Her 'E's' looked like bursting Alcanthia petals rising from a rock garden, and when she wrote her 'T's', she extended the bottom part of the scripted letter to underscore her entire first name, making it appear that both names were joined. Joined together. Joined in spirit and soul and marriage. It felt natural — the way the letters left the pen, the way the syllables sounded together in harmony. *Ember Trayth. Ember Autumn Trayth. Mrs. Trayth. Mrs. Ember Trayth...* That was not to be, though. The feelings she had for Tannen had to be squelched. Abolished. Demolished. Obliterated. As if they were never there in the first place.

On the outside, she had to maintain her stance of defiance against the Council in their pairing of her and Sturd. Even though she had resigned to the marriage, with good reason, she didn't want anyone to suspect that she was up to anything. She had confronted the Council with a request for change of assignment, as everyone probably expected her to do. She had approached Councilwoman #2 in her personal office, hoping her inherently gentle nature would cause her to feel some sort of empathy for her plight. Cerissa Lux had sat at a small metal desk. Her shoulders had bopped up and down, an uncontrollable reaction to her shaking leg. And just as Ember had anticipated, Ms. Lux's final answer was to "put it in writing for formal review." That night, for good measure, Ember wrote an entire dissertation to the Council, outlining all the cons of a Sturd/Ember pairing. Days later, she received her letter back with a stamp on the envelope that said DENIED.

Denied. Denied. But she was determined. She wrote another letter the next day, longer than the first, only to get the same response. Then she wrote another. Then another. Then Barkuss chimed in and wrote one. All returned with the same response. DENIED.

This was good. This was very good for her plan.

With her pen, she feverishly scribbled *Ember Ruprecht*, for the hell of it. Just writing the words together made her sick. The letters sounded harsh. Guttural. She pressed the pen so hard against the paper as she wrote, she nearly tore a hole into the page.

Ember Ruprecht.

She said it out loud, emphasizing the last syllable of the last name with a deep throat rattle, a gagging sound that wasn't entirely intentional.

Sturd...

Of all the elves in the Mines, it had to be Sturd.

From day one, there was always Sturd. The year she apprenticed under Corzakk, she *lived* with Sturd. After her training was complete, she was eventually assigned to work under Sturd. Now, she was going to spend the rest of her life as his elfwife?

When she first met him, she was a naïve elfling of ten, and his appearance had frightened her right away. She had gasped when Corzakk forced him to shake her hand; the unusual coldness of his touch had sent an icy shiver throughout her body that startled her to the core. But Nanny Carole had admonished her to hold her tongue and to be mindful of the Coal Elves' differences, so taking her nanny's advice she looked past his un-elflike appearance. And although she was surprised at the way his eyes glared red and the way his ears pointed straight up like razors, his jet black hair hung shaggily around his brow and down his neck, and when she caught a glimpse of his side profile, it made him look almost... *normal.*

Their year together was definitely an interesting one, to say the least. If their interactions back then were any indicator of what their life together was to be...

Ember winced, trying hard to remember a good memory from their past. Something calm, or sweet, or civil, to give her the slightest bit of hope for the future, but it was no use – any memory of her time living with Sturd that was remotely decent always ended the same way... in chaos...

Corzakk was done giving lessons for the day.

His group of three apprentices were packing up their gear and getting ready to make their way back to their assigned dens. Sturd was with them, too. Two years their senior, he was in a different training program – one that would prepare him to quickly move up the ranks and become a Manager. He tucked his pencil behind his ear and folded his notepad over.

It was almost night time, and Ember jumped when the Graespurs began rousing in their nests throughout the cavern. She had been only a few months into her stay in the Mines and was still getting used to all of the strange surroundings. The two other elflings in the apprentice group talked in hushed whispers and glanced at Ember every now and then. They sniggered and kicked at the rocks beneath their feet in her direction. This made Ember uneasy, but by now she was used to certain derision, having experienced much from the Land Elves for nearly a year. She ignored them and continued putting her tools in her pack.

"Hey Ember," one of them said. "Why so jittery?"

The other laughed and continued in on the teasing game. "Yea. Why so jittery? Something scare you?"

"No. I'm fine," she had replied meekly, trying to avoid eye contact.

"Scared of some little Graespur, are ya?"

"No," she answered. "Just leave me alone, okay?"

The both of them started kicking more rocks and dirt at her; a cloud of rock dust rustled up and into her eyes.

"Stop it!" she coughed.

The two laughed and teased her some more. "Oh, poor little Ember. Scared little Ember. Can't hack it down here like us Ceffles, can ya?"

"Leave her alone," a quiet voice said. It was Sturd.

The elves continued to chuckle, as if not hearing the warning from Sturd. One of them reached into his coal sack, rubbed his palms on top of the black substance, and ran over to Ember. He smeared his hands all over her face and throughout her hair. The other, taking a cue from his friend, did the same thing. They were both pawing at her with their coal streaked hands while she bucked wildly and tried to fight them off. "Now you really look like us," they were saying. "Get down and dirty like a real boy!"

"Go away! Go away!" she screamed as she swatted at them.

Suddenly, the assault stopped. Sturd had quickly stepped in and shoved the boys away. "I said to leave her alone," he growled. The boys scrambled to their feet and apologized to him.

Ember was left in a state of confusion. Sturd had been nothing but cold and cruel to her from the moment she set foot in the Mines, and now he was coming to her defense? Was he having a change of heart?

They didn't speak the entire walk back to Welfort Den, and when they reached home, Sturd went to his room and Ember went to hers. Corzakk called the two for dinner later that evening, and as they sat down he said, "So, I hear there was a little scuffle before we left the cave."

"It's fine. I handled it," Sturd replied.

"Good. Let's not have any more of that out there. If any of the higher ups were evaluating us, it wouldn't look good for our crew."

Sturd began picking at the food on his plate. "Yes, Father," he answered before putting a slice of meat in his mouth with his hand. Ember kicked at him under the table getting his attention, and he looked up at her with furious eyes. Her questioning look made him sneer, his lip curling up over his ragged teeth. "Because," he said, as if reading her mind, "any of your torments are going to come from me."

You certainly were right about that one, Sturd.

She rose from her bed trying to shake off the memory of him, and began to walk into the kitchen. There was a little leftover grulish in the refrigerator, and she thought that maybe a small teaspoon would help ease her mind and let her sleep. But when she passed by her oak vanity, her own reflection made her do a double take.

The elf in the large central mirror stared back at her. A semblance of her former-self, her elflinghood-self, poked through but once again she could see the slow transformation of her appearance starting to take shape. Her frequent trips Aboveground had lessened the effects on her complexion from the Mines. She could once again see the creamy white color of her skin — her cheeks now plumping up with a rosy shade of health, no longer gray and sunken in with malnutrition.

The figure of her side profile was more pronounced, meatier than in previous years. No longer could she see the outline of her ribcage when she lifted her arms into the air. She thought of her sister, Ginger. The last time she had seen her, she was heavy with child — her stomach protruded from her housedress like a giant rubber ball. Poor Ginger! Taken far too soon from the Sickness, her only child left to be raised by Nanny Carole. Even though the sisters had not gotten on very well, there were things about Ginger that Ember missed. Ginger was a constant in her elfling world. Ember remembered that every morning before they got ready for school, Ginger would stand in front of the mirror and make an awful clacking noise with her mouth. Not like Sturd's trademark "tsk," but more of a squishy sounding, air sucking noise. She would only do it for a few minutes, but it had grated upon every one of Ember's last nerves. But when Ember had gone to the Mines and had woken up lonely in her den, the *absence* of that horrific sound was worse than the sound itself. As days went on, and Ember had started working in the Mines, the sound of her pickaxe chipping away at the rock walls was rhythmic, soothing, melodic... like a mouth making a ritualistic clicking sound in front of the mirror... Now there was no more Ginger to make the clicking sound, and no more chipping away at a rock wall.

Time to find a new constant. Time to get me to sleepy-land.

Ember placed her hands on top of the vanity and dipped her neck closer to the mirror. She examined her long hair from the top of her skull to her wrists. The once ashy-black color that had been a staple of her time in the Mines was now reverting back to its natural blonde hue. Another indicator that she had been spending more and more time Aboveground. *Long blonde hair, again. Except for...* She tilted her head forward and fingered through her scalp. "Another gray?" she commented as she plucked a white strand from its root and continued searching for more.

Two, three, four white hairs sprinkled throughout her tresses and Ember vigorously pulled out each and every one, letting them flitter to her floor.

"Great. As if I don't have enough problems." She sighed.

She left her bedroom and finally made her way to the kitchen. She had a sleep-date with some blackberry grulish and she didn't want to waste any more time. The thought of restful sleep tantalized her every movement. Even though it was only a little, and a very mild batch that Barkuss had prepared for her after her Big Night debut, she knew the sweet elixir would give her just enough of the push she needed to quiet her thoughts. She coughed a few times, as if there were someone around to whom she needed to justify her usage of the drink. When she felt like she was "in-the-clear," she opened the container and brought it to her lips. Just as she was about to cock her head back and indulge, she thought of Banter. He would have been so disappointed in her at that very moment. After all he had done for her… the look on his face when she had come out of the grulish-coma wouldn't have been nearly as heartbreaking as the one he would have had on now. She closed her eyes, straightened her head, and placed the cap on the bottle.

"Only when I need it, Banter. I promise."

Closing the fridge, she turned around and made her way back to her bed where she fought against her racing mind the entire night, but did so with a clear conscience.

Chapter Thirteen

THE THIN AIR WAS COLD, BUT NONE OF THAT MATTERED TO KYLA AS SHE leaned her body forward and nuzzled her face between Asche's thick antlers and into his dark, shaggy fur. There was a certain freedom in riding a reindeer, and she trusted Asche so much that she didn't even bother to harness herself to the saddle; rather she preferred stretching her body to a near laying position and allowed her legs and arms to dangle freely against the cold and racing wind. Asche's swift and gliding movements were so smooth that it made it hard for her to judge exactly how fast he was going. He dipped and circled in the air so gracefully for all his massive weight. It almost lulled her into a safe and happy dream.

The sun was cresting on the horizon, creating an arch of pink and gold against the gradually changing black sky. Below her, the city looked like ink spots on a child's painting – spatters of reds and blacks and blues randomly splashed on a snowy white canvass. She stretched out her hand with her palm turned outward and let the harsh wind filter through her fingers. *"Julchen!"* She called in Elvish for Asche to go faster. He pulled back slightly, his strong neck curved upwards, and in one quick motion shot forward like a cannonball. She buried her face in the spot between his antlers and grabbed tight around his neck, giggling all the while. She was *flying*, and she was *free* – free from the constraints of her Life Job, free from the memories of her lost family, free from paint splotch of a world below her. If only she could stay in the air like this forever with the miles upon endless miles of open sky – beauty untouched and unscarred from the hands of elvenkind. Just her, and Asche, and the cold morning air pounding against her ears, and the sun rising to start the glorious and free day. There would be no more training and judging and threat of illness and loss of family and rush of a holiday season.

Kyla dreaded her return to the stable, for today was the launching of the Christmas in July campaign, but the sun crept higher in the sky, telling her that there was much work to be done. "That's my boy," she said, stroking Asche's muzzle. "You're still the best. Thank you so much. But we have to go home now." Asche whinnied in disapproval and Kyla smiled. "I know. I know. I don't want to go back, either, but we have a lot of work to do." Asche let out a final grunt and began his descent back to the stable.

Yes, a busy day, indeed.

The launch of the Christmas in July program was a giant undertaking for all the elves at the Pole. The Council had announced that every elf would play a major role in trying to reverse the sudden outbreak of blackened names. And because the workforce had been so drastically reduced as a result of the Nessie Fruit Sickness, most elves would have to pull double and even triple duty. Rumor had it that there were over a thousand black names in the Book, and the number was said to be steadily increasing. No sooner had she questioned what her role would be (what could a simple Reindeer Trainer do?) she was informed that Plumm Stable was to be utilized as a hub station to send out supplies and materials to the businesses inside the cities. Some of her deer would even have to travel to West Bank.

The Council seemed to be a constant presence in her life ever since those Scarf Brothers had temporarily revoked her Training License. Thank Claus for Ember's help in convincing them that she was running a legitimate business, but that didn't stop the harassing visits and letters that were part of what they called their "Inquiry." Apparently, they were mostly interested in her knowledge of Elvish – who taught it to her, how she learned it, how old she was, who else in her family spoke it. A continuous barrage of questions that she answered the same way over and over and over again – she didn't remember exactly who taught it to her, couldn't remember how old she was when she started speaking it, and yes, other family members spoke it, too. She had always just assumed it was a family thing. Many years ago, Plumm Stable had produced one of the Boss's most prized reindeer, Blitzen, and all of the Boss's deer can understand Elvish. She just accepted that as a normal way of life and had never given it much thought. *Until the Council took such great interest in it...*

When they reached the stable, there were already city elves hustling and bustling about in the training field, stacking packages on large wooden pallets and lining them up to be sent off.

An elf with a clipboard in hand approached her. "Miss Plumm, whenever you're ready to get started." He was a tall elf with a deep voice, and Kyla noticed the thickness of his upper arms underneath his tight long-sleeved jacket. "We've lined up the bundles according to corporate need. Fabrics for the Designers, metal and wood for the Toy Makers, crystals and gems for the Jewelers, etcetera, etcetera. The Sled Elves have already delivered the emergency convoy of sleighs. We just need your signature here so we can get the ball rolling." He held the clipboard out for her to sign. "How many deer on your team did you say you have?"

"Eight," she said, taking the clipboard from him.

A surprised look came over his face. "Oh. No wait. That can't be right. The Sled Elves delivered…"

"I have twelve reindeer, but I'm only working eight today."

He shook his head, yanked the clipboard back, and made checkmarks on the paper, reminding Kyla of the scrutiny she had once endured by the Scarf Brothers. "I'm sorry, Miss Plumm, but we're going to need all the deer-power we can get. I just need you to verify…"

She sucked in the morning air between her gritted teeth with an aggravated sound. "Eight," she emphasized. "You're only going to be able to use eight today."

"I don't see how…"

"Listen, the stable was hit pretty hard by the Sickness, and I had a few deer make the Main Stable a year-and-a-half ago. I'm trying to build the team back up, if you catch my drift. There are four that are *indisposed* right now." Asche snorted as if to back her up.

The elf opened his mouth for a typical business-like retort, but paused and scratched his head in confusion.

"Mommas need to take care of their calves," she said with a smile.

"Ohhhh," he sang as he scribbled something on the paper and handed it back to Kyla. "I see. Guess we'll just have to make do with what you have."

She signed her name on a line at the bottom of the page, and initialed three different sections, acknowledging her approval of the use of her deer. She whistled, and within moments the team filed out of the barn and joined Asche in the field. She took a head count to verify that all were present – her esteemed bucks: Asche, Rory, Camden, and Dunkel. And her precious does: Viella, Ellavorn, Reindrop, and Madchen. She stood in front of them, pride swelling in her heart, and gave them a set of final instructions. Then she nuzzled each of their snouts, whispering a last word or two of encouragement, before turning to the head city elf. "I think we're good to go. Hitch 'em on up and move 'em on out!" The team huffed and grunted. Some of them stamped their hooves on the ground in excitement.

The city elf whistled and motioned for his crew to come and collect the deer to ready them for transport. As each of the city elves grabbed a deer's harness and began walking them to the sleds for hookup, Kyla cheered and patted each one on the rear as they passed by her. "Do me proud!" she encouraged.

"Oh, Miss Plumm," the head elf said as he ran back in her direction. "I forgot one thing. I need you to sign this last piece of paper. Right…" He flipped through the clipboard again and pointed at a pink triplicate form. "…here."

"What's this?"

"From the Sled Elves. Something about a Coal Sleigh. They put it in the barn away from the convoy so that my guys wouldn't confuse it. I need you to sign…"

"Yea. Yea. Yea," she muttered as she jotted a giant K and P on the page.

Ember's sleigh is ready.

She jumped with excitement and yelled, *"Aschen, dulkay julchen!"* And raced to the barn to see the sleigh. Asche, who had not yet been hitched, reared up on his hind legs and took to the sky, appearing in the barn in seconds.

The sleigh was set up next to the deer corrals and was covered in a white blanket. Kyla's heart almost stopped as she pulled the sheet down, revealing a shiny black lacquered carriage with fuzzy red velvet interior. There were two sitting rows and the benches were perched high so even the smallest of elves could properly steer. Why they chose to include a double row was a little odd, but she thought maybe the extra room would be for all the coal that needed transporting. Attached to the front end of the carriage were heavy black leather reins adorned with silver buttons. "C'mere, boy," she said to Asche. "Let's try these out. These are for you."

Asche glided to the sleigh and swatted at Kyla's shoulder with his snout in a defiant gesture. "No? Not now?" she asked. Asche grunted. "Okay, okay. You want to wait for Ember, eh? I get it, I get it."

She ran her hands down his velvety antlers and sighed. "Oh, my boy. My Asche. We've been through so much, haven't we?" His tongue darted out and licked the side of her face, a sign of affection that she only got from him. "It was right here, right in this barn, eight elfsummers ago. Stubborn as you are, you had to be born at night, didn't you?" Asche jerked his head up and down as if he were laughing with her. "My momma and poppa and Tyla all in the house sleeping. Poor me out here by myself, not knowing what in Claus's name to do, coaching your momma through the night. Boy, did you give her a run for her money! You came into this world like a rocket, all jet black like the night itself! You stood up straight right away, no tumbling or fumbling on your brand new legs and even started hovering above the ground within a half hour. And you looked right at me with those gorgeous blue eyes of yours. At *me*. And I knew right then and there that you were something else. Something special. You were mine."

Asche licked her cheek again, but a deep pang grabbed at her heart. "But you're not mine, anymore, are you, boy?" she said in a low whisper, and he shook his massive head back and forth in agreement. "You're Ember's now. And that's ok." She patted him one last time. "She needs you." Tears started to swell in her eyes and she blinked rapidly to prevent them from spilling over her cheeks. "Let's go. We got work to do."

Back outside, the elves were frantically stacking boxes into the sleds. Kyla hopped on Asche's back and guided him to a line of city elves who were hauling and lifting and of course, grumbling about it the entire time.

"Got my big guy right here," she announced.

One of the workers looked up and sighed. "Oh, yes!" he exclaimed in relief. "He is a big guy! Can we get him over to the Lumber Station at West Bank for a pick up?"

She nodded. "Whatever you need him for. He's all yours today."

"Great! Let's get him ready. He'll need to make the drop off at the factory."

"That's fine. He can handle…"

Suddenly, the sound of jingle bells made their way to the stable. Everyone stopped what they were doing and looked up. A team of four reindeer was approaching the ranch. They rode in a single file line with a driver at the head. From what she could see, three of them were hitched to an empty sleigh. Kyla gently kicked at Asche's side with her boot, and he took off for the front gate.

"Whoa! Whoa!" the driver said when she approached the stable, bringing her team to a stop. She was a robust elf. Short dirty blonde hair peaked out from underneath a giant straw sunhat adorned with yellow daisies. "This is Plumm Stables?" she said to Kyla.

Kyla dismounted Asche and walked to the gate. "Yes," she answered inquisitively. "Can I help you?"

The driver removed her white knit gloves and shoved them into the pockets of her yellow pinafore. "I'm Fannie Brightly," she said extending her hand. "Of Brightly Ranch in West Bank. We heard that you were being used as a transport station for the launch, and wanted to come by and give you a hand. We're a small ranch. I only got my four lovelies, but they're hard workers and take direction well. Figured the extra muscle couldn't hurt!"

"I'm Kyla. Kyla Plumm," she said, shaking Fannie's hand. "I know you! You used to be our biggest competition over here in East Bank."

"Yea, well, when our daughter got her Life Job, we just couldn't stay around. Too many memories. We relocated to West Bank shortly after."

"Well, we definitely can use all the help we can get. Thank you so much for coming all this way."

"Aw, no bother. I know we Reindeer folk are usually battling it out every year for spots on the Main Team, but if this is one day we can pull together and do something on the same side, well, why not?" Kyla laughed. "So true. Well, it's nice to finally meet you, Fannie. My deer are all pretty much out in the field right now. It's actually a good thing that you came. The head guy was giving me some trouble about how many of mine were going to work today. I told him, I don't work the mommas!" They both chuckled in agreement. "If you take your crew up to the training field, the city elves will fill up their sleighs and send them on their way." Fannie clapped her hands. "Very well! You heard the lady, troops. Let's go." The first three reindeer entered the gates – three hulking bucks with chocolate brown fur. A rather rag-tag group of less than spectacular stock. Kyla just nodded and smiled at them as they strode past her and Asche, their old wooden sleighs creaking behind them.

But when the fourth deer approached the gate, Kyla's heart nearly stopped. She had jet black fur and a dark gray underbelly. Her cream colored antlers were short and wide, and her eyes were a piercing shade of pale gray. As she walked toward them, the harness around her neck that had been laced with bells jingled a sweet tune with her every movement. Asche stomped on the ground, echoing Kyla's own excitement at seeing another Shadow-Deer... a *female* Shadow-Deer, no less.

Fannie smirked and held her head high in the air. "May I introduce you to Boptail."

Boptail stopped in front of Asche and batted her eyes. He bucked his head wildly up and down.

Kyla reached over and patted his back. "I know, I know, she's beautiful, but *Aschen, claugh sonna. Claugh sonna*," she said in Elvish to try to calm him down. Boptail whinnied in response to the words.

Fannie chuckled and pointed at Asche. "Blitzen, right?"

Kyla nodded. Yes. Asche was from Blitzen's direct line. "Great-great grandson." Fannie thumbed her finger at Boptail. "Dasher. Great-great granddaughter."

Asche and Boptail circled each other, huffing and neighing, swiping at each other's snouts and bellies. This was the first time Asche had seen another Shadow-Deer, and by the way she behaved around

Asche, Kyla assumed it was Boptail's first time as well. She smiled as she watched the two playful animals. *So there is someone out there like you, Asche.*

And then it hit her... Boptail was a *Shadow-Deer!* This was big. Huge! Not only that, but she could understand Elvish. If Boptail could speak Elvish, then did that mean Fannie could, too?

Taking a chance she asked, *"Haaden welyach?"*

Boptail's head rose when she heard the words. Asche stopped his playing. Fannie's eyes opened wide with a look of pure terror. She quickly shifted gears, placed her hand over her heart and said, "Excuse me? Oh, I don't speak the ancient tongue." But even though the words that came out of her mouth were saying 'no,' she nodded her head to secretly say, 'yes.'

Kyla was confused. *Why would she tell me no, but gesture yes? Unless she didn't want anyone to know. But why would she want to keep that a secret?*

Her attention was diverted when the deer started playing with each other again. "Okay, kids," Fannie said, walking in between them. "That's enough. We have a long day ahead of us. Christmas in July can't wait."

Chapter Fourteen

W ORK. IT CONSUMED EMBER'S LIFE THESE DAYS. IT TOOK ITS TOLL, worked its way into her body and mind, confined her to her den, and burned up every spare minute of her existence. When she accepted the position of *The* Coal Elf, she knew it would be a major undertaking, but this? Social time with Ember had stopped. She barely saw Barkuss, missed Kyla's twenty-eighth elfyear birthday, and don't even get her started on Tannen — she hadn't seen him in days. *Guess that's the one good thing about having so much work to do.*

And there *was* a lot to do! There were piles of coalcards to be analyzed, workers to keep track of, the blackened names to be periodically checked on, plenty of lists and data and inventory to be checked and double checked, and a full-on analysis of how Christmas in July was faring in the human world.

Speaking of lists, the preliminary Naughty List had been delivered to her this morning. Its crisp white paper sprawled out on her kitchen table top. While it was just the first version of the document, it was already longer than the List from last year. She moved her hand over its surface, absorbing the green and red names that appeared, committing them to memory. *Hunter Harris, Emily Hoepner, Jordan Jacobe...* the List pulsated with a strong energy that seemed to tingle her fingertips. Although she felt overtired and overworked, she had to admit to herself that the List was a beautiful thing. She was still as fascinated with it now as she was two elfyears ago when she was first in its presence.

Just as she reached for an inventory spreadsheet on the chair next to her, there was a familiar knocking at the front door of her den.

"E? You in there?" Barkuss called, but Ember heard other voices and knew he was not alone.

"Yea," she replied. "Come on in." Work would just have to wait. Besides, she needed a break, and Barkuss was always a welcomed distraction.

Barkuss bustled in with Bambam and Juju in tow. He was muttering something to them about being on their best behavior. The twins were smirking and nodding at Barkuss and at each other. "Hello, Miss Ember," they sang in unison with their high-pitched, mischievous voices.

Ember grinned. "Hello, boys," she returned in the same cadence. "Sit on that couch over there and don't get into trouble!" Barkuss barked. The boys giggled, but followed their uncle's instructions.

Ember got up and began clearing away the papers from the table. Barkuss hustled over and gave her a hand. "How ya doing, E?" he said. "Look at all this! You're swamped! You sure it's okay that we're here?"

"Oh, sure. No worries. And yea, 'look at all this' is right!" she huffed. "Got the new List this morning and..."

Barkuss's eyes twinkled and he bit the knuckle of his chubby forefinger. "*The* List?"

"Yea. It's just the first version of it, but..."

He hopped up and down a few times. "Are you so excited or what?" Ember shook her head and rolled her eyes at Barkuss's dramatics. "Yes, yes," she relented. "I have to say it is kinda exciting, but when you look at all this..." She held up a stack of papers. "I still have to get through all this before I can even look at that List with a clear head."

"You need any help? Here, let me..." He reached for the coalcards that were scattered on the floor.

She bent down and stopped him. "No. Thank you." She smiled. "I'll be okay. Besides, you look like you've got your hands full." She pointed her thumb towards the boys sitting on the couch.

Barkuss exhaled heavily, blowing puffs of coal dust out of his orange corkscrew locks. "Puh-leeze, girl. You don't know half of it!"

"Well, why don't you put on some hot cocoa and enlighten me."

Barkuss clapped his hands. "Ooo, child, now you're speaking my language!" And he turned toward the cupboard to search for a kettle and some mugs.

"We're bored, Uncle Barkuss," Bambam whined from the couch.

Barkuss slammed a metal kettle down onto the countertop. "Bammy, I swear if you don't..."

"It's fine," Ember interjected, raising a hand in Barkuss's direction to calm him down. "Boys, if you open up the top of the coffee table, there's a box that says 'Reindeer Games.' Inside are different board games you can play. It's a special prototype from Aboveground."

"Whoa!" Juju exclaimed as he pulled out the box. The boys scrambled to the floor and began chattering quickly about the new treasure. Barkuss cocked one eyebrow. "Prototype?"

She raised her shoulders. "Yea, it's something the Importer Elves had on their sleigh. I kinda lifted it."

He laughed and continued to prepare the cocoa. "Oh, E! You're too funny, girl. You handle those kids so well. Maybe make ya think twice about being an elfmommy?"

Ember shot him a look of death. "Don't you even..."

"Relax! Relax! Just kidding. It's just that you seem to have more patience for them, that's all I'm saying."

"So, you gonna tell me why you don't?"

"Bommer's all about these Brotherhood meetings lately. Balrion and Bulder, too. So now, he thinks I'm babysitter deluxe! I mean, once, twice, fine. I'll be good Uncle Barkuss a couple of times. But this is getting out of control. I'm running out of ideas for things to do with them. There's only so much Hide-and-Seek I can take, ya know? And their mother, Jacinda!" He huffed. "She follows Elfwife Law to the letter! Since the boys are under apprenticing age, she's with them all day. But at night, she's entitled to two elfhours alone. Those two elfhours just *happen* to be when those Brotherhood meetings go on. So, Bommer has to find a sitter. And because I could give a reindeer's butt about those silly meetings, *I* am the go-to Uncle. Like I said, every once in a while is fine, but this is becoming a nightly thing." He paused for a moment and waved his hands in the air. "Whatever. I guess I shouldn't complain. I'm helping my family, and that's the main thing, right?"

Ember shrugged her shoulders. What did she know of family? The only family she had left was an elfling nephew who lived in the care of her former Nanny. In the language of family, Ember was practically illiterate. She looked over at the boys playing quietly on her floor. They moved the pieces of the game they were engaged in without speaking a word to each other, as if they were in brotherly-sync, their heads of curly orange hair flopping up and down in syncopated rhythm. Then she looked over at Barkuss. He was stirring their mugs and preparing their drinks with the utmost of 'Barkuss love and care.' The boys. Barkuss. They were a family — a family who resembled each other, who spent time together, who got on each other's nerves, but who ultimately loved each other. She paused and wondered. Had *she* ever had that type of family?

Barkuss lifted up the sugar sphere container and dangled it in the air. "One coal lump or two, Mz. Coal Elf?" he joked.

She chuckled and held up two fingers. "And a peppermint swizzler, please. Top drawer."

Barkuss fixed up the drink to her liking and made his way to the table. Ember lifted the ceramic mug and drank. "Jeez, Barkuss, why on Earth didn't they make you, like a chef elf, or something like that? You have such a natural talent for cooking."

A pink blush rose up from behind Barkuss's gray cheeks. "Aww, sugar. You're too kind. But you know how it goes."

Ember nodded. Yes. She knew all too well. "Coal," she said. "Probably one of the most disgusting things on the planet. Why coal?"

He took a sip and folded his hands on the tabletop. "What do you mean?"

"Just what I said. Why coal? Why did the higher-ups decide that we were to give the bad kids coal? I mean, I get it, coal is filthy and useless and I guess serves as a good punishment, but why not, say, rocks? Rocks are just as useless to humans, and I think gathering rocks would be much easier for us elves…"

"Oh, honey," Barkuss sighed. "You mean, you really don't know?"

"No. What are you talking about? Know what?"

Barkuss closed his eyes and shook his head. "Oh, you poor, sweet, thing!" He reached out to grab her hands across the table. "It makes perfect sense to me now."

Ember's face twisted up in confusion. "What makes sense? Why are you being so weird?"

"Baby, baby," Barkuss continued. "Coal is more than just *coal.* Yes, it's dirty and filthy. It makes us sick if we breathe in too much. Leaves marks all over everything and they hardly ever come out. But the meaning behind it? The *message*. Coal can ignite. Burn. Heat. Give light. And most importantly, *hope*. When a child is bad, sure they get punished with the coal. But the coal says, 'hey, there's a light in your darkness and there's hope for you next year, yet.' See? Coal is actually not useless. It's to help them light their way for a better year. I don't think no rocks can do that, now can they?"

She hadn't thought of the coal like that before, and it took her a few moments to absorb the gravity of what Barkuss said. The two sat sipping their hot cocoa in silence.

Ember tried to clear her mind of all extraneous thoughts and focus solely on the message of the coal, but she found her concentration broken by soft whispers and giggles. She looked over at the boys. They were still busy with the board games and weren't making a sound, but yet the persistent giggling and whispers seemed to fill her ears — giggles and whispers of elflings nearby. She studied the two, watched them as they interacted. Soon, she started to hear what sounded like Elvish chatter — low at first, then slowly more clear and distinct.

"*Geshten platther,*" a voice said, and Bambam moved his game piece forward on the board.

"*Hysther platther,*" another voice said, and Juju rolled the dice and picked up a card.

Yes! They were speaking to each other in Elvish! But their mouths weren't moving. No words were actually spoken, yet she could hear them speaking the ancient language *in their minds!* She sat up at attention, tilting her head in their direction as if her physical position would help her to hear them better. Barkuss gave her a look, but she ignored him, focusing on the secret conversation, and trying to block out her own barrage of inner-thought-questions: *How do they know Elvish? And how can they do that?*

Then it dawned on her. *If I can hear them, and they can hear each other, I wonder if they could hear me?*

She closed her eyes, and with all her energy directed at the two of them, she said in her mind, "*Acklen eysh fwartha!*"

The boys immediately stopped playing. Juju instinctively placed both hands on the game board in a startled stance. Bambam froze and dropped his game piece. Ember watched as the brothers stared at each other, mouths slightly opened. Neither dared to look in her direction. Quickly, they picked up the pieces of the game and put the box back in the coffee table. "We're gonna wait for you outside, Uncle Barkuss," Juju said, and the two left Ember's den.

Ember was stunned. They'd heard her. *But how?*

"What's the matter, E? You seem so distracted."

She snapped out of her thoughts. "What? Oh, sorry, Barkuss. Just so much on my mind, ya know?"

"Ahh, heavy is the head that wears the cap!"

She shook her head with small, quick snaps. "What the hell is that supposed to mean?" she demanded.

Barkuss put up his hands in defense. "Whoa, whoa, whoa! No need to bite my head off, honey! I was just making a joke. I know, I know, you got a lot on your plate and..."

"Like, a lot *a lot*," she said composing herself. "The blacked out names in the Book, this whole Christmas in July is bugging me, don't even get me started on the whole wedding debacle, and now the List. You saw it! You saw how long it is. While it's fascinating in its own right, it's kinda ridiculous. Either the kids in the world completely misbehave, or they end up completely disbelieving!"

"The Council seems to think that this Christmas in July thing is gonna do the trick. What can ya do? Pray to Claus that it works."

Ember stood up, waving her hands in the air almost uncontrollably. "Well, I'll tell ya what I want to do! Give em' all coal. Teach them all a lesson." She paced the kitchen floor. "Just when they think they've skated by yet another year, BOOM, they wake up to the black stuff in their stocking. Even give it to the blackened out names. I bet that'll make them start believing again! Why don't we shake their worlds up a bit? Show them who's boss!"

Barkuss paused for a second and stood up next to her. "Ya know, E., that's not at all a bad idea. Even the nice kids are naughty sometimes, right?"

The idea began to take root in Ember's mind. Yes. *Even the nice kids are naughty sometimes.* How many times had her sister Ginger pulled Ember's hair or snapped the heads off her dolls when they were kids, only to wake up on the Big Day to a stocking spilling over with presents? How many times had Ember disobeyed Nanny Carole, or talked back, or questioned a law, or put mashed up Nessie fruit in Ginger's hair brush, only to wake up on the Big Day to an abundance of presents lined up under their tree? If what Barkuss said about the coal was true, maybe that's exactly what the kids needed. Some kind of mystical wake-up call. Not being inundated with the holiday six months before the Big Day. They needed to be put in their place. They needed to be shown that they can't be bad and then all of a sudden be good and expect to be rewarded. They needed to know that, yes! the Boss sees you when you're sleeping and he knows when you're awake! Not cutesy Christmas movies on their cable TVs while they lounged in air conditioned rooms. It made sense. *Perfect sense.*

"Okay," she said putting a hand on Barkuss's shoulder. "It's not a bad idea at all. It actually just might work. But if you'll excuse me, I think I need to go talk to someone about it."

"Someone like who?"

"Oh, just someone who might have the sense to want to punish every child in the entire world for one Big Night."

Barkuss's hands balled into fists and he clutched them to his chest. He stuck his tongue out at her. "I know who you're talking about, E."

Ember smirked. "Yea? Wanna come?"

Barkuss shivered in disgust. "Girl, I'd rather be the permanent guardian of the twins than go to Sturd's house!"

Chapter Fifteen

THE JAGGED PIECES OF OBSIDIAN ROCK HUNG FROM THE CEILING LIKE A collection of knives that belonged to a murderer, each piece sharp and menacing, ready to fall down and pierce the heart of the elf who slept in the bed below. Sturd found it rather fitting that Corzakk chose to live in Welfort Den. Being close to the Ignis River made the rock floor one of the most unstable terrains in all of the Mines, and with the instability he'd seen over the years with his family, he had to wonder how deep the coincidences ran.

When he was an elfling, he often hid under his covers at night, afraid of the way the stalactites appeared against the low lantern light in his bedroom. The dancing shadows created by the flame gave the appearance of laughing faces watching him throughout the night. It terrified him to think that the jagged pieces could twist and move and break and laugh. Now, they mesmerized him, bringing him pictures in his mind - scenes of chaotic horror and beauty. Sturd seemed to get his best ideas while he rested on his bed and stared at the different black hues for hours.

He clutched *The Dublix Santarae* against his chest, envisioning a yellow light surging throughout his body. Possession of the secret book had been a game changer for him. He knew he wasn't supposed to have it (probably wasn't even supposed to know it even existed) and would most likely be punished if it ever came to light that he had stolen it from the Book Keepers' office. No. Not even Corzakk knew he had it. This secret he kept to himself.

And what a rich and delicious secret it was! He traced his finger along the delicate red cover going over every letter of the embossed title with a gentle touch. It made him tingle with wicked giddiness to press his thumb against the opening of the book and feel each fragile page on his fingertip. He brought the book to his face and inhaled deeply, filling his nostrils with the scent of the old paper. It smelled like power — a power he had only tasted briefly when he had been in charge of the List.

The List.

He had been his happiest when the Council gave him charge over the sacred scroll. And that happiness had come to a screeching halt when the plan changed and Ember was granted its control. Losing the List had made him feel lost and almost naked, but now he was changing the plan yet again. The energy he felt from *The Dublix Santarae* was unlike anything from his wildest, darkest dreams. It was a unique energy – a different feeling of power – because it *wasn't* given to him. He had achieved this knowledge and possession on his own, took charge of his own destiny, and made a judgment based on his own free will and not someone else's orders. It reflected the energy and power deep inside of him that had been screaming to be set free. *And free it was...*

And what of the Council? The perplexing, all knowledgeable collection of elves conformed to their secret societal standards. What would they think if they found out he had snatched the book? Like most elves, Sturd still looked at the Council with a questioning eye. He couldn't quite make heads or tails of their firm intentions. Corzakk had said that the Council had plans for him, but exactly what those plans were, was still unclear. He has the List, he doesn't have the List, he's Manager of Coal Mining Crews, now he's Field Data Collector, he's the golden child of the cadre, he's the outcast bastard being punished. Too many mixed messages. If asked what he suspected their plans to be, he would have answered, "A seat at the Council will be in my future." But why? That would mean that one Council member would either have to step down, be removed, or die. Being on the Council is a pretty high honor, and to be granted that honor as a returned favor or fulfilled promise didn't seem likely. *There has to be more...*

Sturd drew his attentions back to the book in his hands. He had read it cover to cover many times already, nearly committing all of the pages to memory. There were some pages that had little earmarks on the corners, places where he felt he needed to review some more, or that he particularly enjoyed. He didn't mind giving the book those slight imperfections because they served a higher purpose – his higher purpose. He slithered the book back down over his chest, closed his eyes, and began reciting from the text, "...therein, if anything should happen to the child, the sibling would easily and seamlessly fulfill the role before the selection..."

Voices from the living quarters stopped his recitation. Angered, he tucked the book under his pillow, got up, and walked noiselessly to his door. He pressed an ear to the thick wood in hopes of discerning the owners of the voices that had disturbed him so.

"C'mon, now! Is that any way to greet your future father-in-law?"

"Really? When did you turn into a comedian, Corzakk?"

"Don't get sassy with me, girl. Show some respect. Show that you actually learned a little while you were my apprentice. Wasn't I the next best thing to a father all those years ago?"

"No. I'd say you were the next best thing to the worst case of Coppleysites."

Sturd held his hand to his mouth and chuckled. Hearing this exchange between Ember and his father was just like old times. Those two could go back and forth for hours with their verbal disputes. And even though Ember was surprisingly able to hold her own against the old and wizened Corzakk, it was always Corzakk who managed to have the last word. His father's approach to Ember's insolence was far different from his own. Whereas Corzakk thrived on the endless derision, Sturd would have much rather spit in her face and shoved her to the ground. *Good times...*

"Look, is he here or not, 'cause if not I have a ton of things I need to do and..."

Oddly interested in why Ember was gracing Welfort Den with her presence, Sturd materialized from behind his door and entered the living room. She blew out an obnoxious breath of air and rolled her eyes.

"You wish to see me?" Sturd asked.

"Uh, yea," she answered. "Can we talk?"

He smiled a twisted toothy grin. "Absolutely," he dramatically gushed.

Ember shot a look at Corzakk then back at Sturd. "In private?"

Corzakk's eyes widened at Sturd and he tipped his head forward. "Well, well, well, Sturd, my boy, why don't you take your *vivacious* future-elfwife out into the gardens? You'll have tons of privacy back there." He motioned his hand toward the back door.

Sturd turned around and said, "Follow me." With each step, his heart pounded with curiosity as he led her through the den and out to the rundown rock garden. *What in Claus's name could she possibly have to say?*

Once outside, he motioned for her to have a seat on a granite bench, but she ignored his invitation. Her blonde hair fell down her back in wild tangles. He sniffed at the air, catching the underlying strawberry scent of her essence when he noticed that she struggled to catch a satisfying breath. Did she have the onset of Coppleysites again, or... was it possible? Did she actually *run* all the way here? Regardless, she was poised — her back was straight at attention, like a soldier being evaluated by her war general, and she spoke to him with a soft voice.

"Look, I didn't come here for a confrontation," she began calmly. "The Christmas in July launch is coming quickly, and I've been play-ing out all the angles in my head. Don't say anything. Just hear me out. You know I hated that idea from the beginning..."

"Yes, you made that quite obvious..."

She rolled her eyes at him. "Can you not... do *that?* Can you just be quiet and listen to what I have to say?"

Intrigued, he smiled, nodded, and motioned his hand for her to continue.

"I understand you truly believe that starting the holiday in July will be a good thing. I realize that you believe that it will give us a better idea of who is and isn't on the final List by August. I appreciate the fact that you believe an earlier start to the Big Day will stop the black names from appearing in the Book."

Diplomacy? Are you actually coming at me with diplomacy?

"But," she went on, "here's why I think it won't work. It's bad enough the shops in the human world start the hype as early as October. I just think that too much of a 'good thing' isn't a good thing at all. It's

going to backfire on us all. The people are going to be so swamped
with Big Day merchandise and movies and music, that by the time
the *actual* Big Day comes, it won't matter! It won't be special. They'll
start to see right through the marketing ploys, and all they'll see are
dollar signs. That will kill the spirit for them completely and blacken
out even more names!"

"So, I'm going to go out on a limb here and say that you've come up
with a better solution." He rubbed his hand over his chin and grinned
at her sarcastically.

She exhaled and rubbed at the side of her forehead. "Yes," she
groaned, and there was a desperate quality in her voice that was
enthralling to him. "Here's my alternate suggestion. I know we all
need to be on the same page with this thing and I know there's a sick
side of you that takes absolute pleasure in the torment of others…"

An uncontrollable purr-like sound escaped Sturd's throat, and
Ember paused to shake her head in disgust. *Now you're speaking my
language.*

"… and I just think that, well, what if we came straight on out and
punished everyone? What if we delivered coal to them all? Ya know,
even the kids on the Nice List act out. They're not entirely good *all*
the time. What if this year we kinda put them all on notice. Like a
wake-up call of sorts."

Sturd stared at Ember's face for a moment. The kitchen light from
the den bounced off the cave walls and into the open rock garden.
Shadows danced upon Ember's face in fractured angles of darkness
– under her eyes, above her brows, in the space between her chin
and lower neck – creating a warped mask of gloom. Every time she
opened her mouth, or closed her eyes, the shadows changed their
position, and the distorted shapes fused onto her skin, disfiguring the
true composite of her visage with chaotic movements. And she spoke
of chaos. She spoke of pain and suffering and of doling out punish-
ments to kids who might not even truly deserve it. For a second, he
was overcome by her beauty – the beauty of her shadow mask, and
the beauty of her torturous words.

It just might work.

"I got a copy of the preliminary List, and so far, it's really long. Like, super long…"

The List. His former List. Now her List.

But I have my Book. His Dublix Santarae. Once again he superseded her in power and control. He took a step back and threw his hands in the air. "This is ludicrous!" he barked. "What makes you think that this would ever work in a million elfyears?"

"Don't you see? It'll make them believe in *something* again. In something real and magical all at the same time. The spirit will be with them if they are made to endure this. And trust me, they can handle a year of coal. It will teach them to embrace the spirit again and not be so entangled with material things."

"Coal?" he scoffed. "You think giving them all coal will keep them believing?"

She jammed her hands into her jumpsuit pockets and started fidgeting with frustration. Sturd ate it all up. He loved watching her squirm.

"Yes," she pleaded. "Look at it. I believe it will give them hope. That's what the coal is supposed to do, right? Be the beacon of hope for a better tomorrow and all that. It's the hope for a better year. Not just for them, but for us, too. A hope that we can have a better life, a better future, a better…"

"I hope for nothing," he muttered. "And what if *your* plan backfires? What if it outrages all the children in the world to the point where they say 'to hell with this!' and stop believing anyway? What then?"

"You're right," she said calmly. "You're absolutely right. It could backfire. But if we handle the situation delicately, I don't see how it can. I thought about how we would send out the coal. It couldn't be something that the children just woke up and found without some sort of indication as to what was going on. There would need to be some sort of explanation. Like I said before, even the good kids act up every now and then. So we would have individualized notes to the children stating why they weren't getting presents. Like, 'Dear Sally, We understand that you tried to be good, but you teased your brother one too many times. Please be better next year.' Something like that."

Sturd shook his head and cleared his throat. "To every kid? And pray tell, how do you suggest we go about accomplishing that?"

"The girls in West Valley."

His stomach lurched. "The girls in West Valley?" he repeated.

"I know it sounds like a lot, but if we started now, work off the preliminary List, I think it could get done. They could rally together, have them suspend all trainings and postpone all pairings so that..."

Sturd's back stiffened and he cocked an eyebrow. "Oh, I see. I get it." He wagged his crooked finger in the air and snickered. "Your true intentions are finally revealed. I knew if I let you run your mouth long enough, I'd figure this out. You are just trying to get out of your *commitments.*"

"What?"

He began pacing back and forth in front of her. "You're crazier than I thought, Skye! I must applaud you, though. This elaborate scheme is rather interesting. Hidden agenda and all!"

"Oh, trust me. If there was any way of getting out of my commitments, I would have done it by now! Ya know, Barkuss warned me this would be a waste of my time. I should have never come."

As she walked past him, he extended his leg at just the right moment, causing her to stumble forward. She was careful not to fall flat on her face, but her upper body was hunched over, hands planted firmly in the rocky ground. She glared up at him with wild eyes and gritted her teeth. "You sonuva..."

He clicked his tongue on the roof of his mouth with a hideous "tsk" that echoed off the cave walls. "Bowing to me looks good on you," he snarled. "You really ought to get used to it."

Ember quickly shot up, fists clenched, ready to engage him in a struggle of sorts, but when he didn't make another move toward her she dusted off her hands onto her jumpsuit, circled him once, and left.

Chapter Sixteen

I CAN'T SLEEP THIS OFF
      Was it not enough?
   Once is not enough?

Ember wrestled with those questions when she returned to her den, practically kicking herself for even thinking Sturd would listen to her for even a fraction of a second. She couldn't help but feel that he purposefully shut her out, that he purposefully ignored her plea. *Maybe he knows I'm on to something. Maybe this is all part of his plan.*

The blood in her veins screamed to her. The gurgle in her belly shot fire inside of her. The sweat from her palms dripped slick with anticipation. The ache in her heart crushed her soul, but gave her a deeper knowledge and understanding. She knew one thing, she *felt* one thing — she was *right.*

Coal was the light and the hope and the way. Coal was the saving grace for all of the wretched souls in the world. Coal would be the one deciding factor in saving the horrible predicament they all were now in.

"E?" Barkuss called as she walked in.

"You're still here, Barkuss?" she replied.

Barkuss came from the kitchen into the front foyer of Ember's den. The chattering of the children was no longer a constant sound in her dwelling, but there was an outline of a figure seated on her couch. Ember raised her eyebrows, pointed in that direction, and mouthed, "Who's that?"

Barkuss's nose crinkled into a tiny ball on the center of his face as Ember placed her hands on her hips in an annoyed stance. "The twins went home. Bommer picked them up after his Brotherhood meeting and…"

Tannen suddenly stood up from the couch and faced Ember. "I walked with Bommer. I wanted to come see you. Hope that's ok?"

Ember nervously bit her lower lip. "Um, yea, sure. I guess so," she muttered, practically fumbling over the words. Her heart felt like it was a piece of perforated paper that was starting to slide apart at the seam. Her first instinct was to rush up to Tannen, throw her arms around his neck, and smother his face with a thousand gentle kisses, but she composed herself, took a deep breath, and fought against her automatic reactions. "How have you been?" she asked coolly.

Tannen smiled, not just with his mouth, but with his eyes — his magical and wonder-filled eyes that sparkled like bright green gems in the deepest, darkest depths of the Mines. His green eyes were hypnotizing — so much that she nearly felt herself give way to the swoon. The meeting with Sturd was all but a blur until...

"How'd it go with Sturd?" Barkuss blurted, interrupting her timeless daydream.

She shook her head quickly. "Not well. But I shouldn't have expected anything more than what I got."

"He shot your idea down?"

"Completely. Barely gave me a chance to explain myself."

"I think it's a great idea," Tannen added.

Ember shot a look at Barkuss and cocked her head to the side.

"I told Tannen all about it," Barkuss confirmed. "We both think it's a great plan."

"I know I'm right about this one. I know this is our best shot at stopping the names from leaving the book. I don't know how I know it, I just do," she said in a faraway voice.

"Well, honey," Barkuss began, "if anyone knows anything about anything, it would be *you*! You've got that *something* — like a sixth sense. Some freakish intuition. When Sturd went and tore up the List, you just *knew*. And better yet, you were *right!*"

"Is that what it's like now?" Tannen asked. "Is that the kinda feeling you're getting from this idea of yours?"

Ember nodded, slowly at first. She dug deep down into her well of memory and tried to pull forth the feeling of seeing the pieces of the torn up List sinking from the top of Sandstone Shelf - one by one, in slow motion. And that sense of urgency and alarm bubbled up inside of her - *screamed at her* – to move, to act, to recreate. She recalled the way the back of her neck had tingled with gooseflesh, and the how the tips of her ears felt tight at the tops. "Yes," she declared as Barkuss squealed with excitement.

Tannen winked at her in approval. "Well, then," he said slyly, "what are we gonna do about this?"

"No, no, no!" Ember protested. "*We,*" she motioned her arm in a circle in front of her, "are not doing anything! I need some time to think about this. To plan."

"I don't think so, Em," Tanned said. "Time is not on your side, in case you haven't noticed. And I refuse to let you shut me out from another one of your missions."

"Missions?" she said in surprise. "I don't plan for these things to happen, you know."

Tannen took a step towards her. "I know, I know. I just want to help you in any way that I can. You know that, right?"

She smiled at him and nodded.

Almond tall struthers.

"Tannen's right, E. This is a much larger thing than you putting a puzzle back together," Barkuss piped in.

"Yes. I know. You're both right. And my list of elves-I-can-trust is not exactly a mile long, if you know what I mean."

"So, what are you thinking?" Tannen asked. "What's your gut saying to do?"

Ember paused.

"Why not go straight to the Boss? Or at least the Boss Lady?" Barkuss suggested. "Cut the chin-chi right at the knees, or whatever the heck that stupid saying is!"

"No," she immediately responded. "I don't trust them, and you shouldn't either." She eyed them both hard with a cold stare. "Trust is in these four walls – right here, right now. And trust is Kyla up Above. Does that make sense?"

Barkuss gave a quick nod.

"Perfect," Tannen answered for the both of them.

"Now, of course, I'm not all too keen on the details, but the basic idea is to give them all coal. All of them. The whole lot of them. The good, the super good, the bad, the super bad. But there needs to be that personalization, ya know? A message. A note. Something to say that we really are here. We really are watching."

Barkuss crinkled his nose again and stuck out his tongue. "This is a lot, E. There's a whole slew of kiddos out and about in that big ole world up there."

"Yea," Tannen added, "and how are we going to go about making these 'love notes'. And that's not even mentioning how we're going to go about organizing and hiding..."

"Yea, E," Barkuss interrupted, "scooping up pieces up paper and hiding them in your kitchen drawer is a lot different than hundreds of thousands of individualized notes to go along with a sack-full of coal."

Ember exhaled in frustration. "Well, I had an idea. What about the girls in West Valley? If we enlisted their help, say we call it some kind of charity mission, then we could pull it off. Maybe? I don't know!" She waved her hands frantically in the air. "Look, even if we can't get to *every* kid up there, if we could at least reach *most*..."

"I think we'd be in good shape," Tannen answered, completing her thought.

All three paused, contemplating the logistics of it all.

"I still think we should present this to the Boss," Barkuss said after a few moments of silence.

"No, Barkuss!" Ember yowled. "I promise you that's not a good idea."

"Yea, but, I'm not so sure I like all this sneaking behind his back. Like, this is major sneaking, E! Major!" Barkuss threw his hands up in the air and curved his palms forward. "What if we get caught? How will we be punished? The Boss – and everyone else for that matter – will be extremely mad and..."

Ember and Tannen sighed simultaneously, forcing Barkuss to end his paranoid rant.

"West Valley," Tannen said, contemplating out loud. "Ya know, Em, my, um... um... future elfwife is from there."

Ember glared hard at him, her heart feeling the sting of his words. "And?" she prodded.

"You know how all those girls are, and…" he stammered, fidgeted.

"And…" she pressed, nearly losing her patience.

"That's actually a good idea, T," Barkuss interjected.

Ember closed her eyes and shook her head in confusion. "Wait, what's a good idea?"

"Once Tannen gets hitched, he'll have her get all her girlfriend elves to help us out."

"Like, maybe we can send her with a folder of names and info to the girls to work on the notes in their spare time."

"And you have your List, and access to the Book. You could collect the intel as you wish, E." Barkuss said.

Ember walked over to the couch and sat down. Tannen sat down next to her and placed his hands on her knees. She lovingly put hers on top of his, intertwining their fingers. "Coal," she said, looking into Tannen's eyes. "We'll have to get lots of it."

"That's actually not a problem," Barkuss said as he sat on the chair across from them. "We still have plenty in reserve from the Coal-less Night. I can manage that end, but…"

"Tannen has to smuggle it," she said, responding to Barkuss, but her eyes still trained on Tannen's.

Tannen nodded at her. "And the notes," he said.

"And the notes," she repeated.

"Do you guys think this'll work? Do you think we'll get away with this?" Barkuss said as he blew a curly lock of orange hair from his eyes.

"It has to," Ember answered. "I mean, we have to at least try."

Ember and Tannen's stare was unbroken. They looked hard and deep at each other, as if they were staring through each other's souls. Barkuss broke the tension when he clicked his tongue on the roof of his mouth. "But that doesn't solve the problem of *you* two."

Ember's heart sank again. She didn't think anything would ever solve the issue of Tannen. *I just want something I can never have.* "We can't worry about that now," she said, still looking at Tannen. "We have to go with the flow of everything for the time being. I need to marry Sturd, you understand that, right?"

Tannen nodded again. "I do. I get it."

Ember broke her gaze, and shifted her eyes to Barkuss. "I'll say this much — I refuse to live with him!"

Barkuss clapped his hands. "Oh, girl! That's an easy fix up! Demand two things: Corzakk needs to find his own den, and you go nowhere until you find someone willing to take over yours."

A smirk creeped its way on Ember's face. "I could kiss you right now, Barkuss! That's brilliant!"

He smiled, folded his arms over his chest, and sat back in the chair. "Yea, what would you do without me?"

Ember and Tannen chuckled. "Less than six months out, boys. We have much to do."

The three went silent again, anticipating the long and dangerous road ahead.

Chapter Seventeen

ONE BY ONE THE RAFTS LEFT THE DOCKING STATION ON THE BANK OF THE Ignis River. Every individual boat was decorated in bundles of white and purple material that draped in scalloped loops on the side of each vessel. The water splashed up onto the gossamer fabric, leaving sprinkle marks, like a polka-dotted design. Each raft carried an elfmaiden donning an extravagant and colorful dress. Their hair was styled neatly and covered with a sparkle spray. Their faces were painted with shimmery makeup, highlighting their best facial features. They all sat on the bench of their rafts, facing forward, while on the opposite side sat an unlit lantern waiting to be sent aloft as part of the Wedding Union Ceremony.

Ember had never witnessed a Wedding Ceremony before; they were always private affairs. But now, as she watched the procession of prospective brides drifting in their boats on the Ignis, it struck her odd that the ritual very much mirrored that of the Funeral Rite. The similarities were uncanny. Death and marriage so closely intertwined and celebrated with near parallel ceremonies. Her heart sank in her chest as she pictured her raft as a ball of fire meandering on the water. If anything felt close to death, this was surely the moment. *Is this to be the death of me?*

She crossed her legs, rested an elbow on her knee, and cradled her chin in her hand. Wearing her black work jumpsuit, and her hair twisted up in a braided bun, she looked more like she was ready to mine coal than be united in elfmarriage. She reminded herself that this union was to be in name only, and while they could force her to take the Ruprecht name, they couldn't force her to do much beyond that. This is all part of the larger plan.

There were mixed messages on the faces of the girls who drifted by in their boats. Some had looks of sheer excitement in their eyes, some looked nervous, others terrified. Her own expression of indifference must have registered with the others, because as she met the gaze of each and every one, they all gave her a questioning look.

When they arrived at Sandstone Shelf, each girl took her lantern and set it on the edge of the river. Head Mistress Shella Arabighymm stood waiting, and greeted her students with a wide glowing smile, her mouth looking like a white circle outlined in bright red lips. She wore a dark purple gown (a color probably chosen to hide any coal stains she would eventually pick up in the cave) and her gray hair was slicked at the top and tied into a tight ponytail. As she handed each girl a small bouquet of pink and yellow flowers, her silver bangle bracelets jangled a tune throughout the cavern - a sweet wedding song that made the elfmaidens giggle. Not Ember. There was no bouquet for her. Because of the "unconventional nature" of Ember's mere presence in the Mines, certain liberties were to be taken in the ceremony. And because Ember had not trained in West Valley, Shella couldn't rightfully serve as her witness. So, Ember was permitted one elf to stand by her side throughout the proceedings, and when she stepped off her raft, Barkuss swooped in, making a fuss over her as if she was royalty.

He took her lantern and placed it with the others for her. "Okay, okay," he said, flitting around her, speaking quickly and quietly, "I'm not sure where your head's at with your work clothes, but..."

"Barkuss," she scolded, "you can't be serious."

"Oh, E. It's just that these other girls are dressed to the nines, and..."

"Because they have something to celebrate. I don't."

"I know. I know. But, what about keeping up appearances? Don't you think someone will get suspicious? And you know, you're so much prettier than..."

"Enough."

"... these other girls, and I really want..."

"Enough, I said."

"... you to shine, and..."

"Enough! Give it a rest!" Her voice boomed in the cave, startling the other girls. All heads turned in her direction with frightened glances.

Barkuss raised his hands and smiled at them. "We're good over here. Just swell."

She grabbed his hands and tugged them to his sides. "Would you give it a rest already?" she growled through clenched teeth. "They all know how extremely angry I am about the set up. No one will think anything of it. This is me being me. Kinda expected."

"I'm sorry. I'm sorry." His bottom lip puckered out. "I know. This is a horrible day for you. I get it. But, sugar, there's something so exciting about us being officially family. I can't help myself sometimes... Sissy!"

Family. Barkuss's family. Clouded by the task at hand, she hadn't even thought about what her marriage to Sturd would mean to Barkuss. In fact, she didn't think *he* had even given it a second thought. Being an official member of the Melithoro Dwin'nae Ruprecht conglomeration meant so much to him. Barkuss and Sturd being half-brothers and all would technically make her Barkuss's half-sister-in-law. She shook her head and smirked at him. Barkuss's frame of mind never ceased to amaze her. He always managed to take the most dreadful situations and find some happiness, some goodness, some shred of optimism within. "You just want to call me Sissy," she teased. "I bet Jacinda wouldn't stand for you calling her that."

"Puh-leeze!" He arched his wrists forward. "I wouldn't dare!"

"Oh yeah? And what makes you think it's okay with me?"

He smiled and drew her in for a tight squeeze. "Cause you're my E. And you love me no matter what I call you."

"Oh, cut it out!" She laughed and wriggled from his big brother embrace.

Barkuss dug into the pocket of his jumpsuit and pulled out a small plastic bag. "Okay, stay still and let me do my thing."

She stepped back, examining the contents. "What is that?"

He made no reply as he came in close and started fiddling with her hair. "Flowers? You're putting flowers on me?"

"Please, Ember, I'm serious. Let me just..."

"Give me that." She took the bag from him and looked inside. "Alcanthia? Moon Glow? You do know that these are *poisonous* flowers, Barkuss?"

He continued to decorate her. "Yes," he replied. "Fitting, isn't it? Now stop fidgeting and let me put these on you. It's what *they* expect from *me*, right? Let Barkuss do Barkuss's thing!"

"Eye on the prize, eye on the prize," she answered breathlessly.

Soon, Shella was clapping her hands and the girls were lining up in a single file. Barkuss gave her a reassuring nod.

"Name only," she said.

"Name only," he replied.

Shella walked at the front of the line, guiding them to the meeting place. Ember looked up at the ridge that loomed above them – the very place where Sturd, not too long ago, created his own brand of chaos and horror when he tore up the List. The ridge was now vacant; only the memory of that day prevailed.

The elfmen were in their own single file line, and the maidens were lined up directly facing their counterparts. Parson Brown, the elderly Cleric Elf, stood before the males behind a podium. The ceremonial pickaxe was placed on the ground next to the podium. The set-up very much resembled an old elfling game Ember used to play called 'Blue Cowhide.' Two teams would line up arm-in-arm and stand face to face against each other about thirty feet apart. The captain of one team would call, "Blue cowhide, blue cowhide, we want so-and-so for our side." And the elfling whose name was called would rush to the other side, trying to break their chain- linked arms.

Shella approached the podium, shook hands with the parson, and began the ritual. "Elves. We gather here today to bind you in elfmarriage. This is a joyous day for all as you embark on the next journey of your elflives. Gentlemen," she turned her head to the left to address them, "I assure you that your counterparts have been properly trained and have met all the requirements for life as an elfwife. The elfmaidens have worked very hard to the best of their capabilities, and I am confident that they will make you a happy home." She turned to the right and spoke to the girls, "Ladies, you have accomplished a great deal in your studies, and I have no doubt that you are at the top of your game. There have been some... bumps in the road," and she shifted her gaze directly at Ember, "but I know in my heart that the match you were given is the most decent, proper, and well-suited one for you."

Ember glared hard at Shella, locking her eyes as if they were the teeth of a Chyga digging deep into the throat of its prey. For a brief moment, it was as if they were the only two elves in the cave, staring each other down, but Shella regained composure and continued with the formalities. "In accordance with Regulation Five, all elf-unions are to be..."

Regulation Five. What a joke! She tuned Shella out, only picking up bits and pieces of her rehearsed diatribe. Did the Aboveground elves hold these cattle-ceremonies, too? Was this what it had been for her parents? For her sister, Ginger, and her husband, Vonran? This mass 'binding' of elves through ancient symbolic acts – was it always like this? Assignments. Regulations. Provisions.

"... and from that union, any and every effort to produce an elfling is to be made for the preservation of the Elven race..."

What about Barkuss's parents? They had been a self-pairing. Borthen and I'len had fallen in love of their own accord. How and why did the Council allow that match to go through and not others? Was that decision made, too, by picking a name from a cap? Why were some elves granted autonomy, and others held to the strictest letter of the law? She glanced across to the line of male elves. Sturd stood directly in front of her, hands behind his back, teeth curled over his lower lip as he bit down. He was staring at the ground, taking in the seriousness of Shella's words, nodding in agreement of the law. She shuddered to think that very soon she would be forced to hold his hand and...

Eye on the prize.

"... the couple will then join hands and step over the ceremonial pickaxe together as a symbol of their new life in the Mines. Joined as elfhusband and elfwife, both will bear the honorable burden of the trials and tribulations that come hand in hand for our people..."

A few elves over from Sturd stood Tannen. She caught a glimpse of his sandy blond hair from the corner of her eye and forced herself not to catch his attention.

"... in accordance with Provision Nineteen, and subject to rulings by the Council, can they so reassign an elfwife should a particular event or need arise." Without realizing it, she caught Tannen's attention. There was a pained expression on his face, and behind a meek smile, she could see a hint of sorrow, an apologizing look of despair and regret. He gave her a reassuring wink, quickly so that the others wouldn't notice, and she smiled back at him. Again, Ember had the feeling of a perforated piece of paper slowly being torn apart. One half of her rejoiced in the fact that she was taking control of her destiny (albeit, in a clandestine manner); the other half crushed that Tannen couldn't be the elfman standing before her, waiting to take her hand in the most sacred of unions.

She craned her neck to look down the elfmaiden side of the line. Holly Adaire was bright-eyed and beaming at Tannen, smiling at him, trying so desperately to get his attention. Her golden curls shimmered and fell loosely around her made-up face. Her pale pink eyes reflected the soft glow of the cave light, creating an ethereal aura around her. No matter how beautiful, or enthusiastic, Tannen's gaze was fixed on Ember. She looked back at him, and nodded her head in Holly's direction as if to say, 'she wants your attention.' Tannen, picking up on the gestures, shook his head in refusal.

Shella stepped down from the podium and Parson Brown took his place next to the pickaxe. His feeble legs barely guided him to his mark. A few times, one of the male elves made a move to help him, but the parson waved a defiant hand in the air, shooing the youngster away. "When you are called, you are to join hands and approach the axe. Together you should simultaneously step over the axe. Then, you are to go to the podium and sign your names on the contract. Ms. Arabighymm will then guide you to your raft, hand you your lantern, and send you on your way. Once in the boat, you are to light your lantern and release it into the cave." The words came out of him slowly and delicately. They sounded garbled and brittle, like old pages in a book. He began calling the names of the elves, and one by one they stepped out of the line, clasped hands, and continued the ceremony.

Ember froze like a statue. Her knees locked in place, and a dizzying sensation made her head feel fuzzy. "Just breathe," Barkuss said from behind her. "Name only, right?" She gave a thumbs-up sign as Parson Brown said, "Sturd Ruprecht and Ember Skye," and stepped forward, face to face with Sturd.

Sturd aggressively seized her hand, and she flinched from his icy touch. His fingers slithered down her palm, interlocked with hers, and clamped tightly over the top of her hand, forcing them together. His touch was cold and clammy, as if there was a complete and total absence of life from within. So unlike the way she felt when Tannen lovingly held her hand. She remembered the touch of *his* hand – the smooth skin against her own, his thumb gently massaging the inset of her palm. Tannen's hands were tired and calloused, but somehow they always managed to feel vibrant and alive when in her grasp. But Sturd? His touch was so un-elflike it almost scared her.

She looked over her shoulder and saw Tannen's worried expression. It was almost as if he was saying, "Don't do this. Run. Flee. We'll go together." Sturd jerked her forward with a grunt and they came up to the pickaxe on the ground. Again, a frozen feeling crept its way over her and for a second, she hesitated. In that moment of hesitation, she stumbled, nearly dragging Sturd (who was fiercely locked on to her) over the axe and on to the floor. Chuckles echoed from some of the other elves, and Ember heard a distinct Barkuss gasp.

"You clumsy thing!" he growled. "Watch where you're going!"

She didn't respond. She couldn't. Everything was happening in slow motion, like some surreal out-of-body experience. Sturd dragged her to the podium, signed his name, and forced the pen in her hand. "It's Ember Ruprecht now, remember that," he hissed into her ear. Ember held on to the pen like an elfling just learning how to write. She scribbled her name on the line. Parson Brown furrowed his brow when he saw the elfling-like penmanship on the page. Ember looked at her name for a few moments, soaking it all in, trying to memorize how the letters of her old name looked on paper, knowing that this could very well be the last time she would draw out the name 'Ember

Skye' for herself. Then it dawned on her — she wasn't 'Ember Skye' anymore. Not the 'Ember Skye' of the Aboveground, not the 'Ember Skye' of the Mines. Her name was taking on a life of its own, with expectations and... what did Tannen call it? *Missions?*

Sturd grabbed her wrist and dragged her around the line of elves where Shella was waiting by the bank to present them with their candle and lantern, and to send them on their way. He stood behind her and shoved her into the raft. "Would you stop pushing and pulling on me!" she scolded. "If I had been wearing a dress, I would have tripped, ya know!"

Sturd grunted. "You tripped just fine before! And you *should* have been wearing a dress!"

On the raft, she crossed her legs and sat gazing at the others finishing up their nuptials as the cavern was beginning to sparkle with the colorful lights from the other elves' lanterns. Barkuss was nowhere to be seen amongst the throng. Ember raised her head up in time to see Tannen and Holly stepping over the pickaxe. In an overwhelming rush of exhilaration and glee, Holly hopped up and kissed Tannen excitedly on the cheek. The remaining elves on the line sighed and ahhh'ed. Ember's heart all but broke. She inhaled deeply, stifling a deep sob from within her chest.

"Light it up," Sturd instructed, pointing to the lantern. He unraveled the raft's tethers and pushed them from the dock. "Ya know, you're going to have to move into the den sooner or later," he said when they were adrift on the Ignis.

"Yea. I know. As soon as your father finds a place of his own, and as soon as I can get someone to move into mine. Those elves worked so hard to build and customize my den that I want it to go to just the right person." She smirked.

"Deny it all you want - *stall* all you want – sooner or later you're going to have to live up to your responsibilities as my wife."

Ember lit the lantern and lifted it into the air. "Whatever helps you sleep at night, Sturd."

But the lantern never took flight. It fell haplessly to the water, the igniter fizzling out.

"Are you kidding me?" Sturd roared. "Why did you throw it into the river?"

"I didn't throw it!"

"Did you even light it up like I told you to?"

"Yes! Didn't you hear the flame thingy fizzle?"

He threw his hands up in frustration. "You can't do anything right, can you? Falling! Stumbling! Can't light a stupid lantern! And to think, they actually put *you* in charge of something!"

Ember turned her head from him and gazed at the water. What she wouldn't have given for the igniter to have caught a shard of their wooden boat and set it ablaze. She removed the flower petals that Barkuss had put in her hair and one by one blew them from the palm of her hand into the Ignis. Sturd was grumbling and mumbling the whole boat ride back, but she remained silent and ignored him the entire time.

Chapter Eighteen

Nestled among the highest mountaintops of Norland, the palace of the Claus sat shrouded in the strongest of magics. To the naked eye, one was able to catch a glimpse of its aura, its outline, a vague sensation that something was there but not — the exact location of the sacred grounds of Lapis Hall forever to remain a mystery. But this is exactly what Docena M'raz feared. She suspected that the end of days for her people was quickly approaching, and the last shred of hope she clung desperately to was slipping from her fingertips like reaching for icicles atop the highest peak of a roof.

Dressed in a lush white fox fur cape, she sat at the frozen table in the center of her grand dining hall. Made entirely of ice, the walls and furniture glittered with a frosty sheen. Blueice archways supported the vaulted ceilings; its magical color made bolder against the white of the snow and illuminated the entire room with a soft cerulean radiance. Large ice portraits of woodland creatures decorated the walls. In the center of the room, above the frigid table, hung an ice chandelier – diamond shaped ice crystals refracted the white and blue lights. The Ice Room sparkled, and Docena took solace and comfort in its frozen glory for she was of the Frost Clan, and the cold had little or no effect on her.

The lunch plate before her consisted of a fantastic meal prepared by her personal Chef Elves: hallyhack meat thinly sliced and smothered in a glazzleberry and Nessie fruit sauce, frozen snowsnap peas with warm buttercream lightly drizzled on top, and peppermint crescent bread. They must have sensed she was tense today because for her mid-day drink they presented her with her favorite spirit, a Raldivver. Normally, she refused any kind of tonic in the afternoon, but the sweet brew with its chilled pink color and smoky top came as somewhat of a relief to her at that moment. The splendor of the meal, of the drink, still couldn't distract her attention from the transmitter device sitting on the table to her right. She stared at the glowing red switch-light and a heavy sadness overcame her heart. Being the Boss's wife had its multitude of perks and advantages, but it also came with heavy responsibility and tremendous heartache.

Many elfyears ago, when she known as Docena Frost, she would play endlessly in the lake in the back of her parents' home. There was something enchanting about the way the water rippled gently against the snow banks, and she felt compelled to take off her capes and clothes, strip down to her undergarments, and swim for hours. Her mother would scold her for her behavior, but her father, Jack, had indulged her. He encouraged her to swim to see just how much cold her body could withstand. He urged her to hold her breath under the frigid water to see how long she could last without having to rise to the surface for air. Both of her parents had been surprised to see that she could stay submerged for very long periods of time. Then her father had created harder challenges for her to endure. He would tell her to dive underneath the water, and using his magic breath, he would create a layer of thick ice, trapping her below. With eyes wide open, she would marvel at how the sky looked from behind the water and ice blanket. She would tell herself if she could stay there forever, she would.

It wasn't long after those days of swimming under the ice that she received her Life Job. Hoping for something that suited her talents and interests, she was less than pleased to hear she was selected to be the wife of the Boss. Of course, her parents were thrilled at the announcement, for her union with the M'raz Clan tied the Frost family to the ultimate position of power. As an elfling who only wanted to swim wildly in frostbitten water, Docena was underwhelmed at the prospect of being the Boss Lady.

However, her feelings immediately changed when she met Jolenir M'raz for the first time. Undeniably, she fell head-over-boots in love with his dashing goods looks, his air of confidence, and his charming ways. The responsibilities and duties that came with being the Claus and the Claus's wife were a piece of cake for them. When a couple is *that* happy and *so* in love, there's a feeling of being unstoppable, of being immortal in a way. There's a sense of being able to take on the entire world with an actual smile on your face. And that's what they did. Jolenir and Docena merrily served Norland, their subjects at the North Pole, and quite literally the entire world. She enjoyed power and riches beyond her wildest dreams. Just raise a finger, or clear her throat, and an elf or two were immediately there to wait on her hand and foot. Yet, after all these elfyears, the love the two of them had for each other never waned or shifted or faded — she still loved and cared for him just as much now as she had back then. But the toll the job was taking on her – on the both of them – was becoming almost too much to bear.

She was well aware that for some time now, Jolenir had been unhappy in his position as the Claus. There was a certain level of disappointment in his demeanor, he seemed easily agitated, uneasy, disgruntled. At first she thought it was due to his age – Jolenir had always been grumpy around birthday time, acknowledging that he was no longer a "strapping young buck." But his discontent went beyond his ever graying beard. She heard it in his voice, and through the words he spoke. It was the social shift at the Pole and in the world that was hardening his heart, and he was so set in his old-school ways that she was afraid he was throwing in the towel. The last few years he had kept mostly to himself, locked up in his chambers, not one for making merry, often refusing food. Of course, the burden of his Job was reason enough for him to resort to reclusive tendencies, but even in his interactions with her, she noticed he had lost the spark of life within his eyes.

Docena feared this was the end. No. She knew this was the end, but it was not the end she'd always envisioned she and Jole would have. She'd always imagined the two of them touring the country-side of Norland in the Bayglade Train. The windows of their coach would be open, remnants of the heart-shaped train smoke blowing in with the fresh winter breeze. They would sit and reflect on their life together, talking about their many journeys, various memorable Big Nights, but most importantly how much they loved and appreciated each other. At onset of twilight, they would eat in the dining car, feasting on their favorite meals and feeling the dizzying effects of their favorite spirited drinks. Then, when they retired for the night, she would lay her head on his chest and fall asleep to the rhythm of his heart until the Mists of the North came and incorporated his soul into the essence of the universe. And although she would wake up on the train alone, she would smile at the pink sunrise, knowing the elf she loved was now a part of something grander than being the Claus.

The Mists of the North come rolling by,
As I spot them from the corner of my eye.
Changing yellow, to pink, to purple, to black.
I hope they soon will roll on back.

The elves of the Pole knew the words, recited them in school or as lullabies to cranky elflings without much thought to the actual words themselves or the meaning behind them. Like a child's nursery rhyme performed from instinct, there was a long forgotten meaning of an ancient time and place. The Mists were very real in relation to the Claus. They were the higher power *above* the Claus, unseen and without form of body. The Claus was just the vessel for them, the spirit of the holiday, and when the presiding Claus had completed his Life Job, his soul united with the souls of thousands upon thousands of Clauses since the beginning of time.

Docena feared this was not to be. Jole was bitter, and angry, and discontented. She saw a frightening darkness in his soul and dreaded the day the Mists would come for him. She knew that day would be soon.

The doors to the Ice Room swung open, and Senara Calix, her assistant, burst into the room. Her high-heeled shoes clacked on the ice floor with careful determination, her face a stone mask trying to hide her anxiety. "Madame," she said and handed Docena a dossier.

Docena took the gray folder and unraveled the string fastener.

"I apologize, Madame, I know this is your dining hour, but you said when the first reports came in to find you at any time of the day and..."

She waved her hand in the air. "It's fine, Senara, thank you."

"You were insistent, Madame."

"I said it's okay." She removed the papers from the file and started reading. It was the early reports from The Christmas in July Initiative, and just as she had suspected the results were dismal. The blackened names in the Book had seen an initial decline, but within a week they were back up at an alarming rate. She put the papers back into the file, handed it back to her assistant, and glanced at the transmitter with a worrisome heart. "Is there anything else, Senara?"

"Madame, I… I'm sorry to have to report this, but in the Lumber District they're saying that a few acres of evergreens have disappeared. I… I didn't know how you wanted me to word this to the community for damage control and…"

Docena looked up at the icy ceiling then over at Senara. In a far-away voice she muttered, "Yes. Yes. Certainly squelch the rumors. Make something up if you have to. We don't want everyone to get in a panic months before the Big Night."

"Yes, Madame. Absolutely not. I'll work up a formal statement right away." Senara leaned in closer and put a loving hand on her shoulder.

"Anything else, dear?"

"Yes, Madame. The elfmarriages went off without a hitch. Above and Under. Smooth as silk." Senara gave a small, forced smile.

"Above *and* Under, you said?" Docena questioned.

Senara nodded quickly. "Yes. All on schedule and as planned."

Docena caressed the collar of her fur coat, deep in thought.

"Is there anything else I can do for you right now, Madame? Anything that you need?"

She smiled weakly. "No, dear. I'm fine, thank you."

"Thank you, Madame," Senara said with a quickstep bow and clacked out of the room. When the door shut, Docena's smile straightened out on her face to a frown. She had anticipated that the plan to market Christmas in July would fail, but at the time it was presented to her, she was desperate — desperate to do something, desperate to save her husband.

It was the same desperation she had felt when the Council had approached her about the Coal-less Night. In her heart, she had known it was the wrong thing to do. She had known the consequences, known the risks, but had agreed to the plan anyway. "Do as you will, just leave me out of it," she had told Una, and the rest was history. Was it selfishness that drove her to give them her approval? Perhaps. But at the time, what other choice did she have? Jole had been getting worse and worse on a daily basis, and she justified letting the Council proceed with the Coal-less Night as a means to force her husband into action. She had thought when he heard of the plan he would have stopped it before it got out of control – he would have jumped up, realized the possibilities, swooped in, and saved the day. She wanted him to feel needed and important and *in charge* again, give him a reason to be excited about being the Claus again. But, on the contrary, that's the exact opposite of what actually happened. "Let Una and her minions do what they want," he had said. "Let her have some control. It's what she's always wanted anyway, right?" Thank someone he had the sense to take action when the Sickness threatened to decimate their race.

All that was still not enough to motivate Jole. There was a part of her that had hoped he would hear about the Christmas in July launch and come up with a solution of his own, but when she told him, he had shrugged his shoulders and said indifferently, "If the names black out, they black out." That's when she knew that he was done. It wouldn't be much longer now until the Mists of the North would be coming for him, and it seemed as if he could care less about receiving the greatest honor an elf could ever dream to receive. And to make matters worse, he hadn't even chosen a successor, much less spoken about one!

If a successor isn't chosen by the time he goes, then...

None of that mattered anyway. The blackened names threatened to destroy everyone and everything. The North Pole, Norland, Lapis Hall – everything... gone. Without belief in the Claus, their lives and everything in it would cease to exist and become a distant memory to a faithless world. It also meant that thousands upon thousands of souls of the Claus would no longer roam the world instilling happiness and joy in others. She couldn't stand the thought of Jole not being a part of the universe in some capacity. He was a good and noble elf who deserved to transcend just as much as those before him. If what Senara said about the evergreens was true, then the effects of the blackened names were already starting to take shape, and she felt the true extent of her powerless-ness weigh heavily on her shoulders.

The light on the transmitter flashed green. Docena pressed a button, and a mechanical voice came through from the other end. "Madame Claus? Where are you, Madame Claus?"

She chuckled and said, "It's just me. I'm alone, Jolenir."

He gave a small laugh, this time in his own hearty voice. "Where are you, my love?"

Heat rose to her cold cheeks with a warm blush. After all these elfyears, he still gave her goosebumps when he spoke sweetly to her. He was always such a charmer. "The Ice Room," she said, unable to wipe the smile from her face.

"Ah," he sighed. "My Frost Queen is in her Ice Room."

"Where else would I take my lunch? Certainly not in the atrium!"

He chuckled again, the sound rising up from the pit of his belly. "Gardens too warm for you this time of year, my dear?"

She playfully rolled her eyes. "Oh, my dear Claus, wait 'til I find you! You'll be going on the Naughty List for sure if you don't stop teasing me."

He paused for a second. "Why don't you come find me?" he said, and there was a certain loneliness in his voice that made her heart melt.

"You seem to be in good spirits today, eh?" It had been ages since they had been playful with each other, let alone spent some quality time together.

For a split second, she thought – *this is it, the Mists are going to come for him tonight,* but as if reading her mind, he deepened his voice to his "Claus voice" and said, "You're not getting rid of me that easily, Docena!"

She nearly doubled over with laughter; a laughter that had been absent from her for too long, a laughter that felt good and warm, and somehow like her older, younger self. "That's it!" she threatened into the transmitter. "You're gonna get it now! Hope you're warmed up, 'cause when my frozen hands get a hold of you, you're in for the ice tickling of your life."

He was laughing now, too, the sound filling the Ice Room with a musical din. "I dare you," he said playfully and turned off his end of the receiver.

She had no idea where this youthful behavior was coming from, or why it was there. Was he aware of the inevitable failure of his Council's latest agenda? Was he aware of the disappearing trees in the heart of his kingdom? Could it be he heard the news of the successful pairings? Whatever is was, she wasn't about to let the moment pass! She got up from the table and raced through the palace like a reckless elfling with no cares in the world.

Chapter Nineteen

THE LAST RAYS OF LIGHT FROM THE SUN'S DESCENT STRUGGLED TO FILTER
into the Meeting Room. The glow from the picture windows
made the crimson walls gleam with an eerie orange light. Blood
dripped from the black ornate picture frames into red goopy pools
on the beige carpet, and slumped in their chairs were the bodies of
the nine elves presently seated at the table – their eyes open wide
with a look of pure terror from seeing the last horrific moments of
their pathetic lives come screeching to a sudden halt. *All dead.* Sturd
envisioned himself planting his hands face down onto the table and
stamping his palms with their blood. What a lovely decoration his
handprints would make for the walls! Sturd smiled at his demonic
vision. He felt lightheaded, faint. The images in his mind put him into
a euphoric state of near giddiness. Lately, he had found himself often
daydreaming about gruesome scenarios of death and destruction and
liking it. His favorite color had always been red…

Mrs. Claus and her assistant entered the room and broke him from
his murderous trance.

The Quarterly Meeting was set to begin, and an evaluation of the
Christmas in July Initiative was the topic of discussion. It mattered
not to Sturd — he already knew what the progress was, and in his
newly prepared report for the cadre, he had outlined the Initiative's
results thus far.

Sturd had concluded that the operation had invoked a four- stage
effect with the people. The First Stage he called *The Smile.* When
people were first exposed to holiday items showing up in stores and
on televisions, they smiled. And it was a genuine one. A legitimate
one. The people thought ahead to the coming Big Day fondly because
of their positive past experiences. It stirred up nostalgic feelings with
lots of *ooohh's* and *aaahhh's.*

The Second Stage he called *The Anticipation.* This is when the real-
ization sets in that the Big Day really isn't that far off. People begin
their initial plans for their celebrations – travel destinations, hosting
parties, taking on extra work so as to have extra money.

The Third Stage he named *The Fear.* The people start to feel an overwhelming sense of fear when they reach this stage. During the planning process, they began to make comparisons between past holidays and become terrified that their current plans will not meet the past expectations. Maybe this year will be too costly? Maybe this year will not be as memorable? Maybe this year will be a complete and utter failure?

Then, there was a Fourth Stage, which he named *The Resentment.* Overall, he began to see something close to a rejection of the holiday by the people. Essentially, they griped that that holiday was being rammed down their throats, and they were sick of the constant barrage of movies and ads and decorations in the stores. He would never admit that Ember was right, and conveniently left the Fourth Stage out of his official report to the cadre. Besides, keeping the Fourth Stage to himself added to his growing power. It increased his potential dominion over each and every elf, even over the Council themselves. If he was the only elf to know, then he would be the only elf to "fix it" when the system ultimately broke. And break it would. This plan of his was surely taking them down a path of irreversible destruction, and he alone would be the savior of the New Age. He licked his lips at the thought...

Everyone at the table rose to greet Madame Claus. When she sat down, she began to read off the names of the present elves, "Jolevana Ruprecht. Zelcodor Ruprecht. Cerissa Lux. Quisto Calix. Trelson Castleberry. Orthor Castleberry. Ogden Castleberry. Senara Calix. Harold Pennybaker. Sturd Ruprecht. Ember Ruprecht." To which they all responded, 'here.'

Ember Ruprecht... The name grated off his tongue with sharp and jagged sounds. Like the sound a pickaxe makes when striking the cavern walls. It gargled in his throat, and both sickened and fascinated him at the same time. He looked across the table at her new wooden wedge nameplate. There were still sawdust flakes on the edges from where the letters had been freshly carved. She glanced up and their eyes met for a split second before she rolled hers and looked back at Mrs. Claus. He smirked.

To an outsider, their first few months of elfmarriage would appear to have been going horribly. Ember had refused to move into Welfort Den while his father, Corzakk, was still living there. So, Corzakk had plans drawn up for a den of his own to be built, but the project was going to take a few more months to complete. Sturd had suggested he and Ember move into a completely new den so the two could have a place to *call their own,* but she wouldn't budge. Their separation had been a strain on what was supposed to be a typical elfunion. As an elfwife, Ember was required to take care of their den, cook, clean, attend to his needs and whims, but she had justified her refusal to do any of that by saying she was *not* a typical elfmaiden, and theirs was *not* a typical elfunion, which actually wasn't so far from the truth.

The only thing that had changed between them was the Law of Property, which Sturd had been well-versed in. The Law of Property stated that as elfwife and elfhusband, any belongings and/or property owned by one was automatically the property of the other. Ember had nothing Sturd desired, but this allowed him *freedom* in which he found endless hours of delight. According to the Law, her den was his den, and he had the freedom to come and go as he pleased. There was nothing he enjoyed more than entering Ember's den at all hours of the day and night. He stalked her, barged in while she was working, and interrupted her while she was taking tea with Barkuss. She screamed and berated him whenever he waltzed in, which only made him cheerier to do so. He would laugh and say things like, "you know you need to get used to this when we finally move in together." Or, "You can't stay away from your husband forever, you know. You do have duties to perform." She would scream some more, throw things at him, even spit at him, much to his deranged amusement. It pleased him to the core to see her get so completely unglued.

Corzakk, on the other hand, was not quite as amused. He had scolded Sturd for his actions, saying that he should alert the Council of her disobedient nature at once. Legally, any elfwife who is found to be insubordinate by the Council would have to face harsh punishment, but Sturd chose not to tell the higher-ups. He enjoyed tormenting her. Watching her squirm was always a highlight of his day.

"Good evening, darling," he whispered at her from across the table. She swept her eyes in his direction and narrowed her brow. "Really?" she said sarcastically.

Sturd smiled, flashing her a mouthful of animal-like teeth.

"Let's begin, shall we?" Mrs. Claus announced before Ember could respond to Sturd's vile gesture.

The cadre sat up at attention. Sturd picked up the papers in front of him and tapped them into even edges on the table.

"We've been reviewing the effects of our Initiative," Mrs. Claus continued with a sad voice, "and it's not as completely disastrous as we first thought. Mr. Ruprecht has come up with a Three Stage Observation Report that outlines what he has found."

Sturd fidgeted with the papers. *That's what you think. It's actually Four Stages, but...*

"Yes," Una chimed in, "as Field Data Collector, Sturd has observed, researched, and will present his discoveries. While they are not as outstanding as we had hoped for, I think with a little brainstorming, there's always room to tweak for next year."

He passed his reports around the table so everyone had a copy. When Ember received hers, she banged a fist on the table top, getting the attention of everyone present. "Wait. Next year? We're actually considering doing this *again*?" Her insolent tone was enough to make Sturd reach across the table and squeeze the life out of her, but he controlled his instinctive urges with a deep inhale and exhale heard by all.

Councilman #5, Trelson Castleberry, spoke out. "Yes. This should be at least a three elfyear plan. Let the data speak for itself. We'll never know the true effects if we don't give it a fair enough shot."

"It's just that..." Ember angrily tried to interject. Sturd felt the heat of her aura flaring out across the table. He closed his eyes and allowed her irritation to wash over him, through him. He absorbed her budding fury, incorporated it within his own. It felt delicious.

"Easy, dear niece," Zelcodor interrupted, trying to calm her down. "We're all family here, now. No need to get defensive. We don't mind hearing what you have to say as long as you say it in a respectful manner."

Ember breathed in again, and Sturd knew she was desperately trying to calm herself down. He watched the way her tiny nostrils flared upward as she drew the air up into her nose, and wished in the pit of his stomach that she *wouldn't* be able to settle her rage down. He wished to see her lash out with an unadulterated wrath. He wished to see the black storm chaos that he knew resided deep within her soul unleashed on the cadre, creating the crimson walls of death and destruction. Oh, how he wanted to dip his hands in the blood red puddles and paint his face and...

"I'll tell you one thing," Harold Pennybaker said loudly, ripping Sturd from yet another vicious daydream. "I, for one, think that maybe all of this is 'too much of a good thing.' Maybe we need to do a strong and forceful launch, then ease up for the other holidays in between – still have a presence, but not so overtly in your face. Then after the Feast Day, drive it home hard and heavy."

"Good point, Pennybaker," Zelcodor noted.

Senara scribbled down notes in her notepad.

Ember obviously wasn't giving up. "But what about the blackened names?" she asked, and Sturd could feel her fire flare up again.

"Very good question," Mrs. Claus responded. "That leads us into the next section of our meeting. Castleberrys? What is the state of the Book of Names?"

Orthor and Ogden nervously looked at each other and mumbled something. Ogden cleared his throat and began, "Madame, Council, all else present," he said tipping his head in everyone's direction. "The total number of blackened names is close to two thousand."

Senara gasped slightly.

"But as Madame Claus said, it's not as grim as we first thought," Orthor chimed.

"Not grim?" Ember shouted. "Not grim? Are you crazy? That's nearly two-thousand more names in an average year? How is that 'not grim'?"

"It's two-thousand less to worry about," Sturd spoke out. "No gifts. No coal." But Una and Zelcodor shot him a look that forced him to close his mouth.

"Alright, alright," Mrs. Claus said, waving her hands in the air. "Let the brothers continue, please. Thank you, Mrs. Ruprecht. Thank you, Mr. Ruprecht."

"Yes," Orthor continued, "there are a lot of names, the most that we have ever seen in our elflives, but they seem to be getting under control. When the launch first happened, the names stopped blacking out for about a week, and we thought we were okay."

"But then, it went crazy. Got out of control again," Ogden added.

"Now, they're leveling off. We see about three or four a day, but it's not entirely crazy like it had been, and..."

Ogden opened his mouth to add to what his twin brother was saying, but what came out of it sounded like nonsensical gibberish. The room went silent, and Ogden, in a state of panic, clapped his hand over his mouth. Orthor's eyes narrowed. He stared at his brother for a moment, and as soon as Orthor attempted to say something, the same garbled words spilled out from his throat. The same mesh of guttural consonants and heavily accented vowels.

Elvish.

Mrs. Claus remained quiet and stared attentively at the brothers. The Council members shifted noisily in their seats. The expression on the twins' faces led Sturd to believe that this had never happened to them before.

Ember sat in wide-eyed amazement. *"Haaden welyach?"* she asked them.

The brothers had a look of absolute terror on their faces and they both shook their heads. *"Sprake doulin a tay?"*

Orthor shook his head and responded, *"Anoof ca'lain,"* to which he clapped his hand over his mouth in fear.

Ember giggled. *"Wilcowl!"*

The heat of anger began to boil up in Sturd's body. If Orthor and Ogden just magically started speaking Elvish, then that meant...

"Can someone please explain what in the Claus is going on here?" Harold Pennybaker cried out in annoyance.

"It's Elvish," Mrs. Claus said in a faraway voice.

"Yes. Yes, I know that," he answered. "But what are they saying? What's happening?"

Sturd knew all too well what was happening. *The Dublix Santarae.* The glorious text that was safe and sound in his possession. There was a passage about the ancient tongue of Elvish — a passage so monumental that he had come to memorize it in its entirety. *'When the Claus is on the precipice of the Mists, the words of the elders shall awaken in the duos...'*

"Elvish," Una spoke out. There was a curious smile plastered on her face. "And by what Mrs. Ruprecht and the Castleberry Brothers have said to each other, this is the very first time dear Ogden and Orthor have ever spoken the language. Ember welcomed the brothers to what we like to call the 'Elvish Club.' Isn't that right, Mrs. Ruprecht?"

Ember looked up at Una. *"Ashtownen,"* she replied and Una raised her eyebrows.

Sturd sat back, holding his tongue. He was stunned to learn that his Aunt knew the language herself.

"Excuse me?" Harold said. "They just started speaking an ancient language? Out of the blue?"

"Yes. While one can be trained in the tongue, such as Mrs. Ruprecht here," Una motioned to Ember with a sly side smile, "Elvish is a gift that is only given to twins naturally. Isn't that correct, Madame Claus?" She glared hard at the Boss Lady.

Mrs. Claus met her gaze. "You are, Una. Everything is outlined in *The Dublix Santarae.*"

The Dublix Santarae. My Dublix Santarae.

"The hoo-doo whad-do?" Harold scoffed.

"The Dublix Santarae. It's an appendage of the Codex. It references genealogy, bloodlines, Elvish. But we haven't reviewed that document for many, many elfyears," Mrs. Claus explained quietly. "We haven't had cause to."

"But what does this mean?" Ember asked. "Is something about to happen?"

The Council members glanced at each other. Sturd knew exactly what it meant. *Yes, my dear wife. Something is about to happen that will rock our very existence.*

"Don't worry, dear," Councilwoman #2 said gently, "I'm sure it's noth..." Zelcodor sneered and interrupted her. "Perhaps we need to schedule..."

Sturd froze. *A Meeting? To discuss the Dublix Santarae?* A meeting would mean they would need to collect the document from the Book Keepers' office, and when they found that it was missing...

"Not another emergency meeting!" Harold whined.

Mrs. Claus gave a small smile. "Of course not, Mr. Pennybaker. I wouldn't say an emergency meeting, but more like a review. I will not require the attendance of the entire cadre. Perhaps just myself, and the Council."

"I'll come," Ember blurted.

Hot rage flooded behind Sturd's eyes. He shot her a terrifying look. "As will I."

Councilman #4, Quisto Calix, stood up from his chair to adjourn the meeting. "Settled, then. Sturd, as Field Data Collector, you should check out the *Dublix Santarae* from the Castleberry's office, and be prepared to report back here say... when do you think is appropriate, Councilwoman #1?"

Una shrugged. "A week? How does that sound, Madame?"

Mrs. Claus was looking at Senara's notepad. "Fine, fine," she said dismissively.

"A week it is," Quisto repeated.

Narrowly escaping exposure, Sturd smiled. If only they knew he was already in possession of the Dublix. If only they knew that he had studied it, memorized it backward and forward, and tucked it safely away in his future arsenal. Now they wanted him to retrieve it, study it, and prepare its contents for a meeting?

This was too good to be true.

Chapter Twenty

STURD STEPPED INSIDE HEADQUARTERS AND FRANTICALLY BRUSHED THE
snow from his jumpsuit, but it was no use, by the time he entered
the building the snowflakes had started to melt, leaving him damp
and cold. *Snow!* It disgusted him beyond words! He couldn't stand the
stuff! It was cold and white and wet and clung to his body like para-
sitic flecks of happiness. No matter how he hunched his body over, or
layered his clothing, he still felt the invading effects of the white matter on his flesh. Now, if all this white stuff had been coal dust, that
would have been an entirely different story. He'd much preferred
the noxious fumes of the Mines after a day's work and the way the
ash flittered about in the caves like gray snow gently falling, falling,
falling... Coal dust stayed, left its semi-permanent mark on the elves,
coated them in dirt and grime. It didn't melt on contact like snow.
Snow was fleeting, much like happiness. Coal dust was real. Tangible.
Dark. Settled on the skin, burrowed down deep in the lungs. Much
like the embodiment of chaos itself. It could be washed and scrubbed
away, but it was never really *gone*.

The front desk was vacant, and after waiting for what seemed like
an hour, he made his way up to the Book Keepers' office without
checking in or getting a visitor's pass. The faster he got in, pretended
to get the book, and get out, the better. Besides, the heavy white
clouds in the sky indicated that the snowfall would continue for a
long time, something he did not wish to be around for any longer
than necessary.

The Dublix Santarae was nestled close to his chest in his breast
pocket. His plan was to get into the Book Keepers' office, sneak the
book back onto the shelf, and conveniently 'pick-it- up' to analyze
and present at the next meeting of the cadre. He took little stock
in the intelligence of the brothers, and knew he would be able to do
this quickly. He patted at the book against his chest lovingly, and
breathed in deeply as the elevator ascended. As the cables mechani-
cally pulled the car upwards, he sucked in the feeling of the escalating

motion. The quick ascent felt good. It was jarring at first, but in seconds, he had the feeling of flying. Flying upward. *Rising...*

The sudden Elvish outburst of the Castleberry brothers had strong implications, and he had racked his brain since the Quarterly Meeting with how he was going to handle the situation. If he was right about what The Dublix Santarae said, the Claus was on his way out and a new Claus would need to be chosen. Sturd's thirst for power when he was in control of the List had gotten stronger with the possession of *The Dublix Santarae.* Just what was his ultimate goal? His ultimate agenda? Spreading chaos throughout the Pole? Wreaking havoc among the Elven race? Sure. At first that's all he'd thought he wanted, but now those seemed like the childish thoughts of a vengeful elfling. But now? There was so much more. He *wanted* so much more. Dare he say eliminate the Claus and take over all of the Pole?

When the elevator reached its destination and the door opened with a *ding,* he had to settle himself down from his thoughts of grandeur.

Don't get ahead of yourself just yet. One step at a time.

The door to the Book Keepers' office opened with an echoing creak. The pages of the Book of Names slowly flipped back and forth, indicating that all was quiet and status quo in the human world. The soft yellow glow of the oil lamps illuminated the room; however, he was surprised to see both brothers sitting behind the desk. Usually, one took the day shift and one took the night shift, but here they were – together, talking excitedly in Elvish, and laughing. Bile rose to his throat and he swallowed hard, forcing it back down.

"What the hell are you two giggling like stupid elflings about?" His voice boomed in the room, and Orthor and Ogden stopped sharply and looked up.

"Oh, Sturd," Ogden said nervously. "The front desk never called up to say you were on your way."

"Never mind that." He walked over to them at the desk. Orthor was still smiling from his conversation with his brother. "Why all the jibber-jabber?"

Orthor giggled out loud. "Now that we can speak Elvish, ya know, everything's different."

Sturd clicked his tongue against the roof of his mouth. "No, I don't know. Enlighten me." He lied. Of course he knew. Of course he knew what it meant! He had studied the damn *Dublix Santarae* for months now!

The brothers looked at each other and smiled. Ogden bowed his head, allowing his brother to explain. Orthor straightened up his back and proudly tugged at the straps of his orange suspenders. "We're up for consideration, ya know."

Ogden nodded in agreement.

Sturd stifled a retching sound and continued to play dumb. He put his hand over his chest, feeling the hidden book. "No, I don't know. Consideration for what?"

"To be the Boss!" Ogden declared. "Apparently, when the Boss is ready to be carried away by the Mists of the North, a new Claus must be chosen."

"And twin elves who can speak Elvish are automatically candidates," Orthor interjected.

Sturd coughed, trying to hide his disgust. The thought of one of these buffoons taking the reins as the Boss turned his stomach. "Really?" he said in mock surprise. "How do you know this for sure?"

"Trelson, our father, told us. Ya know? Councilman #5."

So they haven't read The Dublix Santarae... "Right, right," Sturd replied rubbing his hands together. *Once every set of twins has been identified and gifted with the tongue, selection will take place immediately.* Ogden turned to his brother and said something in Elvish. Orthor responded in kind, and the two laughed again. Sturd was becoming tired of this nauseating display. "What was that? What did you say? Forgive me, I unfortunately am not versed in that language."

"Oh, we were just saying how we thought we would look in the red suit," Ogden answered.

"Yea, and I said I would probably look better!" Orthor chimed.

Ogden elbowed Orthor. "I don't think he chooses based on how one looks in the suit."

Orthor rubbed his arm. "Good point. Then, how does he choose between brothers?"

Sturd's hand instinctively clutched his chest and he froze in place. He knew the answer to that question, but if the brothers were asking it, it surely meant that they *didn't* know. They would probably want to...

"Hmm," continued Ogden, "I don't think anyone would mind if we looked that question up."

Orthor took a step towards the book shelf. "Not at all, considering we are in line to the throne!"

Acting quickly, Sturd stepped in front of Orthor, blocking his path. "Allow me, brothers," he said slyly.

"No, no, no," Orthor said, waving Sturd away. "It's fine. I'll get it." He tried to sidestep Sturd, but Sturd followed directly in time with him.

"No, truly," Sturd said, placing his hands on Orthor's shoulders, "let me get it for you. Don't you think you and your brother should start getting used to having others do things for you?"

His snakelike charm fell on deaf ears. Ogden now moved forward. "No, Sturd," he said, "if Orthor wants to get it himself, he..."

Sturd extended one arm and caught Ogden before he could get past him. A panicky feeling stirred within him, and his hands were slick with sweaty anticipation. Ogden eyed Sturd's hand on his collarbone, then glanced up at his eyes. "Why are you here, exactly?" he asked.

Sturd's lower lip puckered out. "*The Dublix Santarae*, of course. You remember. The Council commissioned me to..."

"Right," Orthor said, sliding out from under Sturd's hand on his shoulder. "I'll just be a second..."

Sturd tried to extend his grasp on the brother, and in the process, *The Dublix Santarae* fell to the wooden floor of the office with a loud *thud*. The brothers looked down at it, then back up at Sturd with questioning faces. Ogden stepped to the side, bent down, and picked up the book. He studied its cover, turned it over and over, before waving it in the air at Sturd. "What's this? Where did it come from?"

Sturd froze. He wrestled with all the possible alibis and excuses in his mind, but the only answer he could muster up was, "I…I don't know what you're talking about."

The brothers paused and looked at each other. Orthor turned around and headed back to the desk. "Yea, well, I'm just gonna go call the Council's office just to let them know…"

His words were drowned out by the blood rushing in Sturd's head. He couldn't let him call the Council. He couldn't let his secret be revealed! In a blinding rush, he saw everything crash down around him. Ogden was waving the book in his face, and saying something to him, but the words weren't registering. His entire body felt as if it were descending quickly on the elevator, his stomach lurching to his throat, a weightless sensation of losing control. In slow- motion, he watched Orthor pick up the corded phone handle and begin dialing away, shattering his dreams like broken mirror glass. The pain of certain defeat stinging his open-wound-ego, making him feel numb, making him see red…

Defeat? He knew not the word. It had never existed in the vocabulary of Sturd Ruprecht before, so why would it be there now? Defeat. That wasn't an option for him. Wasn't a viable alternative. He hung his head low in mock defeat and sucked in air deeply, meticulously, his controlled breaths filling him with strength, clearing his panicked brain, formulating the only solution his red eyes could see.

"Yes, I need to speak to a Councilmember. Any Councilmember," Orthor said over the phone, and in a flash, Sturd sprang into action.

With all of his wild energy, he shoved Ogden into one of the desks in the room. The back of his head slammed onto the sharp edge of the corner and knocked him out cold. *The Dublix Santarae* flew out of his chubby hands and skidded across the floor. Orthor turned his head around when he heard the commotion; his mouth dropped when he saw his brother lying unconscious. He tried to mutter something to Sturd, into the phone, but it was no use. It was too late; Sturd was upon him in an instant – his blind rage surging through him relentlessly.

And relentless he was! Sturd pounced on Orthor from behind. With both hands, he grabbed the phone cord, viciously wrapped it around his neck, and squeezed. Orthor's arms flailed and he choked, desperately searching for that relief breath. He tried grabbing at the cord, attempting to pull it from its death-grip, and when he found that was no use, he brought his arms up and tried to swat at Sturd's face. He grabbed Sturd's ears, and in a last ditch effort for release, pulled down hard on them. The pain only increased Sturd's fury as he criss-crossed the cord in the back and pulled even tighter. Orthor gagged now with croaking noises that filled the room, and his arms stopped thrashing about. Sturd pulled harder until he heard a crunching noise from Orthor's throat and the croaking noises ceased. He remained in his tight-noose position a few moments longer so he was sure Orthor's lifeless body would thump to the floor.

Sturd bent forward, his hands on his knees, his head between his legs. His heart beat so fast, he thought it might actually explode in his chest. A feeling of power pulsated through his veins, like pure electricity surging underneath his flesh. He straightened himself up and tilted his head from side to side. The bones in his neck popped down his spine, relaxing the storm within him.

From the corner of his eye, he saw Orthor's face – eyes wide and bulging out, skin blue from oxygen deprivation. The cord was loose around his neck, but the track marks were fresh and deep around his throat like a red and bruise colored necklace. Sturd walked over, nonchalantly unraveled the cord, and placed the phone handle back on the cradle.

He spun around when Ogden began to stir in the corner. He moaned when he came to, and rubbed the back of his head. Sturd knew he would have to take care of him too. Like a predator stalking his prey, he walked slowly over to him and knelt down by his side. Ogden looked up at him with fearful eyes. They were bright blue and so filled with terror. "W… what… what did you do?" he stammered.

Without saying a word, Sturd smiled and motioned his hand to the dead brother.

Ogden let out a horrified squeal at the sight of Orthor's corpse. "Please! Please! I'll do anything you want! Anything!"

Sturd shook his head and clicked his tongue again.

"It's okay, really. I'll… I'll say it was an accident. He attacked you first!"

Sturd chuckled, lifted his forefinger, and wagged it in the air. "Guess you and your brother aren't up for consideration anymore." He bent closer to Ogden and breathed heavily against his cheek. Ogden was breathing so quickly, he was almost hyperventilating. Sturd placed a hand on Ogden's chest to feel the swift rise and fall of his chest, and smiled.

"Oh please! Please, Claus! Why are you doing this to me?" Tears sprung from Ogden's eyes – this act of weakness repulsing Sturd.

At least Banter met his end with some dignity.

Sturd traced the outline of Ogden's face and neck with his pointed fingertips, leaving subtle red lines in their path. Ogden closed his eyes, and sat quivering at Sturd's every touch.

"Please! Please!" he continued to beg. "You can't do this! You just can't. You can't kill another elf. Just show me some mercy, please!"

Sturd scooted in front of him and gingerly placed his hands around Ogden's throat. He was surprised that Ogden hadn't put up more of a fight. "Mercy?" he said. "Why should I show you any mercy?"

"I… I don't know. We… we're probably related somehow. Ya know, kin of kin of kin. My father, your uncle, they're both Council members. We're all intertwined. You can't kill me. You can't kill family!"

Sturd released his hands and Ogden's body relaxed, but tensed back up when Sturd began to laugh. "Seriously? That's your defense?" he taunted. "Orthor, I killed my own brother, what makes you think I wouldn't kill you?"

Ogden's eyes widened with frantic panic as Sturd clamped his hands down on his neck and squeezed. Electricity once again grew in him as he pressed down on Ogden's defenseless body. Ogden didn't fight much as the life was smothered from him, but he did manage to squeak out, "Ogden," in a hoarse voice before succumbing to Sturd's brute strength.

Sturd released his grip when the deed was done and rested his hands on the tops of his knees. His knuckles were white, and the beginnings of bruises on the tops of his palms were already starting to form. Too easy it was. Too easy to see a life, mark a life, and take a life, especially for his own need. And the ends certainly did justify the means. After his body stopped shaking with ecstasy, he picked himself up, and walked quietly out of the office, leaving the bodies and *The Dublix Santarae* behind him.

Nobody knew that he was even in the building that day except for the dead brothers back in the office, and he had wanted to keep it that way. So, Sturd sneaked down the emergency stairwell in hopes of going undetected. Once outside, he got on his hands and knees and trekked through the back alley. The 'four feet' footprints would make any unsuspecting eye think that some kind of animal had been nosing around the dumpster or just passing through. The smell of the snow on the ground made him shudder with agitation, but if it meant a quick and concealed getaway, he didn't mind enduring the white stuff so close to his face. When he felt he was in the clear, he stood up on two legs and began to walk the streets of Norland. He would have to stay in the city for a while because the Official Transport Carriage had dropped him off earlier that day, and he wanted to solidify an alibi for the time spent in the land beyond the rain. And speaking of rain, the thick falling snow had now transformed into a gray mist.

If what the Castleberry Brothers said was true…

Then, the Boss was, in fact, preparing to incorporate with the Mists of the North. A new Claus was going to be chosen very soon, and he wondered just how he could capitalize on that moment of transition and weakness. How was he going to upset the balance between the established order and the replacement candidates to the point of being able to swoop in and declare himself Law? What if there no longer was an established order? What if there no longer were replacements?

No more replacements?

No more candidates?

No more twins?

And in a moment of clarity, a light shone brightly in his mind. The Boss only chose a replacement who was part of a set of twins. *The Dublix Santarae.* *Double Santa.*

But, what if there were no twins to choose from? The Boss has no choice but to fly with the Mists when it's his time, but what would happen if there was no one to replace him? No Claus. *What a perfect scene of chaos that would cause. What a perfect time to glide in and claim all of Norland for himself.*

As the plan developed deeper and deeper within him, he passed by the Main Stable. All was quiet, and he assumed most of the workers had gone inside to wait for the storm to pass. But there were two elves in particular that he was anxious to see, and by some divine intervention, he spied from within a corral the red and green bottoms of red and green scarves.

Chapter Twenty-One

ASCHE STOOD REGALLY AS EMBER HARNESSED HIM TO THEIR NEW SLEIGH. Every time she saw her Coal Sleigh, she was rather excited by it all. She hopped into the driver's perch, wrapped the black silver-studded reins around her hands and tugged. Asche's head reared back a bit and he let out a small whinny. "Too much?" she asked, to which he snorted back at her. "Sorry, sorry. We'll find the right balance of pressure," she said, unraveling the restraint a little. "We'll figure it all out in time to ride." He jerked his head upward in agreement.

The Big Night was coming on soon, and already Ember was feeling a heightened tension in the air. It was almost as if everything else around her had been fading out of focus, and all her attention was slowly but surely fixated on one thing – delivering the coal. All the other things in her life were taking a backseat – *sure, I just got married to my arch- nemesis! Sure, the true love of my life is completely out of reach, married to a pretty bubbly little thing! Sure, there's a revolution brewing in the Mines that I'm kinda ignoring!* – inexplicably, the only thing occupying space in her head was the Big Night.

Coal for All.

Tannen's wife, Holly, had come through on her end. The girls at West Valley were all too eager to get in on a 'covert operation' for the 'legendary Ember.' Every week, they had produced hundreds of notes for the children of the world— hundreds of 'gotcha' letters to put the entire adolescent population on notice.

Barkuss had been a trooper through the whole ordeal, too. Little by little he had set aside extra coal, secretly pulling from the main reserves and fudging his numbers so no one was the wiser. He would carry sack-fulls multiple times a day to the Catta-car and inconspicuously leave them under his trolley seat. Of course, he only did this during Tannen's shift, when Tannen could retrieve the sacks and drop them off to the secret location. Tannen's entire life was spent studying routes in the Mines, and over the years, he had learned a few tricks. Just inside the Forbidden Corridor, Tannen had discovered an abandoned chin-chi tunnel, which in turn, turned out to be the perfect spot for smuggling coal.

How strange it seemed that as a miner Ember did nothing but gripe about her position, her loneliness, and her place in the world. Now, the thought of it all exhilarated her – the paperwork and lists and spreadsheets – and there was something exciting about the ride. There was a rush of energy that pushed through all the grievances, surpassed all the moaning and groaning. There was a sense of freedom and importance.

She hopped down from the perch and released Asche from the harness. He shimmied his body as if he were shaking off fleas. She narrowed her eyes at him and teased, "Aw, c'mon, it's not *that* bad." He bucked his head up and down and Ember laughed. "It's just a few practices and then the Big Night, then you're free the rest of the year. Don't be such an ornery thing!" He snorted at her again, his nose spraying her face. Her mouth dropped open and she wagged a finger at him. "Not nice, my friend. Not nice." There was a playful twinkle in his eye, and she patted his muzzle lovingly. *Freedom.* Asche had to give his up for a few days out of the year, but for her, true freedom lasted for one night…

Kyla came into the barn with a silver pail filled with oatgrains and Nessie mash. The smell alone made Asche snort with excitement. "How'd our boy do with the harness?" She put the pail on the ground in front of him and he eagerly started eating.

"A champ." Ember caressed his antlers as he ate. "He needs very little direction, if any at all. I think I had him too tight at first, but once we're in the air, I'll be able to adjust to a comfortable level."

"Yea, airtime and downtime are two completely different things."

Ember nodded. "Tell me about it!" The girls chuckled and smiled at each other. "They come yet?"

Kyla shook her head. "No. Weird, right?"

"I don't know. How do those Scarf Brother guys usually show up?"

"Good Claus! They're always on time. Actually, a lot of the time they show up earlier than they have to. Ever since they started that

'Inquiry' on me, they have been up my behind pretty much on a weekly basis."

"So, what do you think is up? Could they be finally easing up on you."

Kyla's eyes widened. "On Judging Day?" Her voice startled Asche who lifted his head from his food pail. "No way! Judging Day is only the most important day of the year for Reindeer Trainers. And those guys take their job super seriously. They used to be trainers at one time, but were moved up to Judges, and they are extremely strict, extremely business-minded, and extremely punctual. My troops are all lined up outside and ready to go, but where are the Judges?"

Asche dipped his head back down into the pail and continued eating. Ember shrugged her shoulders. "Who knows? Maybe they're at another stable and are running late. Maybe they're doing an Inquiry on another trainer."

Kyla huffed. "Oh, you have no idea. I wouldn't wish that level of harassment on anyone!

"It's okay. I wouldn't worry about anything just yet. Besides..." The girls paused when they heard a clamoring of bells approaching from a distance. "See. Told ya. They're here. Time to go to work."

Kyla straightened out her jacket and pulled her hat down to her brows. "You coming?"

"I'll walk with you out there, but then I'm going into the house for lunch. This is all you!"

"Yea, yea," Kyla said, shaking her head.

The girls walked from the barn to the training field. Ember had fully expected to see the two brother Judges wearing their red and green scarves, holding their little notepads, stamping their feet impatiently for Kyla to start her deer demonstration. She was surprised to see a plump elfwoman in a lime green coat sitting in a carriage being drawn by a... *Shadow-Deer?*

"Fannie?" Kyla called as she raced across the field. "Fannie? Are you okay?"

The elf pulled on the reins of her deer and skidded forward. She jumped out of her carriage before the deer had come to a complete stop and met Kyla with a tremendous, bear-like hug. She was sobbing and frantic. "Oh Kyla, Kyla! Are *you* okay? Are *you* okay?"

Kyla pulled back and held onto the woman's shoulders at arms-length. "I'm fine. I'm fine. Slow down. What's going on?" She tried to coax the hysterical elf.

"Did they come yet? Did they come?"

"Who? The Judges? No. Not yet."

"Well, then I don't think they're going to, Kyla. Something bad is going on!"

Ember walked closer to them. "Is everything okay? Can I help with something?"

"Oh...oh," Kyla stammered as if suddenly remembering Ember was there, "Fannie, this is Ember. Ember, this is Fannie Brightly. She owns the Brightly Reindeer Stable in West Bank."

Fannie sidestepped Kyla's grip and extended her hand to Ember. "Ember?" she asked in amazement. "*The* Ember?"

Ember shook Fannie's hand and nodded, but her heart sank in her chest when she registered the elf's name. *Brightly? As in Pepper Brightly? Could you be Pepper's mom?*

"You have a Shadow-Deer, too?" Ember asked.

"Yes. This is Boptail," she answered. Boptail neighed and motioned her head in a roundhouse way. When her bells jingled, Asche immediately materialized by her side and nuzzled his face into her neck. Boptail responded by cuddling back – their antlers nearly becoming intertwined.

A Shadow-Deer. Like Asche. So, he's not completely alone in this world.

"Okay, Fannie," Kyla said, grabbing onto her once more. "Tell me what happened."

Fannie took a deep breath and exhaled. Her strong breath left trails of thick white smoke among them. "They never showed, for me. I was all ready and everything. My boys were lined up and set to do their stuff. Boptail was back in the barn. I wasn't about to have her judged because, well, we all know how that one ends for the Shadow-Deer. They never take the Shadow-Deer, so why bother, right? Anyway, Boptail was starting to get a little antsy – they all get antsy on Judging Day – so, I brought her out thinking that she could let off some steam before the Judges came. Time goes and goes and goes. No Judges. So, I decide to take a ride into town. I got things to do, ya know? I tell Randall..."

"Randall?" Kyla interrupted.

"My husband..."

Pepper's dad?

"...I tell Randall, 'Look, I gotta get going. If they show up, you tell them *they* can wait for *me*!' I get on Boptail and off we go into town. So, we get into town and there's kind of a weird stir going on. And as I'm riding passed the Gumdrop Stand I overhear someone talking about some kind of accident involving the Reindeer Judges, and I just hightailed it out of there! I came rushing straight to you to see if everything was okay over here!"

"An accident? What kind of accident?" Ember asked.

"I don't know. All I know is this isn't good. It's downright..."

"Weird?" Kyla finished.

"Exactly. Weird. And something else weird happened the other day."

"What?" Ember asked.

"I didn't think anything of it at the time. I should have said something to someone, though, thinking back to it. Please, Miss Ember, don't take this the wrong way, but the other day a Coal Elf came to my house. He was all dirty and stuff and he was talking about a group in the Mines. The Brotherhood, I think. He told me that they were enlisting the help of Land Elves for a project they were doing Underground. Wanted to know if I would be part of their Nine Ladies Dancing Faction. I was so preoccupied with getting ready for Judging Day that I kinda brushed him off, ya know. And he kept pressing me and pressing me. And I found myself getting angrier and angrier. I found myself hating him. I mean, I know he wasn't the one responsible for what happened to Pepper..."

You are Pepper's mother...

"… Her disappearance was a complete accident, and I know I shouldn't have taken my anger out on him…."

It wasn't an accident, Fannie. She ran away from Sturd, the elf I now call husband. She defected and was caught and…

"…but I lashed out. Screamed and yelled at him. Demanded to see his Pass. When he couldn't produce one, I threatened to get an Enforcer on him. He ran away right after that." She put her head in her hands and began to cry.

Kyla placed an arm around her shoulder in comfort. "It's okay. It's okay."

"The Brotherhood," Ember repeated.

"I remember something about them," Kyla said. "Had some flyers or something going around a while back."

"Yea," Ember replied. "They're a fraternity in the Mines. Barkuss's brothers are real involved with them. I sneaked in on one of their meetings and they're pretty hardcore. They were talking about some radical stuff."

"Like what?" Kyla asked.

Ember paused. The Brotherhood had been awfully quiet lately. Had they been plotting? Interest piqued, she tilted her ear to the side. "Overthrowing the Council. Restoring order. Crazy talk," she said.

"Ya know, Ember, the Scarf Brothers work for the Council. Do you think this Brotherhood group could have done something to the Judges as a way to incite the Council? If Coal Elves are sneaking up, who's to say they're not sneaking to Norland."

"Norland?" Fannie gasped.

"No," Ember said, trying to remain calm. "I don't think so. Only designated elves have access to transport there."

Like Sturd…

"Or deer that understand Elvish," Kyla reminded her.

Ember thought for a minute. "It's possible, but not entirely prob-able. Fannie, do you have any other Shadow-Deer?"

She shook her head quickly back and forth. "No."

"Does Boptail know Elvish?"

Fannie looked at the ground sheepishly. "Yes," she whispered. "But someone is with her practically all the time. There's no way that…"

"I'm not saying anything like that," Ember interrupted.

Kyla rubbed her hands up and down Fannie's arm. "Sturd?" she asked Ember, raising an eyebrow.

Ember tensed up. Hearing Kyla actually say his name made everything click. "Well, I wouldn't put anything past him, but I'm not one hundred percent sure if he's even involved with them."

Kyla slumped her neck forward. "Meaning you have your suspicions?"

Before Ember could think or begin to answer, Asche and Boptail stopped their playing and stood still in a frightening stance. They both reared up on their hind legs and began neighing and snorting uncontrollably, vicious animal sounds that scared her. Kyla and Fannie rushed to the deer, saying, "Calm down, boy," and "Calm down, girl," in both familiar words and in Elvish.

But it was no use, they were clearly agitated by something deep within them. Their grunts sounded as if they were in pain, and their harsh jolting movements looked as if they wanted to jump out of their own skin. Something had spooked them.

Ember called to Asche, who responded immediately to the sound of her voice. He bucked his body toward her, and she reached for his antlers, hoping to steady him, get him out of whatever trance he was in. The second she touched him, a sharp shooting pain raced up her arms like fire dancing in her body. She wrestled with his antlers and against the pain for a few moments before she was able to get him under slight control. He still jerked around, but she had steadied him to where she could press her face against his snout. That's when it hit her — an urgency that filtered its way into her mind, as if Asche were speaking to her through his aura, "Go to Headquarters."

"Go to Headquarters," she repeated out loud.

"What? What are you talking about?" Fannie said.

"You were right, Fannie. Something is going on. Our deer are hardwired to HQ. Something's happening that is making them bonkers. I have to get there, now!"

Kyla put a hand on Asche's neck. "Go," she said.

Ember fumbled to get up onto Asche's back. She nodded at Kyla and Fannie, then called out, "*Oontza ahnga, Aschen!*" And they disappeared into the sky.

Chapter Twenty-Two

A SCHE'S ROUGH LANDING ON THE ROOFTOP OF HEADQUARTERS RATTLED
Ember's teeth. He still showed signs of agitation, and she was
nervous about leaving him alone untethered. She slid off his back,
grabbed his face in both hands, and pressed his nose against hers.
"Be good. I'll take care of this. Stay right here." His blue eyes hinted
at understanding, but his body was still fidgeting beyond his control.
She kissed his snout and went inside the building, taking the main
stairwell to the Meeting Room on the thirteenth floor.

Without knocking or hesitating, she barged through the door just
in time to hear Mrs. Claus say, "They're dead! They're all dead!" Una,
Zelcodor, and Sturd twisted their heads in Ember's direction.

Sturd stood up, planting both palms on the table top. "What are
you doing here?" he barked at her in surprise.

"What are you doing here?" she spat back. She scanned the room to
make sure no one else was present. "What the hell is going on here?
Why wasn't I told about a meeting? And who's dead?"

Mrs. Claus rose and motioned for Ember to take her seat. "Come,
child. You're more than welcome to join us." She sat back down and
ran her fingers through her white hair. She looked tired, frustrated,
and spoke with a certain tone of defeat in her voice. "It was an emergency meeting. Last minute."

Ember walked over to the table, but didn't sit down.

"If you actually lived with me, like elfwives are supposed to, then
you would have known about the meeting," Sturd growled.

Zelcodor looked her up and down in disapproval. "You know you
have your obligations..."

Ember waved her hand in his face. "Forget all that."

"No," Una said. "I have a question of my own. How in Claus's name
did you know we were meeting?"

Ember cocked her head to the side, took a step toward the table,
and brazenly challenged her superior. "I have two very freaked out
Shadow-Deer, and two very freaked out Reindeer Trainers who were

scheduled to be judged today. But that never happened. Why, *Una*? Should I not be here?"

Una balled her fists. "How dare you speak…"

"Una! Ember! Enough!" Mrs. Claus screamed, breaking the tension of the impending battle.

Una and Zelcodor exchanged brief glances as Ember stood down.

"They're dead," Mrs. Claus repeated. "The Reindeer Judges, The Book Keepers. Someone murdered them."

Ogden? Orthor? Red Scarf? Green Scarf? Dead?

Ember quietly gasped and turned to Sturd. "What did you do?" she questioned as if on instinct.

Sturd struck his chest with his hands. "Me?" he shouted.

"Wait a minute! Wait a minute!" Una intervened. "Sturd hasn't had any involvement in this incident. Let's not go pointing fingers here! Besides, what motivation would he have to do such a terrible thing? He has no reason to harm anyone. He's not a twin!"

"So you're saying we have a twin killer on our hands?" Ember barked.

Mrs. Claus wearily rubbed her eyes. "She's right. Apparently someone has bad intentions. Someone knows that the Boss is getting ready to…"

Una extended her hand across the table and pouted. "I'm sorry, Docena."

Mrs. Claus nodded. "And I'm sorry, too. Jolenir is your brother. This mustn't be easy for you, either."

"Um, an explanation would be helpful here," Ember said.

"*The Dublix Santarae* states that the selection of the Claus must come from a pair of twins," Zelcodor began. "Twins are chosen because they are a rarity and are special. It's necessary to ensure the longevity of the Claus's rein without having too many transitional periods. If something were to happen to the appointed Boss, his twin would be able to slip in this role, his life, without upsetting the balance of things. The twin would completely be integrated in his brother's life. Elfwife. Home. It would all be passed along."

"Being the Claus is a very demanding Life Job," Mrs. Claus said in a faraway voice, "no one quite knows what the life expectancy is for an elf with such power."

"So, while the Boss is being the Boss, what is the twin doing?" Ember asked.

"They usually hold a high ranking position in the Pole," Zelcodor said. "Weather Coordinator, Map Maker, even a slot on the Council." He glanced over at Una.

"Okay, so if the Boss is ready to move on, wouldn't his twin just step in?"

"It's not that simple," Mrs. Claus answered. "Jolenir doesn't have a twin brother to take his place." Una cleared her throat and Zelcodor placed his hands over hers.

Ember's head snapped in Una's direction as a veil of knowledge was lifted from her mind.

Una. Una M'Raz Ruprecht. The Boss's sister. The Boss's *twin* sister.

"That's why the selection process has begun," Sturd chimed in.

"Enter the twins," Ember said matter-of-factly, her gaze trained on Una.

"Twins are inherently gifted with the ability to speak Elvish. It's in their genetic makeup," Zelcodor continued. "Once the last set of twins has been granted the gift, then the Claus will officially select the two who will replace him."

"But, then how do they know who becomes the Boss and who gets stuck on some iceberg manipulating the snow storms?" Ember asked.

Una straightened up in her chair and huffed. "Well, that's up to the Mists to decide."

Ember sighed. "But why can't Una take his..."

Una closed her eyes shut and tightened her lips. "It doesn't work that way, Ember! It just doesn't work that way!"

"Enough you two!" Mrs. Claus exclaimed. "We have four dead elves on our hands. Four dead *twin* elves. Two of whom just recently became empowered with the gift. I fear there will be many more if we don't act on this now."

"Then, there's only one thing we can do," Sturd said. "We need to protect all the twins we can round up. Put Enforcers on the streets. Get the twins to safety until the Boss can make a selection."

Ember rapidly tapped her foot on the floor, her whole body shaking with anxiety and frustration.

"There's a group in the Mines," Sturd spoke up. "They call themselves the Brotherhood. We can see if they'll help us ..."

Ember's eyes widened.

"I say we get to the Aboveground twins first, then work our way down to the Mines," he continued.

"My thoughts exactly," Una said.

Because you would be the one elf to gain something from all this, wouldn't you, Una?

Ember shook her head and turned on her heel. When she reached the door, Una called to her back, "Oh, and Ms. Ruprecht, don't think the Council has forgotten about your living arrangements. I do hope you work it out soon. You wouldn't want to endure an Inquiry, would you?"

Sturd laughed quietly. Ember didn't turn around. She placed her hand on the door handle and turned. Before she exited, she said, "No Ma'am," in response, but the words came out in Elvish.

Chapter Twenty-Three

THERE WAS ALWAYS A CERTAIN ANTICIPATION ON THE BIG NIGHT – EVEN in the Mines, elflings could barely fall asleep. Sturd remembered distinctly what it felt like to force himself to go to sleep and then wake up the next morning filled with an overabundance of eagerness. His mother would walk him outside to the rock garden and there would be gifts waiting for him. They were always perfectly wrapped in brightly colored paper and billowing bows with bells attached to them. It always filled him with happiness to tear open the presents little by little – meticulously, methodically. Corzakk would always complain that he was taking much too long, that he wanted to go inside and go back to sleep, or have his breakfast. But I'len would just laugh and scold him. "Let the boy take his time if he likes. I think it's sweet," she would say. Even back then, Sturd was teaching himself a form of self-control. Savor the moment. Relish every movement and emotion. But when his mother left them, Big Days changed. For a few years, he still received presents in the shamble grounds of the rock garden, but there were no bows on them and they were awkwardly wrapped. By the time he was eleven elfyears old, he told his father, "You can stop the charade. I know it's you. I know I'm on the Naughty List." And that was that. Sturd had not received another present since.

Now, it wasn't even the Big Night, yet Sturd was as giddy as an anxious elfling. He didn't even mind having to make numerous trips Aboveground. Everything was falling perfectly into place for him, like the best present wrapped up nice and neatly. The Twin Roundup was coming underway with complete approval from both the Council and the Boss, and he was one step away from inciting his secret coup. The Brotherhood was on point, doing as they were told, fully believing they were doing good for the overall society. End-game was right in his grasp. He could feel it. Taste it. Like a vulture circling a wounded animal just waiting for it to die. The anticipation of the swoop was maddening; he couldn't remember the last time he had felt such exhilaration, such jubilation.

Cerissa Lux and Trelson Castleberry had temporarily taken over the duties of Book Keepers until permanent replacements could be found. It was agreed upon that a new set of twins would be needed to fulfill the position, and with everything going on, it was best that Councilmembers were put on post. The blackened names were still showing up at a rapid pace, and the both of them were keeping post twenty-four elfhours a day. This was a good thing for Sturd. As Field Data Collector, he was able to come and go as he pleased with no harassment from the Councilmembers. He was able to consult all the genealogy books and records, and was able to put together a list of all known twins Aboveground. While the list wasn't very long, there was a lot of ground to cover at the Pole as the records only stated names of families and not specific addresses.

Another piece of information he needed to clarify was whether the registered twins were able to speak Elvish. While some were able to speak from birth, others, like the Castleberry brothers, spoke spontaneously. Some were still unable to speak it at all. This was important to know because once *all* twins were gifted, then the selection process would begin. He definitely had his work cut out for him, but...

All in good time.

Once all the twins were in his possession, he would then be able to have complete domination. Extermination of the twins was inevitable, and he had planned to make it look like a freak accident. Fire, maybe. Roof collapse, perhaps. Something tragic and dramatic. Something that had just enough of 'Sturd flair' but not enough to implicate him in the deed. He licked his lips at the thought of the devastation.

The Mines were always warm this time of year. Even though the snow fell in heavy blankets Aboveground, there was always a dark balminess emanating from the caverns. Even the cool waters of the Ignis River churned with a degree of warmth. At the rafting station, he dipped his hands into the river and splashed some of the water up onto his face. He was headed to Sandstone Shelf to peek in on the latest Brotherhood meeting, but before he could start unraveling a raft tether to launch him to there, he looked up to see his half-brother, Balrion, approaching with some fishing gear and two little children in tow. His nephews. *Twins.*

He chuckled softly to himself. Once the Brotherhood collected all of the Aboveground twins, they would make their way to the Underground, and his lively little nephews would be in his possession. He stared as they bounced gaily beside Balrion – their faces marked with the same splash of red on their cheeks as their grandmother I'len. Balrion stopped suddenly when he noticed him watching them, and extended his arms for the boys to fall in line behind him.

Balrion stood in front of a raft and hesitated before untying the tether. His eyes were fixed on Sturd's.

"Nice night for some fishing, eh?" Sturd said with a phony smile.

"Yep," Balrion curtly answered. The boys poked their heads from behind his back and looked at Sturd with scared puppy-dog eyes.

"Must be nice to spend some family time with your Uncle Balrion, boys." Bambam and Juju stiffened up again so Sturd couldn't see them. "Nice. Nice. Nice. So sweet and nice," the sarcasm dripped like venom from his tongue.

"Is there something I can do for you, Sturd?" Balrion said with an irritated huff.

"Oh no, no, no. You never mind me. Just have some errands to run. Always something to do. You know how that goes."

"Yea, well, you have fun with that."

Sturd chuckled. It was forced and fake and the sound resonated hauntingly in the cavern. Both boys threw their hands over their ears to block the sound.

"Mother always wanted us to be friends, ya know?"

Balrion narrowed his eyes. "Actually, I wouldn't know." He bent down to untie the tether.

"She was always about the family," Sturd continued nonchalantly. "I know she would be so proud to see that you were pitching in and taking care of her grandbabies." He looked directly at the twins and smiled. "Your Uncle here is such a good elf for spending time with you. You should consider yourselves lucky." Their mouths were agape in identical 'o' shapes. Their fear gave Sturd excited goose bumps up and down his arms. "Where is your father, anyway? It's way past working time…"

"Brotherhood meeting," Balrion blurted before clamping a hand over his mouth.

Sturd smiled at the thought - his own brother teaming up with the ones he controlled. They were a low-level force when it came to a power play in the Mines, but their numbers were steadily increasing and they were getting into some interesting territory. Right now, Nim Nim'sim was probably giving some speech about the inequities between the elves Aboveground and the elves Underground. Nim liked to say it was a 'polar opposite.' *What a stupid play on words!* Right now, Sim Nim'sim was probably rallying up a group of elves to continue with their twelve-point plan. They must be up to about ten so far, which was good for him because it coincided perfectly with gathering the twins, and hustling them away.

"Ya know, Balrion, my schedule is pretty wide open today. If you want, I would be okay with babysitting those little ones so you could have a break. What do you say, boys? Want to spend a little time with your Uncle Sturd?"

The boys gasped and hid behind Balrion again, eyes wide with fear. One of them started mumbling to the other, but Balrion swatted his hand in front of his face to 'shush' him.

"What did he say?" Sturd asked. "Kinda sounded like he mumbled something."

Kinda sounded like he mumbled in Elvish…

"Oh, it was nothing," Balrion answered, waving his hand in the air. "Thanks for the offer, Sturd, but I promised the boys I'd spend time with them and…"

Sturd smiled wide, his gnarled teeth jutted out of his mouth. "Say no more!" he relented. "I completely understand. It's surely going to take some time for the boys to get used to good ole Unkie Sturd."

Balrion gave a weak smile and ushered the boys onto their raft. "Come on, guys," he said calmly.

Sturd continued to smile. "You all have a nice time," he said, but his mind twisted and turned with possible ways of how his new allies in The Brotherhood were going to convince Bommer to release the twins to them and into his trap.

Balrion and the boys remained silent as their raft drifted onto the Ignis, leaving Sturd on the bank with a maniacal smile on his face.

Chapter Twenty-Four

The bells that dangled from Boptail's collar jingled every time Ember brushed the comb through her mane. She stood completely still and let Ember lovingly groom her inky black fur. Asche had already been cleaned and brushed, and was eating his lunch at the trough. After the two Shadow-Deer had experienced their psychic freak-out, Boptail had refused to go home to Brightly Stables. It was obvious that there was a connection between Asche and Boptail, and Kyla had suggested that she stay at Plumm Stable. Fannie agreed, and the deer were since inseparable. Ember was happy that Asche had a counterpart, a potential mate, and had even contemplated training Boptail to ride with Asche and her on the Big Night.

Boptail reared her head up and whinnied and Asche stomped his hoof on the ground, as if reading Ember's mind. She pulled back and stared at Boptail's pale gray eyes. "You'd like that, wouldn't you? You *want* to help Asche deliver the coal?" The two snorted in delight, and Ember laughed. "You two, I swear to Claus! Don't think I'll be able to separate ya even if I tried." Boptail and Asche both exclaimed with a high-pitched bleating wail and stamped their hooves thunderously on the floor in excitement. Ember laughed at their display, but stopped when she heard someone screaming over the animal sounds in the barn. "*Caloyinda!*" she shouted at them in Elvish, and the deer stopped their merry making.

"Ember! Ember, come quick!" It was Kyla screaming from across the field.

"Stay here," she instructed the deer and took off at full speed. On the front porch of the house, there were two Coal Elves backing her against the front door. One had Kyla's arm in his firm grip. She was fighting them off, kicking and yelling for them to let her go. "What's going on?" Ember yelled, coming up onto the porch. "What are you two doing here?"

The Coal Elves backed up. One of them lifted his hands in a defensive stance. "Oh, Miss Ember," he said in surprise, "we're representatives of The Brotherhood. We're here to bring Miss Plumm to the safehouse as part of the Twin Roundup."

He's going through with it. He's actually going through with it. Her head spun with suppositions...

"Ember, I tried telling them that..." Kyla began.

"She's not a twin," Ember finished, looking directly at the grimy face of the elf to her right. "Not anymore," she said to the elf on her left.

"Yes, but, it says in our orders that all twins, especially those who speak Elvish, must be taken to the safehouse immediately. It's just a precaution."

This smells like a trap. Don't believe what they say.

"What safehouse? What are you talking about?"

"We have instructions not to divulge that information, Miss Skye. The location of the safehouse is only for those on a need-to-know-basis. It's only for the protection of the twins. I'm sure you understand."

"Yea, well, Kyla isn't in any danger, thank you." She yanked Kyla's arm out from the elf's hold and moved forward to the porch steps, but one of the elves stepped in front of them, blocking their path. Ember scowled and snorted. "Get the hell out of my way."

"I'm sorry, but we must take Miss Plumm to the safehouse until a new Claus has been selected. It's the only way to keep her out of danger."

"Ember, that could be years from now," Kyla whispered.

Ember ignored her, and there was no denying the panic was rising in her chest. She breathed heavily to maintain composure, but the truth was she was near frantic with fear. "She's not in any danger. She's not even up for consideration. Her twin sister passed away from the Sickness last year. Go back to the Mines, boys." Grabbing Kyla's arm tighter, she shoved through the elves.

The Coal Elves followed them onto the field. "She is our last stop Aboveground before we round up the twins in the Mines."

Ember stopped and eased up on Kyla's arms. *Twins in the Mines. Bambam and Juju.* The twins with the fascinating telepathic secret.

Then it hit her like a coal mine cave-in. What if Bambam and Juju were the ones? What if their special ability was the one thing that had marked them for replacement of the Claus?

"No. She's not going anywhere with you!" she asserted.

"But what are we to tell Sturd?" one asked.

She turned on her heel and looked at the Coal Elves. They were short and thin. One of them had high cheekbones that jutted out from the side of his face; the other's ears flopped forward at the tops as if he had been in some kind of mining accident that ripped them to shreds. They were dirty. Filthy. Pathetic looking. Alien looking.

"Don't worry about my husband," she growled through gritted teeth. "I'll deal with him. The bottom line is, Kyla isn't going anywhere with you. Like I said, get back to the Mines, boys, before someone asks to see your Pass."

The two stiffened up and quickly glanced at each other before taking a step back and leaving the field.

Kyla sighed a breath of relief. "Good Claus! What was all that about?"

"Shut up the barn and make sure the deer are protected. Then, go into the house and lock everything up tight. Don't put on any lights, don't even light a candle. Stay away from the windows. Be quiet, like you're not even there. Whatever you do, don't answer the door for anyone except me. I'll be back soon. I think Barkuss's nephews are in trouble. I think you are, too."

Kyla breathed heavily, trying to fight back tears. "How will I know it's you when you come back?"

"*Jingla Boptail gongen.*"

"Bells on Boptail ring?"

"You hear that, open the door. But be ready to leave. I have to get you somewhere safe. Somewhere they won't find you."

"Wait! Wait! But you said that…"

"Just do it. I have a feeling they're going to be back."

Chapter Twenty-Five

THE GUARDS AT THE GATE OF THE MOUTH RAISED THEIR SHIELDS IN order to block the onslaught of Graespurs emerging from the Mines. Ember used the swarm to conceal her position and sneak past them. With her high-ranking position, she had clearance to move from the caverns to the Aboveground whenever she pleased, but for some reason she felt the need to be covert in her actions. Getting back into the Mines was not the hard part; the hard part was going to be getting the twins back Aboveground. She thought about all the different lies she could tell to convince them to let them through and she was certain that some would actually work, but time was not on her side, and the more time passed, the more likely it was that the Guards would be alerted to the impending Round-up in the Mines and not permit their leaving.

The magic of Barrier Holt never ceased to amaze her. The way the cave walls felt with their crunchy faerie dust, the way the light shone in thin ray lines from the shadows of the Gates – there was something mystical about this region; it was no wonder that the higher-ups forbade the Coal Elves from ever passing through here. It was like a delicious secret that only a handful were privy to. But there was no time for fawning over the magical elegance of the sparkly cavern; she had to hurry to Ebony Cragg before the Brotherhood started collecting the Underground Twins for whatever they were doing.

Barkuss's den was empty. It was Adam's Day, the day that Coal Elves threw extravagant parties in celebration for the Big Night, and if Barkuss wasn't at his house, he would most likely be celebrating at one of his brothers' dens. She decided to stop off at her den – just to be sure he wasn't there – before she started her hunt. When she arrived, she was surprised to see that he was, in fact, at her den with the twins. She was even more surprised to see Tannen and his elf-wife, Holly, sitting in her living room as well.

Barkuss was breathless when Ember came through the front door. He rushed up from the kitchen table when he saw her and squeezed her in a tight embrace. "Good Claus!" he sighed. "You have no idea how glad am I to see you! I was wondering when you were going to come back home!"

She rested her chin in the hollow of his neck and patted his back. "We don't have much time. Quickly, tell me what's up."

"I was over at Bommer's den when he said he was going to give the boys to the Brotherhood. That whole Round-up business, ya know. It just completely freaked me out. I don't like it, and I sure as heck don't trust it. Bommer says it's for their safety and all, but it's just all too weird. The Nim'sims came by asking all kinds of questions, telling the boys to put some stuff in a bag for the safehouse. Like, really? A *safehouse?* So, I'm all wiggin' out, the boys are clearly upset by all this, and I finally say to Bommer to leave it alone and let the boys enjoy Adam's Day…"

Bambam and Juju stared at each other, and Ember knew they were communicating. Barkuss was flailing his arms up and down with wild gesticulations and speaking so fervently, she didn't have enough strength to concentrate and listen in to what they were saying. Holly and Tannen were sitting on the couch. Holly's hands were placed gently on his knees and she leaned forward to hear Barkuss's tale. Ember glanced at Tannen and he gave her a half smile. A hard lump rose in her throat, and for a split second, she was breathless, weak. *I just want something I can never have…* She shook her head as to not get lost in Tannen's green eyes, his smile, his presence. She raised her eyebrows and looked back at Barkuss who was still going on with his story.

"…let me and Balrion take them fishing while he could spend time with his wife, cause who knows how long the boys are gonna have to be in that safehouse. So Bommer thinks it over, and thank Claus for level headed Jacinda, cause she got all up in Bommer's grill saying I was right, let them enjoy the festivities. Balrion grabbed the fishing gear and told the boys to run to the Ignis, and I took his cue and came straight here." Barkuss had exhausted himself and sat down at the table, taking in deep breaths. His barrel chest moved up and down, quickly at first then to a more steady, calm rhythm.

"And that's when we saw them," Holly said.

Ember's head snapped in her direction, startled by her squeaky voice. She pursed her lips in frustration, but Holly's soft pink eyes seemed to burn holes of adoration through Ember's heart, and all she could do was nod at her.

"Yes," Barkuss continued. "I didn't know what I was going to do. Balrion did take them fishing, but they ran into Sturd, so he turned around and brought them right here. I swear I was just about to run away with them in a hot flash..."

"But I convinced him otherwise," Tannen interjected.

Barkuss nodded his head quickly. "Yes, yes, and that was a good thing. Tannen suggested we come here to your den to hide out until you got back and then we could figure out what to do."

"Good thinking," Ember said directly to Tannen.

"I try sometimes." He smiled and the gleam in his green eyes sent shivers down her spine.

Holly threw an arm around his shoulder and kissed his cheek in a seemingly territorial gesture. Heartbroken, Ember turned away again and looked at the twins who were sitting on the kitchen floor. "You boys okay?"

They nodded in unison, but their faces told a completely different story. "Those Brotherhood guys are bad news," Barkuss said.

"Yea, even more so now that Sturd is working with them."

Barkuss gasped. "He is?"

Ember ran her hand fingers through her hair. "They're in his back pocket doing his dirty work for him. The Brotherhood has been very vocal about shaking up the Council. Sturd's always been the wild-card elf – looking out for himself under the guise of the Codex. The blackened names are still increasing, which is a whole other animal to be dealt with. Maybe the failure of the Christmas in July thing kinda threw him over the edge and..."

Barkuss cupped his hand around the side of his mouth so the twins couldn't hear, "Do you think Sturd killed those elves?" he whispered.

"It's possible. Either him or someone in the Brotherhood. Or someone in the Brotherhood acting on orders from Sturd."

"Or the Council?"

Ember leaned back in her seat. The legs of the chair lifted up then crashed back down against the rock floor with a *clang.* "Everything is just spiraling out of control right now."

"It is!" Holly agreed. "The Boss should totally step in and get everything under control."

Ember closed her eyes and giggled softly. *Totally.* "I seriously don't think that's going to happen anytime soon. Guess I married Sturd for nothing! I didn't even get a chance to get close enough to gather information. All this was never part of the plan! This is all happening so fast!" Ember exclaimed.

Holly's face twisted inquisitively, which Ember ignored.

"The Brotherhood guys were also asking if Bammy and Jujy spoke Elvish," Barkuss said. "And I told them that was the craziest…"

The twins stiffened and Ember opened her eyes wide at them as if to say, "Be quiet." Barkuss stopped in his tracks and looked down at the boys and back up at her. His head tilted downward as he raised one eyebrow. "What aren't you telling me, E?"

A croaking sound came from the boys' throats as they held their breath. "It's fine," she said to them in Elvish. Barkuss pounded his fist angrily on the table. Holly jumped in her seat from the sound of it. "Barkuss, relax," Ember began seriously. "I have good reason to believe that Bambam and Juju are candidates."

"Of course they are candidates! They're twins!" he roared.

"No! I mean, like, *the* candidates. They have a very special gift." She looked down at the boys and smiled. "I never even knew it was possible, but they can talk to each other just by using their minds. And they speak in Elvish."

Barkuss looked at the boys. "How long?" he whispered.

They shrugged their shoulders.

"Probably from the time they were born," she said, still smiling at them. "They never told anyone because they liked having a secret between them. Am I right?"

They both smiled back and nodded.

"Well, I'll be damned," Barkuss breathed.

"Which is why we can't let the Brotherhood or Sturd get them. If they are the replacements, and there is some kind of evil plot going on, we need to keep those two as safe as possible."

"Yea, but the Underground is definitely not a place of safety," Tannen added. "There are only so many places you could hide out before you get caught... or worse."

"What are we gonna do, E?" Barkuss begged, the desperation in his voice like a hollow bell.

"I have to get the kids out of here. Like now. Somewhere where they can hide out just long enough for this to blow over. Some place safe. Some place underground, but not the Underground."

Then it hit her. The catacombs that ran beneath Skye Manor would be the perfect spot. That would be the last place that anyone looked. On the outside, Skye Manor was abandoned — overgrown with callixus and other foliage, left to rot away until the structure crumbled to the ground. The only other elf alive who knew of the secret passageway beneath the mansion was Nanny Carole.

"I need to get them Aboveground to my old house in Tir-la Treals. It's the safest place I can think of. But I don't know how I'm going to get past those Guards. They're going to give me static for sure."

"West Valley," Holly interjected. "The girls have helped us out so much with the letters and all, I'm sure they'll take care of the boys for as long as you need them!"

Ember rolled her eyes. "I can't take them to West Valley, Hol..."

"There's a Mouth there, too, but there are also many secret spots. Openings to Aboveground. A bunch of the girls used to sneak out from time to time to visit family or go to the market for treats."

"You know where these passages are?" Tannen asked.

"Sure. There are dozens of them. Right outside the gates to the compound. I could show you. Of course, you'd be up by West Bank, but..."

"Doesn't matter," Ember said.

Barkuss grabbed Ember's hands across the table and looked deep in her eyes. "Take them. Go now. Bommer's gonna be so pissed off, but I'll take care of it."

Ember nodded and motioned for the boys to get up from the floor. "You ready to ride the rails, Tannen?"

Tannen and Holly stood up. "Don't you know it!" he answered.

"Good. We gotta move."

The five of them sneaked through the pathways of the Mines taking every corner and turn swiftly and cautiously. Rollicking parties and lavish feasts were being held this Adam's Day, and laughter and music echoed throughout the cavern walls. Even with the festive distractions, they were careful not to make too much noise and were vigilant in keeping to the shadows.

At the Catta-car station, Tannen started up the engine from the driver's car while the twins hopped into a carriage of their own, not leaving any space for Ember and Holly to join them. Holly motioned for Ember to get into the car behind the boys, and jumped onto the seat across from her.

Ember didn't know how to react to being alone with, and in such close proximity, to Holly. There were so many conflicting emotions in her heart and in her mind, that to look at Holly Adaire Trayth sitting right there, right in front of her, reflecting the life that she had dreamed of having for herself, was downright heartbreaking. Holly smiled at her, but Ember turned her head and watched the scenery of the Mines as they whizzed through on the trolley.

"We love you, Ember," Holly said after some time of silence.

Ember looked at Holly, tilted her head to the side, and furrowed her brow.

"We all love you. You're so strong. You're such an inspiration," Holly continued.

Ember shook her head. "No. You don't have to say that. I'm really not as strong as you think."

Holly grabbed at one of her blonde curls and nervously wrapped it around her slender finger. "He loves you, too," she said in a quiet voice as she motioned her head toward the driver's car.

Ember's heart sank. "What are you talking about? That's crazy," she said, not wanting to believe it, but wishing to Claus it was the truth. "I know he does, and I know he could never love me the way he loves you. He says a name in his sleep sometimes – Em – and I know he's dreaming of you." She hung her head low.

Ember stared at her, but Holly looked up with a weak smile on her face. "It's okay, though. I'm okay with it. I'm a good elfwife to him, Ember. I take care of him, and in his own sweet way, he takes care of me, too. Tannen and I are a good balance. He makes me laugh. He teaches me new things. I make the most of our marriage. If he was in love with any other elf besides you, I don't think I could live like that. But it's *you*, Ember. It's okay that I can't compare."

Ember's heart went from sinking to breaking at Holly's admission. She couldn't hate her now even if she tried.

"We're here."

Tannen slowed the trolley just outside the West Valley Gates. They were high up on the trolley tracks with no surrounding platform. He hopped out of his side and around to meet the others where he escorted the twins onto the unpaved terrain. Next he went to the girl's cart, opened the door for them, and held Holly's hand as she jumped out. "Follow me," she called over her back to Ember, and guided the twins off-path.

"You're next, milady," he said to Ember, stretching out his hand. She refused his offer and jumped out of the car on her own. "Déjà vu much?" he asked.

She chuckled. "Yea. You could say that."

He smiled wide, his green eyes almost glowing in the dark cave. "You're always getting yourself into these crazy adventures and..."

"I told you! I told you my life was complicated!"

They both laughed quietly.

"We would have never worked out, ya know? My silly self always causing trouble and all," she joked.

"Oh, Claus no!" he playfully agreed. They giggled again, and as Tannen put a hand on her shoulder, a deafening sound permeated the caves. The familiar sound of the Defector Alarm made them wince.

"Ember!" Holly screamed over the blaring sound. "I found the spot! Come on!"

Ember made a thumbs-up motion and looked at Tannen.

"They're playing your song again," he said, still smiling.

"I know, I know."

Tannen moved in closer to Ember and whispered in her ear. "Take care of Holly. She's a good girl. She only means well."

Ember's lips tightened up and she nodded.

"Don't worry, though. I got your back for a little bit down here."

"Almond tall struthers?" she said, referring to the last time he had kept her safe.

Tannen pulled her close and hugged her fiercely. "You know I always will," he said as he kissed her on the forehead.

Holly led Ember and the twins upwards through a hidden sewer tunnel that emptied out into West Bank's main promenade. Under the cover of darkness, they lurked in the alleyways between the city buildings, searching for a remote spot to rest for a few minutes. The twins were tired and had begun whining as soon as they reached Aboveground, but Ember scolded them in Elvish, and ended their complaints. In one of the alleys, the boys spotted a sled with a team of two Poledogs hitched to it. "Look, Ember! Look!" Bambam said as he raced over to the dogs.

"Bambam! Be quiet!"

"Is there anyone around?" Holly whispered.

Ember looked up and down and side to side. "No. Not that I can tell. The owner probably works in one of the shoppes."

"You thinking what I'm thinking?"

"Do we have any other choice?"

Holly shook her head.

Ember called the boys to her. "Okay, here's the plan: Holly is gonna *borrow* the dogs and get to the Plumm Stables in East Bank. We're gonna walk it to the Manor."

"Awwwww," the boys groaned. "Why doesn't Holly just drop us off?"

"Because, if she gets caught, we get caught. We don't want Holly to get in trouble, either."

"But won't she get in trouble if she's caught on a *stolen* dogsled?" The boys said in unison.

"Silly, silly," Holly said laughing. "I'm not stealing it. I'm borrowing, remember?"

Ember smiled. She hated to admit it, but she was grateful for Holly's help. "Holly, when you get to the Stable, get Kyla. I told her not to open the door for anyone but me."

"So, why would she open it for me? I'm not you."

Ember breathed deep. "Because you have the password I set up with her. You need to say, 'Bells on Boptail ring.'"

Holly looked confused. "Um, that's not how the song goes."

"Just trust me. Say it! When she comes to the door, tell her to get to Skye Manor as soon as possible. No deer. Just herself. Then, drop the pups back here, and get back to the Mines."

"Got it, boss!" Holly winked at her and smiled.

"Thank you. For everything."

"No problem. That's just what we do for each other."

"Okay. Come on, boys. Stay close to me. We got a little ways 'til we get home."

She said the words without even realizing it. Yes. She was going home. To the place that she had been shut out from for all these years, just waiting for her to swoop on in and reclaim its territories as her own. The place of her elflinghood that had made her feel safe and protected, free now of judgmental and disillusioned eyes. The place where she could shelter these important elflings, and keep them safe from harm. For the first time in a long time, Ember felt like she was truly going home.

Home. *Home.* HOME!

Chapter Twenty-Six

T HE BIG NIGHT
    The sun began to poke its head up over the horizon. The swarm
of Graespurs making their way back to the Mines temporarily blot-
ted out the light, giving the appearance of total darkness for twenty
more seconds or so. When they finally passed, the white fluffy clouds
had already begun to take on a pink and gold hue just above the line
of sight. The air smelled heavily of that gray smell – the one where
the clouds are filled to the brim with frozen water particles and are
ready to burst open and unleash a thick blanket of snow. There was
no doubt in Ember's mind that today would be laden with whistling
wind and dense snowflakes, which in turn did not bode well for her
Coal Ride tonight. *The All-Coal Ride.*

She and the twins had trekked all night through West Bank to get
to Skye Manor. The road to the Manor's gate was windy and steep. The
large golden gates that towered around the perimeter of the property
had once glowed gold; now they were rusted over with corrosive reds
and oranges. Flecks of iron chipped off the handles, and the S emblem
that had held the gates tightly together had been robbed of its rubies
and emeralds. The landscaping was much neglected. The large topiaries were beasts of their former selves, overgrown into snarled ani-
mal- like figures. What were once kittens and ponies and puppy dogs
had been transformed into hideous monstrosities – ogres and white
headed chygas. The flowerbeds were packed with snow but brown
weeds were wildly pushing through the white blanket. The wooden
guardhouse was abandoned – its roof beveled in from the weight of
the heavy snow. No sense of life emanated from the property, and
in any other circumstance it would have made Ember sad to see her
former home in such shambles – but now, she was comforted by the
desolate and uninhabited terrain.

Kyla was already there, waiting for them. She was perched on
the front steps, concealed behind a trellis overwrought with callixus vines. Ember embraced her when they reached the doors of the
home. "You made it," she whispered in Kyla's ear.

"What? Did you think I wouldn't?" Kyla smiled and reached for the twins' hands.

Ember lifted up the door mat and fetched the spare key. She opened the door and led them into the dark and desolate house. *House*. That's all it was now – a house. Not a *home* with laughter and love and warmth. This was merely a shell, a structure, a building so barren that every breath they took echoed through the hollow hallways.

The room that was just beyond the butler's pantry was her father's old office, and Ember distinctly remembered the day she had been snooping around his blueprints. As a child, his job as Toymaker had fascinated her, and she was always interested in his new and whimsical creations. That particular day she'd thought he was off on business, and having snuck away from Nanny Carole's attention for a few stolen moments, she decided to go have a peak at Father's latest ideas. When the bookcase behind his desk creaked open and Father emerged from the secret section, she had nearly stopped breathing.

Now, she stood there opening the door of the bookcase with the same heart-stopping creak. Her hands searched for the light switch on the side of the stone wall and the dome light on the ceiling sputtered to life when she found it, revealing the spiral staircase that wrapped down into darkness.

"W… what's down *there?*" Bambam said nervously.

"Yea, Ember. That looks kinda… *unsafe*," Kyla added.

"Trust me. It's fine. My father used to be a Toymaker and did all his experimenting down here. Apparently, he was super secretive about what he was inventing, and when I was an elfling, I came across this room by accident. This room isn't even logged on the house's floor plan. The only other elf alive who knows this space exists is Nanny Carole."

"Are we gonna be okay?" Juju asked, his voice trembling.

Ember placed both hands on his shoulders and looked into his eyes. "Yes," she said confidently. "Kyla is going to take care of you. I know my father kept supplies down there, so you should be okay with snacks and stuff for a little bit."

"Yea, guys. It's gonna be fun. Just think of it as a campout!" Kyla tried to encourage.

Bambam and Juju looked at each other and rolled their eyes. "We're in trouble, aren't we?" Bambam asked.

"No, you're not in trouble," Ember began.

"*You're* in trouble!" Juju interjected. "*We're* in danger!"

Ember chuckled a little. "Yea. I suppose I'm in trouble." *Again.*

"And yes, you guys are in danger. Kyla too. See, she was a twin, and the Brotherhood wants to take her away as well."

Wide-eyed, the boys turned to Kyla. "Ember's right," she smiled. "Now, let's go. Let's let Ember do what she's got to do. *Adleng gofrem.*"

The boys smiled at each other and cautiously walked down the stairs.

"Kyla, thank you so…"

"It's fine. We'll be fine. Don't thank me yet. How long do you think you'll be?"

"Well, I want to keep everything status quo tonight, ya know what I mean? Then once I can get a fix on where Sturd has the others… I'd feel more comfortable watching over them. Does that make sense?"

"Why do you think Sturd is up to no good with this?"

Ember cocked an eyebrow. "Has Sturd ever worked in the parameter of good?"

Kyla huffed. "I guess not. From what you've told me…"

"That ain't even the worst of it. I'm afraid of what he's capable of. I'm afraid that he's got this crazy idea of having power and control. The things he would do used to scare me, but now I'm even more terrified of what he might be planning on doing."

Kyla took a step down. "Well, like you said, you have a job to do tonight. Worry about that for now. I'll be able to manage with the boys for a while."

"Good. I'm going back to the stable to get Asche ready. I'm going to take Boptail with me tonight, too. I can definitely use the extra deer power."

"Boptail? She was never approved…"

"I don't care, Kyla. She's a good deer, and she and Asche work well together. I need her to be on my team."

"But I don't think she's ready for..."

"Were you? Was *I*? Are we ever *really* ready for what we need to do in this life?"

Kyla stopped and nodded. "Touché, Coal Girl," she said with a wink.

It was mid-morning and already a pulsating liveliness was filling the streets of East Bank. Shoppe keepers were stringing colorful lights on the outdoor trees, and fantastical wreaths covered in plastic wrapped candy canes were hung over door thresholds. The ice skating rink was set up in the middle of the Town Square, ready for the revelers to carve their blades along the icy surface. Ember lingered through the alleyways, watching the preparations, soaking in the energy and excitement.

The Candlemaker's Shoppe was at the corner of the Square, and as she rounded a corner she heard the elves working within. She bent down and peered into the basement window and watched as the workers heaped shovelfuls of coal into tall black furnaces. They were singing a lively song about the Big Night festivities with large smudgy smiles on their faces. The sound of their jovial song filled her ears and heart with a happiness that she welcomed heartily. For so many years she cursed coal, and now, watching these elves – *Land* elves, no less – merrily sing while working with it, made her eyes open even more to the truth. She finally understood its worth and value in this world. *Life force. Hope.*

When she reached the Stable, she went straight to the barn to ready Asche and Boptail. The deer bucked wildly and grunted at her when she entered. She waved her hands in the air and spoke softly to them. "Easy everyone, easy. Ky's helping me with something, but it's going to be okay." They groaned some more, but calmed down. "Alright, alright. Don't get all ornery with me. We need to be extra supportive today! Boptail is going to make the ride out with us, Asche."

The silver studded reins felt as if they were better suited for Boptail. Ember attached the two deer using one of the harnesses hanging from the barn wall and the materials that were left in the carriage. Asche and Boptail excitedly neighed together, much to Ember's delight. Just as she was she was finishing up, an ominous feeling overcame her, like she was being watched. Stalked. She looked over her shoulders as fear began to make its way through her body. It was a familiar fear, bordering on hatred. Like how she felt whenever...

Sturd lurked into the barn. Ember instinctively gasped when she saw his figure come into view.

"What are you doing here?" she spat.

"What are *you* doing here?" he returned.

"Um, I have work to do, remember?"

He slithered closer to her, and she felt his hot breath on her cheek. He extended his ferret paw and ran it down her shoulder, making her quiver with nausea. "Where's the Trainer?" he hissed.

She jerked her head up in defiance. "Dunno. She wasn't here when I got here. I just figured she'd gone with your boys like you wanted her do."

He rubbed his chin and mumbled, "No. Not with them." There was a look in his red eyes, and she swore she could actually see the gears and wheels of his brain turning round and round, like trying to solve a puzzle.

Damn straight.

Not wanting to play any more games with him, she asked, "Well, why don't you just tell me where the safehouse is, Sturd. Where are you keeping all of the twins? What are you doing to them?"

"I'm keeping them safe, for one." He moved closer to her, sniffing her neck. Asche snorted in protest, but Ember remained still. "And I can't tell you where they are. That would be a severe security breach, now, wouldn't it?"

She closed her eyes when his cold cheek brushed up against hers, then she slowly opened them and glanced in his direction. "What? Being your elfwife doesn't entitle me to certain privileges?" she sarcastically cooed.

He hissed his hot breath on her neck and sniffed at her some more, like an animal readying itself to pounce on its prey. "Perhaps," he snarled into her ear. "Perhaps if you acted like a proper elfwife. 'Name only' is only going to last you so long, ya know."

"'Name only' is about all you're gonna get," she replied.

He took a step back and licked his lips before he laughed with his deep and fractured sounding chuckle.

"I don't see what's so funny," she said, annoyed. "I would think, if anything, you would be super pissed off right now 'cause you can't call me a Defector. You can't chase me down, cook me up, and serve me in a platter for Sunday night dinner."

He continued his laughter. Rollicking belly laughs that doubled him over. "You can only see what's in front of you, little girl. And that will be your downfall, won't it? After all this time, you still fail to see the bigger picture at hand. I had that problem once, but as soon as I saw things for what they really are, I became... enlightened!"

She narrowed her eyes, trying to understand his message. "What are you talking about?"

"The bigger picture. Beyond all this." He motioned his hands in large circles. "Beyond all us. Hell, beyond the *rainbow*, even!"

Ember stopped and took in his words. For the first time, she felt as if a veil had been lifted, as if some dark coal cloud had finally blown out of her vision. As Sturd stood before her, laughing his maniacal laugh, holding his side from the giggle-pain, she finally – FINALLY — understood. All this time – it's never been about naughty kids and Lists, never been about blackened names in magic books, never been about elfwives and true loves destined to be torn apart forever. There was something much more sinister at hand here — a bigger picture that had begun to take form on the Coal-less Night. Everything else had just been a distraction. Chess pieces lined up in position, just waiting for Sturd to get the jump on them all and declare *check-mate!*

Sturd wants beyond the rainbow. He wants to have supreme control.
And if that's the case, just how far is he willing to go?
Is the Council in on all this?
Is this the Boss's way of "getting out"?

Just how much of a role does this Brotherhood play, anyway?
The Pole under Sturd's command would be complete and utter chaos.
The way he likes it.
He wants it all. He wants this all.
He wants to be the Claus.

The thought of Sturd's rise to power sickened her. Sensing the imminent danger, she quickly turned on her heels, hopped into the sleigh, and grabbed the reins of her Shadow-Deer.

Sturd settled down — his spirited laughter calming to labored pants. "Leaving so soon?" he joked, the last remnants of his laughing fit bubbling through.

Her cold glare was answer enough.

"Oh, well, I think I'll hang out a while. Wait for the Trainer to come back."

You're going to be waiting a long time, Sturd.

"Fine, then," she said. "I have an actual job to do. My List is two elfmiles long this year, and it's going to be a long night."

With that, she tugged on the reins, and they were off to the Mouth.

Chapter Twenty-Seven

THE PURPLE HAZE OF A TWILIGHT SKY WAS FRECKLED WITH DISTANT STARS. It hadn't snowed as she had expected, which would surely disappoint the merry makers and their festivities. For Ember, the absence of snow was a blessing.

At the Mouth of the cave, the trucksleds were already packed with bags of coal and sat waiting to be hauled onto her new sleigh. When she pulled up, some of the Importer Elves applauded her arrival. Balrion was front and center to greet her and get the ball rolling with the whole process. "You made good time," he said, shaking her hand as she remained in the carriage.

"I guess I did. What's the old saying? Two deer are better than one?"

"Well, there's a lot to put into the sled. Looks like you got your work cut out for you tonight!"

She smirked. "I was just telling someone else that very same thing! The List is unusually long, and..." Ember's hands reached to her jumpsuit side and she patted down her pocket.

The List!

She swooped her hand in to feel for it, but it wasn't there. The List was gone. A hard lump formed in her throat and she jumped down from the seat and scoured the front and back floors of the sleigh on her hands and knees.

"Everything okay, Ember?" Balrion asked.

She panicked. She knew she had the List on her at all times! Maybe Sturd had pickpocketed her when he had gotten so close? Her hands got sweaty as she tried to recall the names – *Alexia Welton, Olivia Whitaker, Jake Lemon, Mariah Legge* — all jumbled in her brain like name soup.

"Lose something?" a voice said.

Ember's head popped up from the back of the carriage. Barkuss was smiling at her, waving the List in the air. She shot down and raced over to him, grabbing it from his hands and clutching it to her chest.

"Thought you might need this?" He smiled.

"How did you…"

"Just had a feeling. With everything going on, it had been a major afterthought for you."

"But how did you know?"

"I remember. When we did our thing last year. The List drove you, ya know? It was important to you. This time around, you barely mentioned it. Barely gave it the recognition it deserves. We've been so preoccupied with doubling up that coal, ya know?"

She smiled. "But not you. You're still attached to this thing, aren't you?"

"I'm saying! I don't know what it is, but…"

"Wait! Barkuss!" she screamed, interrupting him. "You came! You're here!"

"Uh, does the cold weather make all elves brains go bonkers, or just you?"

She threw her arms around him in a fierce embrace. "Silly Barkuss," she whispered. "You're Aboveground, right now. You know that, right?"

He laughed and squeezed her back hard enough to lift her off the ground. "Shhh…don't tell anyone, sugar. I'm certainly not going to make a habit out of it either!"

"Baby steps, Barkuss. Baby steps."

"Ember?" It was Holly. She came up from behind Barkuss with her hands behind her back.

Thank Claus, she made it safely.

"Holly!" Ember broke from Barkuss's embrace.

"The letters are packed up on your sleigh and ready to go. It was the first thing I did as soon as I got back." She fidgeted as if she were looking for Ember's approval and gratitude.

Ember nodded, thankfully.

"Holly and I *volunteered*," Barkuss said, putting air quotes around the 'v' word. "Big List. Lots of hauling. Lifting." He winked at the girls. "Moral support needed."

"Yea, we're all in this together, right?" Holly continued. "We're all Coal Elves."

"I suppose so," said Ember. "Thank you both so much," she looked at Holly, "for everything."

Holly nodded back and brought her hands forward, revealing a floppy black velvet cap with white fur trim and a white fur ball dangling from the top. She lifted it to show Ember. "I made this for you. I didn't know if you had one already. But by the looks of it, you don't. I was going to make it pink and sparkly, but Tannen said it would be better black. That you couldn't have any kind of distractors or something like that. It kinda looks like..."

"Coal." Ember said matter-of-factly.

"Yea, coal!" Holly's pink eyes brightened with happiness. "Do you like it?"

Ember took the hat from Holly. "You made this for me?" she repeated in disbelief.

"Yes. I told you, Ember. We all love you. May I put it on you?"

"Of course you can."

Holly smoothed Ember's blonde hair behind her pointy ears and narrowed her eyes.

"What?" Ember asked, panicked by Holly's expression.

"No. It's nothing. It's just... *how* old are you Ember?"

Barkuss started laughing and Ember rolled her eyes. "Eighteen. Why?"

"Eighteen and a half!" Barkuss snorted.

Holly looked confused. "Oh. It's just that... um... do you know how many *gray* hairs you have?"

Barkuss nearly fell to the ground in hysterics. Ember sighed. "Would you just put the darn thing on my head, please!"

Suddenly, there was a rumbling from deep within the cave, like the approach of a deadly maelstrom. The Importer Elves began to race frantically back and forth, and Balrion screamed, "Graespurs!" over the din. It was time. The sun had set. Ember kissed both Holly and Barkuss on the cheek, and ran to the sleigh. Within seconds, the swarm circled in the nightsky. It was time to ride. With the List in one hand and the reins in the other, Ember shouted "*Oontza ahnga, Aschen oft Boptail!*" And they ascended into the air.

The world always seemed so peaceful and serene from up high. In the distance, she heard the boom of the Boss's sleigh as he too made his way into the night. Beneath her, Land Elves were celebrating and singing and lighting trees and decorating cookies, and below them, the Coal Elves were tucking themselves into bed after a long and stressful day. It still boggled her mind how the same race of beings could hold two completely different lifestyles. Beneath her, somewhere, all the twins of the North Pole were being held – *captive?* – by Sturd and his goons.

Beneath her, two special Coal Elf twins were being watched over, in secret, away from Sturd's deformed clutches. Beneath her, lights dazzled and sparkled for the festivities of the Big Night. Beneath her, the evergreens in the Lumber District were looking sparse, and *didn't there used to be a snowbeach just North of there?*

Regardless of what was happening below, she was flying and free at that very moment. And her view of coal had so drastically changed – that there weren't sacks of black dusty balls in her sleigh, no! There were sacks upon sacks filled with light and hope and life. The promise of a new day. She reached up to touch the black hat that now rested on her head. Her ears were tucked underneath the warm material, and she remembered how the tips of her ears had been frosty for days after her debut ride.

"Pink and sparkly!" she called to the deer. "Can you believe she was going to give me some glitter infested thing?" Asche and Boptail made a sniggering noise. "Thank Claus Tannen had the foresight to stop that one! Wouldn't want to intersect the Boss!"

And what about the Boss? What did he have in the back of his sleigh? Goody goodies for ungrateful children in the world who eventually grow up and turn their backs on him? No wonder he was over it! No wonder he was done! He got glory for one special night, and the rest of the year led a thankless existence. But that didn't excuse him from being their leader. That didn't excuse him from 'checking out,' hiding behind some ambiguous Codex, and giving power to the Council. How selfish could he really be to allow the fate of his people to go careening out of control, to what? End up in the paws of someone like Sturd? If he was the supreme Boss, the guy in charge of it all, why did it take a lowly Coal Elf like her to dream up the perfect fix-er-upper plan? Wouldn't Coal-for-All just kinda seem... seem... *obvious?*

This whole situation was far from over. She knew she would catch slack for going behind the Council's back without their permission, but she had had enough. *They* had had enough. All of them. It was about time someone stepped up to the plate and took charge, and it was blatantly obvious that Sturd was slowly slithering his way into that void left by the uncaring, ignorant, tone-deaf leader they had now.

No. We deserve better than that.

No more Councils. No more cadres. No more Codexes, and Lists, and books, and rules and regulations. After tonight, I'm going to see Him. I'm going to confront him. And so help me, I'm going to force him to get off his fat ass and take a stand!

No one ever dared go against Santa Claus?

Well guess what? This Coal Elf is about to.

About the author

Maria DeVivo is the author of the YA dark fantasy novel, *The Coal Elf* – the first book in a series centered on the darker, more obscure aspects of the holidays.

Originally from New York, Maria now lives in Florida, with her husband, Joe, and daughter, Morgan.

www.mariadevivo.com

www.facebook.com/mariadevivoauthor

Made in the USA
Las Vegas, NV
21 September 2022